THE STRANGE

Vivian Lane

THE STRANGE ALLIES SET

THREE BOOKS, ONE PRICE! Contains SEVEN AWAKENED, STRANGE ALLIES, and SAVING CHARLOTTE.

Della discovers she's a paladin at sixteen after a vampire attack, surviving due to her skin burning the undead to ashes. Graduating to Agent at eighteen, she embarks on missions to save the world, or at least as many people as she can.

When the mysterious vampire Adam starts helping her cause, Agent Seven doesn't trust him. Every vampire is evil, right? Will Adam prove her wrong, or be Agent Seven's downfall?

This series is a spin-off of *Children of Ossiria* following the lives of Della, Adam, and the people they care about most. Urban fantasy.

All Rights Are Reserved. No part of this book may be used or reproduced in any manner whatsoever without written permission, except in the case of brief quotations embodied in critical articles and reviews.

By Vivian Lane

Copyright 2015 Vivian Lane

Edited by K.C. Taylor

Published by Phantom Ridge, a Willowick Publishing imprint

The right of Vivian Lane to be identified as the Author of the Work has been asserted by her in accordance with the Copyright, Designs and Patents Act 1988.

This book is a work of fiction. The names, characters, places, and incidents are products of the writer's imagination or have been used fictitiously and are not to be construed as real. Any resemblance to persons, living or dead, actual events, locale or organizations is entirely coincidental.

Children of Ossiria

Dive into a world with modern-day paladins, secret organizations, demons, vampires, magic, seers, and curses. Our heroes will have to learn how to save the day, or die trying.

#0.5 - **The First Vampires**
#1 – Protector – Jan. 1, 2016
#2 – Goddess
#3 – Outcast
#4 – Mate (August 1, 2016)

Strange Allies

#1 – Seven Awakened
#2 – Strange Allies
#3 – Saving Charlotte

SEVEN AWAKENED

The people we save look at us like we're superheroes, or guardian angels, but we bleed.

We break.

And sometimes, we even die.

Della thought she was a normal sixteen-year-old until the night she met a vampire behind a drugstore and discovered a deadly power. Now The Agency wants to recruit her, but who are they, and where does this power come from? How do you choose between a destiny to save the world, and the people you love?

CLASSIFIED

Sacra Aedes Archive: Ref. No. 4302.

Agent File: Seven, "Della Garvison", Vol. 1

Contents: Journal entries dated May 2004 — May 2007

Librarian Note: This is the personal account of Agent Seven's training in her own words and therefore subject to interpretation and personal perspective.

References: See Biography — Thornhill, Amelia; Biography — Agent Thirteen.

Chapter One
May 2004

The story of how I got drafted into the world-savin' business isn't so complicated. Amelia Thornhill directed a vampire at me. A normal girl would probably have been killed, drained of her blood and possibly even turned. By grace of God, I hadn't been *normal* since my sixteenth birthday last month.

It was a warm night in Guthrie, Oklahoma, but not so warm to be uncomfortable for walking home. I took the turn off Main Street and cut behind the drugstore. When I say "drugstore", I don't mean a Walgreens or anything like that — it was a Mom-and-Pop store same as most of the businesses in Downtown.

"Little girls shouldn't be alone in the dark at night," a voice said.

Turning in a circle, I looked around me. "Who's there?" Gravel on the asphalt crunched under my shoes.

A man came out of the shadows, tall and gaunt. He was dressed like a homeless person, his clothes dirty, tattered, and torn. Tightening my grip on the strap of my backpack, I prepared to run, backing away toward the public street. Suddenly, he wasn't in sight anymore.

"Boo," he said behind me.

I jumped and screamed. Pretty quick on my feet, I thought I could make it inside the drugstore. A sharp tug on my backpack pulled me backward and I almost landed on my butt. The man pounced, smelling like garbage, something rotten and metallic.

I pushed his face away. He howled in pain—maybe I'd poked his eye—and came at me again. His eyes were red—not bloodshot, but with *red irises*. They were nothin' like movie eyes with the contacts you still know are fake.

Some instinct within me said *you're going to die if you don't do something now*. He kept trying to bite me and it was all I could do to flail my arms, trying to scrabble back from underneath him. My hands landed on his face again and I pushed, my heart pounding in my ears to the point of making me deaf.

Bright light, heat, and no more man. Ashes floated down on my clothes and the asphalt. "What the *hell*?"

"You tapped into your power." A woman walked into view from the corner of the building. "Well done." She wore a tweed suit, wire-frame glasses, and her hair pulled back tight. If she told me she was from The Watcher's Council, I was going to hunt down whoever put acid in my soda.

I scrambled to my feet. "Stay away."

She held up her hands to show they were empty. "There is no reason to fear me, Della."

"How do you know my name?" For every step she took forward, I retreated.

"I was sent to find you. I represent an agency dedicated to protecting humanity from evil. You have a gift, Della. A higher purpose."

"No offense, lady, but I think you're off your meds. I'm goin' home and you can go back to England or wherever it is you came from."

"Please," the blonde said. "We can teach you to harness your talents. You just reduced a vampire to dust. Aren't you the least bit curious how you did that?"

I laughed. Doubled-over-belly-hurting-on-the-verge-of-manic kind of laughter. A *vampire*? How could she possibly expect me to believe that? "Lady… I don't know what happened tonight. I just wanna go home." I got maybe five steps, when she added an incentive.

"We'll pay for your education."

I sighed. She had done her research, somehow. I wanted to be the first woman in my family to go to college. Much as the diner was home, I didn't want to work there all my life like my mother and the generations before me.

The blonde handed me a business card.

I told her I'd think about it, and ran home. It was a relief to get safely inside our little house with its *Country Home* décor and the scent of Pledge. Mama must've dusted before going into the diner today. Parched from my run, I went straight to the fridge and guzzled an orange pop. The adrenaline started wearing off, and despite it being May, the sweat on my back started to chill. My hands shook.

Doing my best to convince myself none of what happened before I got home was real; I showered and went to bed early.

It wasn't real. There was a logical explanation that had nothing to do with monsters from the movies. In the morning, I'd continue sophomore year like the average middle-of-the-country kid I was and this would only be a blip. A stupid little memory. The business card would disappear in tomorrow's trash.

My days started early. Mom dropped me off at 7:00AM on her way to the diner. Breakfast service started at nine (except Sundays), but restaurants required a lot of prep work. After school, I'd walk to the diner to put in my shift until sundown, and then walk home, or sometimes if it was a quiet night she'd let the staff run the dinner shift and we'd come home together. I wasn't going to be valedictorian, but I got good grades, participated in activities, and did some volunteer stuff.

Like I said — normal.

My focus was on college. Didn't know what came after that.

By the weekend, there had been no more weirdness and I started to breathe easier.

Until Mom came home Saturday. The crazy lady met with my mother, spinning a compelling tale about representing a summer camp looking for smart teens with a penchant for service. Humanitarian aid training, focus on the downtrodden...all the right buttons to push in a Bible-believin' mother. Bonus: they were offering a scholarship so I could attend for free.

"Mom, don't you think it's kinda weird she shows up out of the blue with offers on a silver platter?"

"Oh, Della, it's just a summer program. This'll be good for you! You love hearing about faraway places when the missionaries visit."

"I don't wanna go. I don't think she's tellin' us everything."

"You've gotta trust people sometimes, Della Garvison. Now quit fussin' about it. I already filled out the release form and that's final. If you want out of Guthrie, we're goin' to need some help and this will look good on your college application."

"Yes, Mama." There was no arguing with her once she made up her mind. She wanted me to save the world with good intentions.

Little did either of us know, it would mostly happen at the point of a sword.

I finished out the school year, then got on a plane with Miss Thornhill. Once again, she was dressed like she should be in some fancy office.

"Can you stop fidgeting, please? These seats are too close together for you to keep wiggling about," she said.

"I'm sorry. I can't get comfortable."

"Why in heavens not?"

"I'm nervous, okay?"

"Della, I promise we have the best intentions. You're special to us."

"It's not that—though I want to be clear I'm here because my mother said so. I've never flown before."

"Really? At sixteen? Hmm."

"If you noticed, we're not exactly rolling in dough. Never had the occasion, okay?"

"No judgment. You know, statistically speaking it is safer to fly in an airplane than be in a car on the highway."

"Swell." The car still had the advantage of being on the *ground*. But of course I was worried about where I was going, which I had no clue about. The brochure didn't include an address. Was it a cult? A child slavery ring? Something worse?

My fingers rubbed the cross pendant I always wore and I sent up a silent prayer this wouldn't end in tragedy.

We landed in New York, then Miss Thornhill escorted me to a car and we drove into the boonies. From the driveway, the property was nothing special—just two long buildings made of red brick and decorated with ivy. It looked like an old private school.

"What is this place?"

"Our US training center." She parked the car. There was only one other visible, a black SUV. "Come."

I followed her inside and through the basement door. It led not to a cellar, but a huge underground installation. The corridors were wide, walls and floor made of thick concrete. An endless amount of gray.

"From now on, you'll be known as Seven," Amelia said, showing me to a dorm room.

"My name is *Della*."

"And you'll forget it if you want to survive. A name isn't merely a word, it's an identity, and therefore has power. There are many things in our world that would use that against you."

"But why 'Seven'?"

She paused at a door and handed me the key. "Because you're the seventh active we have at the moment."

"Six people? That's your organization?"

Amelia averted her eyes and tugged on the hem of her jacket. "At the moment, yes. Some of the agents were injured recently. Others were forced to retire from field service."

"Why?" Probably wanted a big raise.

"You can ask them yourself when we go to London." She walked away, shoulders stiff and dress flats clicking on the concrete floor.

I had the feeling I'd just offended her in some way.

My room was cozier than I expected. The walls were papered in textured light blue and I had white wooden furniture, except for the armchair in the corner. A print of the Serenity prayer hung above the lone bed. I missed having a window, but figured I wouldn't be in here much except to sleep. With my clothes put away in the drawers, I followed the map Amelia gave me to the dining hall above.

My first meal away from home.

Picking up a tray from the stack in the corner, I walked to the buffet station. They *had* to be kidding—plain chicken breast and steamed vegetables? I glanced at the tables in the center. Not a single salt shaker in sight. My stomach growled, complaining about the lack of breading, gravy, or pie. A single bowl of apples and oranges sat at the end of the cart.

"Ah, there you are," Amelia said. She was followed into the room by three young people: two boys maybe in college and a girl just a hair over five-foot tall. Couldn't place her nationality besides Asian.

"For the love o' Pete, Thornhill, you brought us a *redhead*?" That came from the guy on her left. He was shorter than the other, with a stocky build.

"It won't show when she's in uniform," she said. "Seven, these two gentlemen are your trainers."

"Hi." I groaned internally. Dealing with the opposite gender had never gone terribly well before.

She placed her hand on the girl's shoulder. "This is Kaede." The girl remained silent, standing with her arms crossed under her breasts.

"I thought names weren't allowed here?"

"She hasn't been tested, yet."

Ah. No wonder the girl looked like this was the last place she wanted to be. I'd had to relive dusting a vampire in my dreams every night for the past month to have it sink in as real. Or, as real as I could trust a memory to be. People who hallucinated usually thought their visions were real, too, didn't they?

The boys walked through a swinging door to the side. I caught a glimpse of the kitchen. Might there be real food hidden away in there? Amelia nudged Kaede up next to me and handed her a plate. The girl slapped food on it and stomped to the table farthest from us.

"How did you get her here?" I asked.

"Her brother came to us a couple years ago."

"Oh. You're hopin' whatever this is runs in the family."

"It's not unheard of. Fill up your plate. Suppertime is limited."

I chose a chicken breast and stuck to carrots, since they were the only veggie offered I could swallow without seasoning. Stocky Boy came back first, carrying a pitcher of milk. He set it down at Kaede's table.

"I can't drink that," she said.

"Why not?"

"I'm lactose intolerant, duh."

He placed his hands on the table and glared at her. "That's 'sir', little girl."

"I don't call white boys 'sir', meat-head."

Wow. If Mama heard something like that, I would have gotten my mouth washed out with soap.

Stocky Boy pulled Kaede out of her chair by her arm. "Twenty push-ups. Now."

"Go to hell," she spat.

"*Forty. Now.*"

"You can't touch me," she said. "My father donates too much money to your stupid organization."

Stocky Boy shrugged, bent to toss her over his shoulder, and left the room with her upside-down like that, kicking and screaming.

"What's he gonna do with her?" I asked Amelia.

"Confine her to her room. Part of the reason her parents agreed to send her is this, her attitude."

"You're not a reform school, though." Institution for the mentally altered, I could believe.

She sighed, and sat down with her own plate. "No…but sometimes a favor is worth the cost. Doing what we do isn't cheap."

"Oh." Made sense, I guess. "May I ask somethin'?"

"Yes."

"Will all the food be this bland?"

She pushed her glasses up her nose, attempting to hide a twitch of amusement. So, she *wasn't* pure British stiff-upper-lip. "The menu is part of our lessons on discipline, Seven. Pure body. Pure mind. Pure heart."

"Yay…" The chicken felt dry in my mouth, leading me to drink more milk with the meal than I'd done at age five. Tall Guy entered, drying his hands with a dish towel.

"Seven, this is Thirteen."

Thirteen offered me a handshake. "I thought there were only six," I said

"There were fifteen," he said.

Were… "Oh. I'm sorry." And *gulp*. Past tense meant people *died*. "So, I'm takin' someone else's number."

"We all do," he said. "The Agency has been sending out soldiers for over three hundred years. Don't worry—no one's sending you out unprepared." He had a kind, friendly face. Looked like a California surfer. I liked him a lot better than the other one.

Better than Amelia, too.

She smiled when I cleaned my plate. She'd been watching, studying, since we left Oklahoma, cataloguing everything I did. I'm not that fascinating.

Thirteen asked me to put on running shoes when I was done and meet him outside. I was already wearing what I had, basic tennies. He led me to a track.

"You're gonna ask me to run after eating?"

"You never know when you'll have to run," he said. "Stretch your legs then do a lap as fast as you can."

I'd rather do the push-ups. Mama didn't raise no whiner, though, so I did what he said and warmed up. He nodded at me to go, holding a stop watch, and I ran. The stitch in my side that always came in PE didn't appear.

It felt good.

I felt *fast*.

The dusk air was cool on my cheeks, but I wasn't sweating. I skidded to a stop in front of Thirteen.

"Not bad," he said.

"Not bad? I was *flying*."

"It was alright for your first day."

I pouted. "You're gonna be the 'I never give out A's' teacher, huh?"

He smiled at my assessment. "We don't assign letter grades."

"Whatever. So, what do you really do?"

"You don't believe Amelia."

I stuck my hands in the pockets of my hoodie. "I don't know, but come on…vampires and magic and crap? It's fiction."

"Is faith fiction?"

"What makes you think I have any?"

He pointed at my collarbone. "Saw the cross you're wearing."

"Could be a fashion statement."

"If you had one of those frilly types. That one is plain silver, small and modest." He smirked, looking absolutely confident he was right.

He was. I'd worn the cross every day since my twelfth birthday, even showering with it on. It was the year my faith became something more personal to me, more than stories in Sunday school. "Fine, but believin' in God is different than sayin' old horror movies are based on fact."

Thirteen grinned. "In our world, not so much. You'll see for yourself soon enough. In the meantime, let's get you in shape to beat a human."

"What's wrong with my shape?" I was *not* fat.

He poked my abs. "You're soft, kid." He pointed to the other building. "To the gym."

Though this building was the same two-story height as the other, it was an open space. The side we entered on had various weight-lifting and work-out machines. The center was taken up by a large blue mat. On the far side, a couple gymnastic bars in various heights.

"Learn to love it, Seven. This will be your home for the next month, if you're lucky."

"Lucky?"

"Could take longer." He walked to the weight bench. "Ever lifted weights before?"

"I've carried heavy things." Restocking the diner every week could be back-breaking work during busy season.

"Not what I asked."

"Then no. I haven't used any gym equipment before."

He sighed and muttered something about schools falling down on the job. For the next hour, he explained what everything did and showed me how to do proper form with them.

"How long…have you been doin' this?" I asked while he made me run on the treadmill.

"Five years."

"Does your family know?"

He increased the speed of the machine a notch. "They're dead. Gang of bloodsuckers interrupted their date night."

I was running too fast to reply, but I hoped he could see sympathy in my eyes. Foot in mouth—check.

Twenty minutes at that pace, and my legs felt like cooked noodles. Wheezing, I slid off the treadmill. Thirteen made notes in a little book, then offered me water.

"Do you…still…remember…your name?"

He laughed and joined me on the floor. "That's been bugging you all day, hasn't it?"

"Well…*yeah*." I was Della Garvison, just like my great-grandmother.

"I still remember."

"What is it?"

He shook his finger at me. "Uh-uh…can't say."

"I'm trustworthy."

"Would you keep that secret if you were tortured? Could you hold your tongue under a spell or compulsion? None of us can take that risk, Seven. And none of us will."

My first reaction was to be offended, but then I thought about it. This guy didn't know me. He also believed in the dangers he mentioned; I could tell by the conviction in his voice. Crazy or not, if these people thought their identities had to be secret, I needed to respect that. There was no harm in calling him a number — it was just awkward.

Bedtime was at ten during my training.

Amelia had me up with the sun. My first full day started the routine of the coming weeks. I had ten minutes to shower and dress, then a half hour for breakfast. She ate with me, answering some of my questions and delaying others for my lessons.

From eight to ten, she taught me about the monsters I would face. "Vampire 101 — Kill them with a wooden stake to the heart or by cutting off their heads. UV light burns and younger vampires go up in flames from sunlight."

"Only the young ones?"

"There are reports that the ancient can walk around on a cloudy day, or make short burst runs through sunny spaces, but no one has seen the old ones for many years. We can't confirm they still exist."

"Are they all like that guy that attacked me? A walking corpse?"

She took a photo album off the shelf and placed it on the desk in front of me. "We've catalogued several specimens since photography was invented. You will be taught how to observe without being noticed or caught. Know what you are facing before you attack."

I started flipping through the pages. The vampires were former people from all walks of life, which surprised me. I figured the most vulnerable would be the unfortunate, those who didn't have a safe home or transportation at night. "Can they walk into my house?"

She shook her head. "A vampire needs an invitation to enter a home. There is a distinction between a house and a home, by the way. The dwelling needs to be in the occupant's name, either on deed or lease, and they need to live there often enough to—"

"Believe me, I understand *home*. Is there any other way they die?"

"Sanctified items also burn the undead, though one would need to subject them to prolonged exposure to dust them. Fire works, of course…not many creatures natural or supernatural can resist that. The vampire is not truly immortal, Seven, but you must always remember they possess a powerful innate skill set. They are faster and stronger than you and hand-to-hand combat is greatly discouraged."

"So I'm s'posed to shoot one if I see it?"

"Thirteen will cover that."

"But you want me to avoid them."

"You're not a vampire slayer. The supernatural world is huge and vampires are merely a small part of it. Most of your work will consist of containment, and retrieval of dangerous artifacts."

"Containment?"

"Early interference. Cutting problems off at the pass. People naively mess with things they shouldn't. We handle that."

"Oh. So, are all vampires the same?"

"No…aside from individual personalities based on the people they used to be, there are four families. The vampire's visage changes when their true nature is revealed. Aside from the fangs, their irises shift color."

"The red-eyed man that attacked me."

"Yes. They display as red, gold, green, or blue-white."

"And that's the only difference, the eye color?"

"No, each family has innate traits. The Reds are what you know as the classic vampire. The Golds are not affected by holy items and we don't know why. The Greens are reclusive and rarely seen, so we know little about them. And the Blues are thought to be extinct."

"Thought to be."

"The vampire is a wily creature, so we cannot be one-hundred percent sure, but yes. We are quite certain they were killed off."

"By what?"

"Does it matter? The only good vampire or demon or any other monster is a dead one. Moving on, let's talk about werewolves."

From ten to noon, Stocky Guy kicked my butt with plyometrics. I got a half-hour lunch, then another two-hour lecture on the history of killing demons. Amelia let me have a half hour in my room to do what I wished, then Thirteen took over at three with weapons training.

He started with the Bo staff.

"I'm not hittin' you with that."

"You can't damage me any more than I've had in the field. Besides, it's padded."

"Yours isn't."

He smirked. "I know what I'm doing." He twirled the staff around his fingers, all fancy like. Jerk. "Attack already."

My arms already felt like jelly from the workout earlier. Couldn't they alternate days? I dropped the staff. "I'm not a violent person."

"This isn't about *violence*. It's about protection. Every martial art is about disabling your opponent quickly so you can get away alive. You have the talent, Seven. Learn to use it."

"Talent? *Talent?* All I know is a man with red eyes disappeared after I pushed on his face. It was weird and it was scary and it was *dark*. I only came because my mother insisted on me going to summer camp." I turned to leave. Got as far as two steps when my legs were swept out from under me and I landed on my butt.

Thirteen stood over me with the end of his staff pressed into my chest. "I did not give you permission to go." He jabbed the staff at my face.

I caught it before it struck my nose. What the hell?

"See? The instincts are there, Seven."

"Let me up." He backed off. I reached for the padded staff, setting my hands slightly wider than shoulder width. "I'll try this *once*."

He grinned and bounced on his toes. "Sure…"

I started circling him so at least I was moving.

Thirteen moved with me — step, crossover-step, step. He kept grinning at me, making part of me want to knock that smile off his face. "Gonna swing that thing, or what?"

"I'm thinkin' about it."

Sighing, he dropped the staff tip to the floor. "Maybe we should start you with Aikido and add weapons later."

I jabbed his chest with my staff, like staking a vampire. "But then I couldn't do that."

Thirteen was instantly at the ready again. "Oh, is that how we're playing it." He swung for my head.

Turning my head so he didn't hit my nose, I narrowly dodged the strike. "Hey, that was close."

"Be even closer when you're fighting for your life." He went low to sweep my legs again. This time, I saw it and hopped over the staff. "Good. Faster." He had me on the defensive, trying to block his moves from hitting my body and driving me backward. My foot slid off the mat and I fell, landing on my back. "What should you have done there?"

"Not fall down?"

He shook his head. "Don't get forced into retreat. Either retake control, or run. If I was something that wanted you dead right now, you would be."

I held my hand out for a hand up. He backed off to the center of the mat, leaving me to get up on my own. My back hurt from hitting the tile.

He stood poised to attack. "Again."

That night, I lay on my bed bruised and sore, and homesick. This place was so empty. Cold. I missed the chatter of the diner, the sounds of sizzling burger patties and bubbling oil. Missed Mama's contagious laugh and buttermilk biscuits. Rolling over, I faced the wall, wrapped around Muffy, my bear.

Could I take years of being away? That's what *they* wanted.

Summer would be long enough.

****

I progressed rapidly my first week, though my muscles felt like they'd been through hell.

Stocky Guy turned out not to be an Agent. He was ex-military, drummed out for insisting he saw demons in some backwater jungle. They didn't want anyone "unstable" around demolition equipment. He rode Kaede hard, making her run on the track until she puked and kept going. After seven days of punishment, she stopped hurling insults.

"Why is it only the five of us?" I asked Thirteen.

"Truth?" He moved his hands to spot me at the bench press.

"Always."

"We're at war, kid, and grossly outnumbered. It's why people like Amelia are searching for people like you. There was a time when we had a small army."

"And?"

"Something has made it their mission to wipe us out, one by one."

"Not good."

"That's the reason for the hard sell. Every recruit is essential. We're hoping your generation has a lot of potential."

No pressure.

I pushed my twentieth rep up and set the bar back on the stand. He dropped a hand towel on my face. He was a good teacher, only getting on my case when he thought I wasn't doing my best. Amelia was a lot harder to please, impatient little sighs escaping her lips every time I fumbled over the name of some obscure demon.

I looked forward to the end of summer when I could go back to high school.

As the days went on, Amelia's lessons stuck to demon species identification and awareness of supernatural practices. She drilled me on photos, sketches, scents, and names.

It took me a bit, but I started noticing she side-stepped all my questions about The Agency. What were they an order *of?* Who started it? How were they allowed to operate in the modern world?

Frustrated, I went to Thirteen. "Amelia won't answer my questions."

He stopped stacking the weights and turned to me. "What do you want to know?"

"What exactly *is* The Agency?"

"Just what she's told you: a secret organization committed to protecting the human world from supernatural threats."

"And nobody cares that you walk around armed with swords and crossbows?"

"We have the permission of most governments to do what we do as long as it's quiet. No one needs a public panic. Amelia is cautious with newbies because a lot of how we work is sensitive information. Our lives and the lives of our families depend on being invisible. Secretive." He tossed me a shenai for sword practice.

I caught it with one hand. "Are you saying the President knows vampires and werewolves exist?"

"I don't know, but someone on his staff does. You think too much. What have I said about coming to practice with a clear mind?"

"'Focus keeps your head on your shoulders'...yeah, yeah, I got it."

He got into battle stance. "Begin."

This first month was about the basics of everything, a little here, a little there. I shot arrows, bolts, and darts, was forced to master weapons in both hands, and lost count of how many times my knuckles were rapped by a bamboo sword. At least he hadn't made me pick up the hardwood boken, yet.

"So, if we have this power in our skin, why is most of my training about staying at a distance?"

"You've listened to Amelia's lessons, haven't you? Your touch only burns *the undead*. Everything else can kill you up close and personal and they'll try. That's why we use these." He opened a case and picked up two rifles, one long and one shorter.

"*Guns?*"

"Ever fired one before?"

"Pellet gun, and my cousin's .22. But I'm not killing anyone!"

"I'm not asking you to, at least not anyone human. We tranquilize humans and werewolves. Killing demons and vampires is doing the world a favor. So, today you're going to learn cleaning and operation of firearms."

"Are these yours?"

"God, no. They're from the armory. No rookie is touching my babies when they're sighted in perfect."

"Spoken like a man…"

"Seven, provided you don't wash out of the program, one day your weapons will feel like part of you, too."

Shuddering, I followed him outside to the target range. I didn't want to be that person. Learning to protect myself was one thing — becoming a bringer of death another.

Chapter Two

July

"Congratulations on reaching your first month," Thirteen said at breakfast.

"Yay. What does that mean?"

Amelia poured milk into her coffee. "It means I'm taking you to London."

"What's in London?"

"Headquarters. Currently for the entire Agency."

I swallowed a bite of unsweetened oatmeal. "I don't have a passport."

"It's been arranged," she said, and left the dining hall.

"Weird," I said, watching her go. "She didn't eat this morning."

"She was up early on the phone. Reporting in."

"'Yes, sir, Kaede is still an obnoxious brat'," I imitated.

He choked on a piece of toast, cleared his throat, and laughed. "They're sending her home tomorrow."

"Really?"

"She doesn't have it."

Ah, the freak-of-nature gift in his blood and mine.

This many weeks of mastering physical challenges later, I couldn't deny something extraordinary was going on. I didn't tire when I should, ache for as long, or stumble over the constant influx of new techniques. In only a month, my body was visibly different—leaner, stronger, and defined. I hit bull's-eyes on eight of ten of my targets—nine on a good day—and could best Thirteen with the Bo half the time.

"What happens in London?"

"Proficiency tests, then more training. Lots of people to meet."

"Lots?"

"Sure. Researchers, agents, the administration...you know, book people and field people."

I pushed my oatmeal around in the bowl. "Sounds big."

"Four stories." Did I mention I was shy around crowds? Noticing my discomfort, he patted me on the back. "You'll do fine."

I smiled for him. "Where do you go next?"

He shrugged. "Where they send me. Maybe searching for more of you."

"I heard Amelia talking about prospects the other day."

"Yeah? Hope so. Come on." He stood. "I have one more lesson for you."

I put my dishes on the tray. "Where are we going?"

"Into the woods."

Uh-oh. I'd never liked the look of the forest behind the school. It was the height of summer, yet that wood still looked dark and foggy, like an evil fairytale forest. The thought of going in there gave me the heebie-jeebies.

"What's the objective?"

"Find me," he said, and grinned.

Yeah, *right*. "Hey, I'm no Indian."

"Tracking is at least seventy percent of our job, Seven. Can't escape it." He pushed open the door to the outside and took off running for the trees.

I started to chase, then remembered a lesson he'd been hammering into my brain—never go into the unknown unarmed. Detouring for the training building, I grabbed a small sheathed knife, a crossbow, and a tranq pistol. I attached the knife to my belt loop, slung the crossbow over my shoulder, and resumed course to the wood.

The air was cooler when I neared the trees, and all light seemed to be soaked up below their entangled branches. No person in their right mind would want to venture into that forest. I found the clearest path between the trees and followed Thirteen in. Dry leaves crunched under my feet. My pulse beat faster the further into the darkness I went. Wings suddenly fluttered overhead; I crouched and aimed the crossbow at the sound.

Calm down, Della, or you'll be wandering this forest all day.

Sure, easy to think it. Try telling my heart it can slow down.

Remember your training, dummy.

Deep breath. Observe your surroundings. Deduce.

I got in control of my fear and looked around me. Unless Thirteen could fly, he had to be crunching leaves like I was. The whole forest floor was covered with them. I spotted his trail and followed.

Checking my watch, it'd been ten minutes since I entered the tree line. The hairs on the back of my neck stood on end. "Who's there?" Nothing answered but the breeze shifting the leaves above.

Just run-of-the-mill paranoia.

Walking another five minutes, keeping my eyes on the crunched leaves, I had the sudden feeling of being watched. Put my back to a tree and waited.

Nothing. Hated this place.

"Hey, Teach! Really funny, tryin' to scare the apprentice and all, but this is getting boring."

Somebody laughed, and it was *not* his voice.

"Screw this." I turned back the way I came and set a brisk pace for the open field.

My teacher stood waiting for me. He glanced at his watch. "Not bad. You lasted twenty minutes."

"You…you were never in there?" I could kill him. "What *is* that place?"

"*A forest.*" He grinned. "Some think it's haunted."

I pushed him. "What if I got lost in there? How dare you send me on a wild goose chase?"

"The lesson is conquering fear, Seven. Had you not given up, you would have seen where I doubled back and knew exactly where to find me. You're going to be looking for the innocent and helpless, kid. They *need* you to stick to the task at hand no matter what."

"I'm not ready," I said, and stomped off for the residence hall.

"Hey, you're dismissed when I say you're done." He stepped into my path, making me bump into his chest. "You better *get* ready. Like it or not, this is your destiny."

"Says who? You? Amelia? Try sending an archangel, then it might be convincing."

I stepped around him and resumed my course. Thirteen grabbed my arm. I decked him with a right hook. He went down. I stared at my hand.

He rubbed his jaw. "First time I've felt you mean it."

"I'm sorry."

He didn't deserve that. Striking out of anger went against everything I believed in. I ran, full speed, and didn't stop until I'd locked myself in my room.

****

I awoke to someone knocking on my door. Three more taps—knock, knock, knock—while I decided to answer it. "Who is it?"

"It's Amelia. May we talk?"

I rolled off the bed to my feet and unlocked the door. "Is it important, Amelia?"

She fidgeted with the ring on her right hand. "About today…"

"I let my temper get the best of me, and I'm sorry. If the world really is in danger, Amelia, you need someone more mature than me. I just want to go home."

Her mouth tightened into an angry line. "Fear is not a reason to quit, *Della*." She turned to walk away.

"Hey. This isn't about fear. I'm a sixteen-year-old girl from a small town. Not a soldier. I didn't sign on for any war, and at my age in the US of A, you can't press me into service."

She paused, her back rigidly straight. "You're determined."

"Yes."

"Very well. We are not heartless, and we will not force you against your will."

"Thank you. You'll send me home."

She sighed, and her shoulders slumped. "Yes."

The ride to the airport was silent. It didn't take me long to pack my duffle bag. It'd never been completely emptied in the first place. She bought me a plane ticket and sent me to the gate without a goodbye.

Made me feel guilty for not being the hero she hoped for.

Mom met me in Oklahoma City. I wrapped my arms around her and squeezed. She squeaked. "Breathing room, honey."

"Sorry." My cheeks turning pink, I let go. "I've been working out."

"I can tell. I'm thrilled to have you home, dear, but I thought this was a three-month camp?"

"I… I got homesick. The place was too quiet and all they had me do was work. Rather be in the diner if I'm gonna do that."

She wrapped her arm around my waist and steered me to the car. "Aww, that's what I like to hear. You know, you're back just in time for the ice cream social on Sunday."

"Sounds perfect." Never been so happy to see my hometown in my life. Not that we'd ever been farther out than an hour or two before, but to see the old houses, big ol' trees, and Victorian-age commercial buildings of Downtown…just this side of Heaven. I couldn't wipe the grin off my face.

Made her laugh at me. "Think you'd been away a year, Della."

"Kinda feels that way, Mom." I rolled the window down. "Nothin' smelled right!"

She drove straight home.

Mama was "country when country wasn't cool" and our house reflected it. Lots of gingham in the living room and kitchen, and her bedroom was decorated in florals and lace. An old quilt hung on the wall behind the sofa, and an afghan my grandmother crocheted was draped over the armchair. Our house still had wood floors, so knotted-rag rugs kept the furniture from scratching them. It was small, but we didn't need much.

"Do I smell a roast?"

"With carrots and little white potatoes, and those pearl onions you like so much."

"Mama, you're spoiling me."

"Just happy to have my baby girl home! Go freshen up and put your things away."

I grinned. "Yes, ma'am." For her roast, I'd scrub my clothes clean by hand.

I closed my bedroom door to change into something comfy and caught sight of my reflection. The girl looking back was me, but not me...or rather, a changed me. She had a bit of color from the days running outside and no longer looked like a young kid, but that was superficial. It was the look in my eyes that made me pause—the absence of total innocence. I *was* young, and sheltered, yet there were things I knew now.

Things I couldn't erase.

What would I tell Mom when she asked? 'Cause she was definitely going to notice. Mama didn't miss a trick when it came to my moods.

"Deal with it when it comes and not a moment sooner," I muttered, and changed into shorts and a loose tee. Anything dirty got dumped in the hamper. I stopped at the bathroom, then walked out for dinner. The wood floor felt good on my hot bare feet.

"Mom, you made too much food." Besides the roast with veggie trimmings, she had a bowl of green beans with bits of onion and bacon on the table and a full basket of rolls.

"No such thing. Gives us leftovers. Sit."

I sat. My stomach gurgled. After a month of plain chicken, this was going to taste as good as water to a parched man. The moment Mama said "amen" for grace, I reached for a slice of beef.

"Did they feed you?" she asked, her eyes a little wide.

"Yeah." I stuffed a chunk in my mouth. Pure nirvana.

"Slow down, Della. You'll give yourself belly ache."

"Sorry," I said, mouth full of potato. It was just so *good*.

"S'pose it won't hurt you much. You're too skinny, anyway."

Hey… I hadn't whittled away my curves, thank you very much. My boobs were actually perkier thanks to the new muscle underneath. Once my stomach was convinced the roast wasn't going to disappear, I asked Mom about the diner and the latest town gossip. That got her talking until my eyes started to droop and I was ready for bed.

Mmm, my own bed…

****

I got a week of peace before my ear started catching weird things about town.

Pets disappearing where there'd been no coyote sightings.

Tales of the ghosts at Stone Lion Inn being not-so-friendly.

The kicker was meeting *another* vampire on the way home from a friend's house. Only this time, I had a stake. "Can't you guys leave me alone?" I watched his body crumble to dust.

"It's about balance, kid."

I spun around. "You."

My teacher stepped out from behind a tree. "Good and evil, light and dark…the world is meant to have a balance. When you have a gift, you're meant to use it."

"Why are you here?"

"You left before receiving your reward for stage one."

"Reward? Like a certificate?"

He stopped beneath the street lamp. Under a black leather long coat, he wore tactical gear. Silver threads glinted here and there in the light. Combat boots were on his feet, giving him nearly an inch more of height. He handed me a small box.

"What's with the get-up?" I opened the jewelry box. A silver ring lay inside, plain except for the Greek letters alpha and omega engraved in the center. "What's this?"

He held up his right hand to show an identical ring. "Whether you want to be or not, you're one of us now, Seven."

"Oh... I don't think I can—" I looked up from the ring. He was gone. "Accept this. Yeah, that isn't weird at all..." I shoved the box in my pocket and continued home.

Knowing vampires were in my town, even just occasionally, didn't sit right with me. I started doing sweeps at night after Mama went to bed. Found one maybe once a week or so...well, they seemed to find me. They were all gross and no one I knew, thank God. Little more than rabid animals. A high-powered crossbow was my friend.

A week before school was going to start in August, Mom came down with a flu-like bug, feeling really wiped out. When she was still really fatigued at three weeks, I made her go to the doctor. Diagnosis: lupus. For a woman working ten hours a day at her own business, she was *not* happy to discover a disease requiring her to rest more. Looking at the list of drug, diet, lifestyle, and supplement suggestions, my head spun.

They wanted her to come in for frequent tests until it was in remission. "Mom, can we afford your treatment?"

"Probably. For a while."

"A *while*?"

"Don't raise your voice in the car, Della Garvison."

"I'm sorry, but I'm worried. I know how stubborn and proud you are."

She stopped at a light and scratched the rash on her arm. "You're my daughter. Don't need you takin' care of me until I'm old and gray."

"You're going to have to hire more help at the diner or you won't reach 'old and gray'."

"Della!"

"I listened, okay? This can get serious if you don't take care of yourself."

"I'll make it work. End of discussion."

"But—"

"No buts. Zip it."

I sighed, knowing there was no use when she was in this mood. "Yes, ma'am." We didn't have much extra, I knew that. She had savings, but it wouldn't last for a life-long disease.

In my room, I pulled out a wrinkled business card and dialed the number.

"Hello?"

"Amelia, this is Della… I'll come to London if we can make a deal."

"I didn't expect to hear from you again."

"This agent gig… I get a salary, right?"

"Of course. We support every member of The Agency in all the ways they require."

Going by her tone, I'd offended her again. "Look, I'll speak plainly. My mother is ill and I don't know if we can cover all the medical bills to come. She's all I've got and I want to take care of her." Needed to.

"I understand. School is in session, yes?"

"Yeah. It's almost October now."

"Then I will come to you and we'll begin in earnest and perhaps your mother will allow field trips on your holidays."

"Field trips?"

"Goodbye, Seven. I'll see you within a day." She hung up.

I hoped I was doing the right thing. We all knew about Hell and good intentions.

Amelia wasn't kiddin' about arriving quickly. She was waiting on the curb when class let out.

I took in her blazer, blouse, and slacks, and shook my head. "Lady, you're as subtle as a gravy sandwich."

"I beg your pardon."

"You stick out like a sore thumb." I started walking home. I needed to finish my homework so I could get to the diner.

"I'm your guide, Della. Not your buddy. My attire is entirely appropriate for my station."

"Really…you kill demons with your good pearls on?"

Her hand went to her throat. "Well, no. That would be impractical."

"Well, I'm as practical as you get and this is a small town. People talk, and they're gonna wonder what I'm doin' with a fancy-pants British lady."

"It is not anyone's concern. We work in secret for a calling that transcends societal norms." Geesh. And I thought my history teacher had a pole up her butt. "This brings me to my recommendation that we not stay in one place very long."

I stopped on the sidewalk. "I'm still in high school."

"You can take the equivalency exam, Della."

"Oh, no," I said, shaking my head. "Mama would kill me if I skipped graduation."

She frowned. "Then I don't know what you expect me to do with you. This isn't a part-time job at the shopping mall. We have all committed to a greater cause. You've already been hunting, haven't you? I can assure you, they'll keep coming."

"Are you saying I put the town at risk by being here?"

"Eventually, yes. You and those like you are like magnets to demonkind. It's part of how we find you."

"Forgive me if I don't take your word on that. I'm stayin' until I finish school." Almost two years from now.

She sighed. "Very well. You will see for yourself by summer." She walked back to her rental car, letting me continue home.

My secret life began the next night. In the hours between Mom sending me home from the diner and her getting home, Amelia tutored me in the ways of The Agency. Wandering the messy parts of town…I felt like I was in a TV show, except without the super strength, blonde hair, and my technique wasn't nearly so flashy. All that kicky, flippy stuff might look good in the movies, but it wasn't practical in real life, and quipping with your opponent just got you dead. Kill quickly and move on.

Most nights, we didn't find anything. Suspicious noises usually turned out to be a stray cat, or a raccoon.

"You haven't told me where this special ability comes from," I said.

"We don't know."

"You don't *know*?" I glanced at her blank face. "I don't believe that."

She'd taken me to the woods outside town, hoping, I guess, for somethin' odd out here. "Curiosity killed the cat, Seven."

"Don't play that game with me, Amelia. If you guys made this happen to me and changed me, I deserve to know."

She glanced up at the stars and stopped walking. "I swear we did nothing to you. There is speculation about the powers of the agents, but no proof. No substantiated facts. Those of us with faith consider it a blessing. Whatever force for Good is out there chose you to be a thorn in Evil's side. Maybe you carry the heart of an angel. Maybe it's a genetic mutation. We don't know. What's important is you have a purpose, Seven. How many people can ever say they know exactly what they are meant to do on this earth?"

"Alright…you ever find out, I'm the first to know, deal?"

She clasped my hand. "I swear it." And met my eyes in the darkness. "I'm not the enemy, dear. I never will be."

I nodded. "Let's hunt some bad guys."

The closer to Halloween, the weirder things got. Traditionally the night where the barrier between the natural and spiritual worlds was thinnest, we'd been cleansing the town of ghosts with rings of salt around the graveyards and anointing the gates with oil.

"Are you sure this is necessary? I've never seen a ghost."

Amelia extinguished the incense she'd used. "Maybe not everywhere, but better to be safe than sorry. There are those that would use the dead for evil purposes. The spirit is eternal and those not in Heaven are vulnerable to dark magic."

"Magic."

She sighed. "Yes, *magic*. Have you not paid attention since I found you, Seven? Why must you be so stubborn?"

"Genetics." Mostly Irish, in fact, with the stereotypical red hair, pale skin, and freckles.

When I said things had gotten weird, I didn't mean actual *events*...it was a feeling. An unease. True, I felt ridiculous skulking around in the dark in a black hoodie and matching pants with weapons in my backpack, but beyond that, nights in October were making my skin crawl and I didn't like it.

Amelia seemed unaffected.

On Halloween night, I put a ghost sheet costume over my camo outfit. "Headin' out, Mom."

"Be good and have fun, honey. Don't forget to save me a few Butterfingers." She was staying home to hand out candy.

"I won't. Don't let any monsters in while I'm gone."

She laughed. "I'll be careful. Scoot! Join your friends."

Friends...ha. Had the same ones from last year, sure, but with this big secret, and so much of my time taken up...well, even tonight wasn't about teenage fun. Amelia was allowing me one hour to trick-or-treat before being on duty, so I carried a small plastic bag with a jack-o'-lantern on it I could stuff in my backpack later, but I couldn't take the risk I'd draw something to the people I cared about. What was that they said on *Buffy*, 'The Slayer is always alone'? While I'd never been the most popular, I didn't want to be a loner, either.

Maybe I'd make friends with others hauled into this crazy service.

Maybe in an asylum where all this hokum belonged.

Would the world end if I gathered candy, bobbed for apples, and went on hay rides?

No.

Screw Amelia. If she was so worried about Halloween, she could deal with the 'spooky' herself. Nothing was happening!

We had a lot of arguments about 'responsibilities' in November.

Other parts of the world might have issues, but Guthrie was quiet as always, so we spent a lot of time walking in circles. I invited her to Thanksgiving as a peace offering, but she declined. Would've been hard to explain her to my relatives, anyway.

Mom caught a cold that hit hard over Christmas break. My first drive with my new license was to take her to the hospital for a breathing treatment. She came home with an inhaler to help clear her lungs. "You're staying home from the diner until you're better," I said, tucking her into bed.

"Della, I have to—"

"No, you don't. I can cover what you do while I'm on vacation. I've spent my whole life there, Mom. Let me take care of you."

"I'd keep arguin' with you, but I'm too tired."

I handed her a mug of tea. "We'll pick it up in the morning. *Rest.*"

"I love you, Della. Do I tell you enough?"

Smiling, I turned off the light. "Always."

Dishes needed washing so I walked to the kitchen, plugged the sink, and ran the hot water. Times like this, I wished my father hadn't run off when I was five. I wasn't ready to be a grown-up yet.

Amelia wasn't happy when I told her I needed to work the diner full time and couldn't run around at night now. "Della, you made a commitment—"

"For *her*. My mother comes first, Amelia. *Always*. That's somethin' you gotta learn about me right now. If it comes to her or the world, I'll choose her every time. Now, once she's well, I'll be happy to wander around town with you chasin' cats out of garbage cans."

"No reason to be cheeky, Seven."

"Just wanna make sure we understand each other. I gotta go."

Had to admit, I was glad for the normality of the diner. Felt ridiculous sneaking around town prayin' I didn't run into anyone I knew.

For two weeks, I could pretend I had no secrets.

Chapter Three
2005

You know how winter can bring a hush over the world? The quiet cold lulled me into a sense of security that my world really was normal, mundane, and safe. Amelia didn't send me out anymore, ordering me to the library instead to study. I read, but usually at a table in the diner. Libraries were too quiet for me.

Spring Break was Easter week in March. I lit one of the candles up front on Palm Sunday, Mama snapping pictures. Her lupus was under control for the time being, and she was respecting doc's orders about staying out of the sun even though the week was full of picnics. Amelia was back in London — she didn't say why they called — so I was free as a bird and hangin' out with my youth group. We were doing a skit for the Good Friday service in a few days.

"Kay, Mom, we'll be at the lake all day, so don't wait up." I kissed her on the cheek and skipped to the door.

"Hold up, who's we?"

"Youth group, fishing, picnic…any of this ring a bell?"

"Oh, gosh…of course. My mind's all over the place this week, honey. Have fun and don't get burned."

"Yes, ma'am."

Moira honked outside. She was the youngest of the youth leaders and the one I felt most comfortable with. I hurried out, climbed in the van, and we were off. Guthrie Lake was only four miles out of town, and bordered by lots of trees. I loved how green spring was here.

"Hey, Garvison, long time no see." My cousin Chris.

"Yeah, I know… I need two of me just to have fun this year."

"Your mother's well?" Moira asked.

"Right now. Think flu season convinced her to take it easy, God willing."

"Well, any night you don't want to cook, hon, come on over."

The smell of hot dogs on the grill greeted us when we parked. Mmm, broad daylight. No monsters.

Most every teen in town was at the lake today, and a lot of them were related to me due to my grandmother having six sisters. Men in my family were soldiers and the women got married. When the boys came back from service, they settled somewhere in the state with a good, respectable job. Mama was the third-generation owner of the diner. I wanted more than Guthrie, but I was afraid to leave at the same time…no Oklahoma, no family.

"Della…"

I snapped out of my big thoughts. "Coming!" Dropping my backpack on a table, I hurried to grab a rod and bait. Almost wished I could stick a fishin' pole in Amelia's hands today. The woman's idea of fun was reading ancient Latin. With any luck, supper would be fresh fish filets…

Amelia had warned me, but I was only a kid. I didn't want to believe one of *them* would search me out.

We were sitting around a campfire telling stories when I felt a hum of energy spread through my body, my internal proximity alarm for a Creature. I excused myself to the girl's room and made a detour for my backpack. A stake and collapsible crossbow had been in there for months. I grabbed my weapons and followed my instincts.

The woods weren't quiet at night, insects and birds chirping their tunes. Traversing the dark without a flashlight was still a part of Thirteen's training I wasn't used to. My night vision was better than average, but it was all still mostly shadows for me. I kept going, and heard murmured voices, and a giggle. Great—necking kids. Prime horror movie bait. If it was a vampire I was tracking, it definitely wouldn't resist a young, fresh meal like that. They sat on a fallen log in a tiny clearing.

I couldn't see any danger around, so I closed my eyes and focused on the hum. When I looked again, I saw *it* across the clearing. Red eyes glinted in the moonlight. He smiled at me, exposing white fangs. This was no undead newbie. It was a predator, a master hunter. This close, I could feel his power.

My heart pounded in my chest. We stood on opposite sides, the teens oblivious in between us, and it was fast enough to make at least one of them dead before I could prevent it, if it wanted. God, please let it want to engage me instead.

I blinked and it was no longer there. What the…? I searched between the trunks, up in the trees… Where did you go, Creature?

"Heard there was a paladin in these parts," it whispered behind my ear. I turned to attack, but he grabbed my shoulders hard enough to hold me fast. "Wondered why one of you would possibly be here of all places, but you're just a babe. Have you even killed one of us, yet?"

"I've dusted my share," I said through clenched teeth. The teens continued making out, still oblivious. Sweat trickled down the middle of my back.

"Then you know you're not dealing with a mere fledge." He had a hint of an accent; somewhere in Europe.

"Yes. Are we going to talk all night or what?"

He chuckled, obviously not threatened by me in the least. "Your generation is so hasty. You can listen, dear Paladin, or I can snap your neck like a twig and have my way with your friends over there."

"Fine." The longer he wanted to talk, the better my chances for figuring a way out of this.

"Tell your superiors that Lady Juliet wishes to keep Los Angeles for herself and finds the attempts to remove her quite rude. If The Agency will leave her alone, she'll leave you alone. Continue this war, and every last one of you will die slowly and painfully. Clear?"

"Who's Juliet?" Never got an answer to that question. A blow to the back of the head knocked me unconscious.

****

OW. My first concussion. *Amelia will be so proud.*

My weapons were gone. I sat up, my head swam, and I squeezed my eyes shut.

The couple on the log... I forced my feet to support me and searched the clearing. I was alone. Something was shiny on the log. A spatter of blood. Oh no... Did it carry them off? Were they ditched dead somewhere? Did they make it back to the group?

It was all my fault...

Breathe...you don't know what *happened.*

"Della?"

Oh, thank God. "Here!"

"Della!" Moira entered the clearing followed closely by Pastor Ken. They carried flashlights.

"Hi."

"Honey, you were gone for an hour. Are you alright?" She ran her hands over me, checking for injuries.

"Guess I got lost."

"Let's get you back to the car. You're shaking."

"Is...is anyone else missing?"

"No, but there was an animal attack. Couple kids ran out of the woods with scrapes," Pastor Ken said.

I almost collapsed in relief. Moira wrapped her arm around my shoulders and guided me home. The back of my head hurt badly enough I knew I had a goose egg, if not blood. The vampire probably head-butted me. I'd never been dazed that bad in all the sparring with Thirteen.

I collected my backpack and really did go to the ladies' room this time. The girl in the mirror was a wreck, with leaves and stuff stuck in her hair and circles under her eyes. I cleaned up best I could and Moira drove me back to town early. Mom's car wasn't in the driveway, so I went straight to my room and called Amelia.

When I told her what happened, she freaked. "You're coming to London immediately."

"I can't."

"Della, it's not safe."

I had questions about who Juliet was, but I was so tired. Amelia's fear was obvious in her voice, but worrying about it had to wait 'til at least tomorrow. "I know, but I can't just bail."

"Why do you always have to be so stubborn?"

"God made me that way. Look, I'm exhausted. You needed to know the message and now I'm going to bed."

"Do *not* sleep when you might have a concussion."

"I'm fine."

"Agent Sev —" I hung up.

After checking all the locks on every door and window, I crawled into bed with the light on and cried.

Amelia arrived the next day.

"You are the most reckless, irresponsible—"

"Can we not draw an audience?"

She caught me at rehearsal at church. "Seven, if you don't take this seriously, you'll wish you were back in the woods last night!"

It was the first time I'd seen her anything but polished. Her hair was pulled back in a ponytail instead of up in a fancy twist, and she wore loafers with plain pants and a button-down shirt, not a suit. No jewelry adorned her ears or neck, and her face was bare.

"Okay, okay...let's get somewhere private and you can ream me all you want."

We walked to her car. "I am deeply concerned that an old vampire chose you to pass on a message, especially if it really came from Juliet. There were several possibilities closer to—"

"Who's Juliet?"

"One of the oldest surviving vampires—maybe *the* oldest. She's cruel, cold, ruthless, and very intelligent, and those she sires are chosen to be the same. It's rumored she was nobility as a human and still thinks she's entitled to rule any city she chooses to inhabit. Her latest haunt is Los Angeles."

"Is she the reason so many agents are gone or in recovery?"

"One way or another, yes. We can only hope the vampire last night happened upon you by chance."

"Or?" She met my eyes, and there was sadness and fear in hers. "I still have two months of junior year. Mom won't let me—"

"Seven, every day here puts those you care about at risk. I can't take you away without her permission, but you need to think about what's best."

"I know, but..."

"I'll do my best to protect you, but you need to decide soon."

Mama decided for me. She was home from the diner with a fatigue flare-up when I arrived. I'd never seen her so tired, so weak. Once I fixed her an early supper, I went outside to talk with my guide.

"Amelia…"

"You're not coming," she said in a flat tone.

"I can't yet. She's really hurtin' and I'm all she's got."

She sighed. "You need to find someone else, and soon. How many might die while you put her first?"

"That's not fair."

"Life isn't fair. Do you think you're the only girl in the world asked to make sacrifices at this moment?"

"I…"

"You're not." She pushed her glasses higher on her nose. "Stay in tonight. Without complete training, you're merely another tasty snack."

I went back inside feeling like the biggest heel in Logan County.

Mom didn't feel well enough to leave the house again until Sunday, and that was only for church. Her doctor ordered her to stay home from the diner for the week, which meant I had to pull shifts around school. Amelia picked me up at sundown each night and took me home.

All through April and May, I walked into the house with dread, fearing my mother would have a relapse. By the time I felt safe leaving her, the school year was practically done.

Soon as finals were over the first week of June, I said goodbye to Mom and moved to London. She thought Amelia was taking me to an awesome boarding school and I hated lying to her. Hardest thing I'd ever done. It sucked to give up my youth, but I knew now I was putting the town in danger by staying. That wasn't something I could live with. With my life in a duffle bag, I flew to England with Amelia.

Whatever kind of ID she had got us past all the airport screening and straight to a taxi. "Welcome to London, Seven."

"I can't believe you stuck me on a plane for a whole day. Couldn't we have gone to the place in New York?"

"Your training continues here." The car stopped in front of a plain brick two-story building. She paid the driver and carried her luggage to the door. It was tall and made of steel.

"Why is everyone walking by like they don't notice we're here?"

"There's a ward on HQ that causes all things to ignore the building unless they're looking for it. Discourages trouble." The steel door opened inward and she walked inside.

Following, I felt a bit of drag when I crossed the threshold. "What the…?"

"Security check. Without that ring you're wearing, you'd be denied entry." Her eyes flicked down to the alpha/omega ring on my right hand.

"A spell that checks for a ring?" Inside, it looked like just another office building, the old type with opaque glass in all the doors.

"A ward. It looks for the design of the ring, specifically. Come." Amelia continued down the long hallway to the back of the building, her shoes clicking on the tile.

"Um, you passed the stairs…"

She went to the left of the T-junction and pressed on one of the wood panels. It slid away to reveal a security access keypad. She typed in a code and the wall revealed an elevator.

How very Spy Central of them. "Is there a basement here like in New York?"

A hint of a smirk graced her lips. "In a fashion."

We stepped in the elevator. The buttons were marked "G", "B1", and "B2". Amelia pressed B1. "Identification," a computer voice said.

"Amelia Thornhill."

"Access Granted." The elevator moved. We dropped down one floor. The doors opened on a major office complex.

Wow…

People walking, talking, going in and out of rooms…the hall was wide open with long wooden tables down the center and doors on either side. Unlike the New York school underground, this facility was fully furnished with carpeting and wall treatments. At the other end of the space were more corridors, people going left or right. Most of them were dressed like Amelia, in conservative business attire.

Two agents were talking to a man in a lab coat. One of the agents turned in profile. A familiar face. I ran and hugged Thirteen before I could think better of it.

"Ooof. Hi, kid."

I let go. "Sorry. I'm just glad you're here."

He smiled that California grin. "Welcome to Sacra Aedes."

"Huh?"

"*Sanctuary*. Heard you had quite the ordeal."

"I failed. I was terrified."

He put a hand on my shoulder. "Hey, no one died. You didn't fail. You just need more training."

"Will you be my Mr. Miyagi again?"

He shook his head. "Not this time, Seven. I've gotta be somewhere."

"Oh." Bummer. "Good luck. And keep in touch."

"Yeah. This is Three."

Thirteen's companion was a tall black man that looked closer to thirty. "So you're the pain in Thornhill's side."

I blushed. "Hi."

Amelia took my arm. "Seven, I want you to meet the Director." She nodded to the agents and led me further into the complex. We entered a chemistry lab. Several scientists in lab coats were at work with beakers or computers. "Sir, excuse the interruption."

An older gentleman turned around. He was bald on top, white-haired, and dressed in a three-piece suit. "Amelia. Good to have you back at HQ. This must be Seven."

"Della Garvison, sir," I said, and offered my hand.

He frowned at me, and didn't shake it. "Indeed. You're finally committed to being trained properly, Seven?"

"Yes, sir. I've done what I felt was right, but my hometown is safer now without me."

"Hm. Amelia, show her to her room, then begin exercises immediately. Too much time has already been wasted." He turned his back on us and went back to talking to the scientist.

And I thought my guide could be prickly...

I followed her down more turns until the hall opened into a common room with sofas. She talked to the clerk at a desk and came back with a key and a card. "This will be your home until training is complete, and your room will be waiting for you between missions." She turned the key in the lock for door "7". "This is your meal card. You are allowed three squares a day. Use your card four times, and the next day only gets two."

I wasn't expecting a suite. There was a kitchenette consisting of a microwave, sink, and mini-fridge, and a private bathroom. No TV, though.

"We expect you to keep the room tidy. Cleaning supplies are in a cupboard. Laundry facilities are down the hall. Change into work-out clothes and be out in the common room in five minutes." She left, closing the door.

"Yes, ma'am." I set my luggage on the bed, rotated my shoulder, and unzipped the bag.

A small city under London...who would imagine? I wondered what was on B2. A lot of the people we'd passed were English, but a lot weren't, too. It really was an international operation.

Dressed in stretchy pants and a t-shirt, I tucked my key into my sock and met Amelia. "What's first, Coach?"

She sighed, not amused by my joviality, and started walking. We soon entered a gym. The Agency had a full sports facility down here with machines and weights. "You will resume your cardio schedule from last summer. I can trust you to self-motivate while I retrieve your schedule?"

"Yes, ma'am." I headed for the elliptical. *Shed*-ule still cracked me up inside. English people talked funny.

Guess I *was* kinda soft. Since last summer, I'd let P.E. be my exercise except for my sweeps around town. I occasionally went through katas when I wanted to clear my mind and was sure to be left alone. Mama would have too many questions about me practicing martial arts.

Without Thirteen kicking my butt, I went through a light routine while I waited.

Amelia walked back in carrying a file. "Prepare to devote your mind, body, and soul, Seven. Since you are still finishing school, you will have to work that much harder to keep up with the others. You will eat, sleep, and breathe training of one sort or another. Are you sure this is your choice?"

"I can't really stay at home, can I?"

"No." She took off her glasses and for a moment, she wasn't my boss. "I do understand what you've had to give up, Della. I know this isn't the life you envisioned, but our calling *is* worth it. And you're not alone." I nodded, a lump in my throat. Maybe I did have a friend here. That said, she got back to business. "Report to Medical first thing in the morning."

"What for?"

"Your physical. It's all very routine. We need a baseline for treating you in the future."

"Oh. Yay."

Medical turned out to be a mini-hospital. Passing an operating room made me uneasy...nothing was going on past the window in the door, but the fact they had one here was a big deal. How bad an injury or illness could they handle? I handed my ID to a nurse at a desk. She ran it through a scanner.

"Ah, Seven. The doctor will see you in Room Two down there. Please disrobe and put on the gown hanging on the back of the door."

"Undress?"

One eyebrow arched. "You've been to a doctor before, haven't you?"

"Yes, but—"

"This isn't a request, Recruit."

"Yes, ma'am." I took the clipboard she handed me and went to the exam room. A family history form and pen were on the board. I stripped down to my bra and undies, put on the gown, and hopped up to sit on the table and fill out the form while I waited, hoping it'd be a female doc. There was a knock on the door a few minutes later and a woman in her fifties walked in.

"Welcome to Sanctuary, Seven. I'm Dr. Lee. Let's get started, hmm?" She took my blood pressure and pulse rate, then stuck the stethoscope on my back to listen to me breathe.

"Cold!"

"Sorry. They're always like that. Do you have any allergies you know of?"

"No..."

"Outstanding injuries or ailments?"

"Not at the moment."

"Hold your breath, please. And, exhale. Good." She put the stethoscope in her coat pocket and pulled out a tiny hammer. "I'm going to check your reflexes." She knocked on my knees, then examined all my joints. "Hop down and stand up straight, please."

I did. "What's this for?"

"Checking the alignment of your spine." Her fingers trailed down my vertebrae. "Good." We continued through the usual eyes and ears check and she asked about my typical diet. Then, she went to a drawer and pulled out a needle and vial. "I'm going to take a blood sample. Sit down again, please."

I didn't like needles. My veins should stay hole-free, thank you very much. When she aligned the needle with my left arm, I turned my head away. It hurt less if you didn't look. The vial filled, the needle was extracted, and she taped a cotton ball to my arm.

"Just a few more questions, and then we'll go to X-Ray. Have you ever been sexually active?"

"No!"

"Don't be afraid to be honest, Seven. I'm bound to confidentiality like any other doctor. Have you engaged in any kind of sexual activity before?"

"*No*. Haven't touched or been touched. What does that have to do with killing demons?"

"This is about your health record, Seven. Teenagers aren't known for taking the best precautions. I'm not here to judge you, alright?"

I folded my arms around me. "Just don't like the implication."

She wrote more notes on her chart. "Have you had a pelvic exam before?"

"You're not going to do that here, are you? Because I do not give my permission."

She sighed. "Under the circumstances, it isn't strictly necessary. Do you have any problems with your cycle? Pain, nausea, etcetera?"

"No."

"When was the onset of your last period?" I told her. This was so embarrassing. I didn't talk about my monthly with Mom, let alone a stranger. "I'm going to give you a prescription of birth control pills—"

"Excuse me?"

"It's standard procedure with our female operatives. Demons have a very acute sense of smell in most cases, Seven. The hormones will make you skip your period and keep you safer out in the field. There are possible side effects, of course, like with any medication, but—"

"You want me to artificially stop my cycle indefinitely? How is that healthy?"

"Seven, you won't be allowed in the field if you don't comply. The scent of blood is a danger to you and your team. You can ask the female agents, but none of them has had a complication. This particular drug is a low-dose hormone. You shouldn't feel any different except in gaining freedom from your period." She handed me a small box. "You'll take one of these every day. When you're about to run out, come see me."

"I have to think about it."

"Noted. Come, let's finish your tests."

I followed her out of the room. The floor was cold to my bare feet, but at least the gown wasn't the backless variety.

A couple hours later, I empathized with lab rats. After the x-ray and a lung capacity test, she had me dress and put me through a stress test on a treadmill, seeing what my heart did under load. I was then sent to an optometrist to check my vision, and another tech who tested the acuity of my hearing. The doc took a sample of my hair, too, before I was done. I wasn't allowed breakfast before going to Medical, so by the time they let me go, I was exhausted and famished. Found the chow hall and thank God it wasn't limited to plain chicken breasts and vegetables.

Since Amelia found me, a new generation of agents was popping up and the dorm was full of new recruits in their first year. It was good news, except we'd all be going out there green. They were all types from all places, and a lot of them just as scared as I was. We were all under eighteen and expected to save the world.

The Agency had assigned the recent newbies in odds for boys and evens for girls. Guess it made easier bookkeeping or something. Ten, Twelve, and Sixteen were the girls' designations. The boys made up Five, Nine, Eleven, Fifteen, Seventeen, and Twenty-one. Not too conducive to nicknames, huh?

Five went to HQ about the same time Amelia found me and he was the only one older than I was. He'd spent months in a cast with a badly broken leg, though, so he hadn't made it out in the field, yet. Eleven was seventeen, a few months younger than me, and still growing into his frame. Poor kid was all limbs and tripped over his own feet half the time. I didn't really know the others.

Most of the kids were alright, though. Some of them were able to meet the agents they were replacing. The wounded Actives lived in a different wing of the complex close to the med clinic, and worked upstairs if they were able. Most of them were using canes or crutches. A couple were missing a part of a limb or two. The attack must've been horrific from the burn scars not all of them could hide. Recruits shied away from them, fear driving them into denial about what they might become.

Thirteen introduced me to all of them before he shipped out. He treated his disabled friends like everything was normal and I wondered if I'd ever have the strength to do the same.

I got up at 5:00AM, ate, ran on the treadmill, then did homework until noon. With Amelia's private instruction of my senior subjects, I was progressing through the school year faster than I would at home. Provided she was pleased with my work, I would be going home to take semester finals before Christmas break.

Lunch was a protein shake — yuck — then I was in Master Takeshi's combat training class until three.

Sensei was a *lot* harder on me than my other instructors. "Learn to like pain. It means you are still alive." He says this while making me do a handstand on wood blocks for who knows how long. He won't let me wear my watch. My arms are shaking, the muscles burning, and I'm fighting to keep my body straight in the air so I don't fall. "Let go, Seven. Stop *trying* to balance and *be*."

I take a deep breath through my nose and close my eyes. My body stops fighting and I feel like I'm floating.

"That's it...now attack."

"What?" I toppled off the blocks and landed on the wood floor hip first. Ow.

"You have to focus, Seven. Your mind can never drift out in the field. All information should flow through you like water as you collect what you need and discard what you don't. A voice should never startle you."

"Well, sorry, Mr. Miyagi, I concentrate on one thing at a time. It's how I'm wired."

He swept my legs out from under me when I started to stand. "Pay attention."

"You just enjoy giving me bruises."

"What does not destroy you makes you stronger, Seven. Ignore pain."

I rolled further away and stood. "To what extent? Broken bones? Severed limbs?"

He sighed. "You chose to be here. Why do you fight it?"

"I... I don't know."

His dark eyes saw too much. "I believe you do."

"Fine, I don't want this... I don't want to be a freak or away from my mother and friends or learning to be an expert in death. I'm only seventeen, sir. I don't want to know monsters exist, or any of it."

He walked to me and placed a brown hand on my shoulder. "Seven, death is what we are. It is our gift to the world. For the vampire, we've released a soul from bondage. But not every part of our work is death. A werewolf can't help being infected. We teach them what they are and how to restrain themselves during the full moon. Our scientists are working on a cure."

"That's...that's good."

"The Agency helps the possessed, the misguided, the enslaved. The supernatural world presents more dangers to humanity than death. It's your destiny to help those people." He turned away. "Lesson over. Go back to your quarters and evaluate your heart."

"Yes, sir."

****

During my time alone, I prayed for guidance and thought about the way I'd been raised. My guidelines. You don't whine, you don't quit, and you don't disrespect your elders. I kept using my youth as an excuse, but it wasn't good enough... I'd asked for somethin' bigger since I was ten, right? Now was my chance, the brass ring. So what if The Agency wasn't part of my plans...God worked in mysterious ways and I knew deep down I couldn't turn my back on what I'd learned.

I decided to grow up and stop pining for what I thought I was missing.

Another two hours of schoolwork, then weapons proficiency for two hours, and supper. At eight, I had tactical class for an hour, then it was back in the gym until eleven.

Then, sleep.

Lather, rinse, repeat.

Six months would have to be endured before I'd see home again.

Sanctuary was a lot bigger than the footprint of the building above it and without my photographic memory it would've taken me weeks of following a map to know where to go, even with the recruits' area all in one section. The Council made sure HQ had all the creature comforts of an above-ground corporation, making you almost forget we were all below the earth. Still, even with the potted plants here and there and natural lighting effects, it wasn't outside air or sunshine. I kept hoping for a field trip or training exercise anywhere else but here.

How did they all stand it? I watched for the staff to go up to dinner or grocery shopping, but people rarely left. Could be my imagination, though. I was in class or asleep every day.

Five shared my common area. The residence section was divided into groups of eight suites, so we were in one-through-eight, the next complex was nine-through-sixteen, and so forth. Our designation was our suite number, so this was one of a few areas where agents and recruits mixed, when the agents were home. Five still did rehab on his leg, so I usually ran into him in the gym.

"How's the PT coming?" I asked.

He was doing reps on the calf machine. "Same as yesterday when you asked. But I'm not limping anymore, so they're finally letting me train."

"Cool, you got clearance? Takeshi is going to make you wish you were still in the wheelchair, just so you know." I started my warm-up on the elliptical.

"The little Japanese dude? He comes up to here." Gesturing to the middle of his sternum, he didn't look concerned.

"Size doesn't matter, Five. Sensei knows his stuff. Every class is pain so far. I think he's a sadist."

"A what?"

"A guy that enjoys the pain of others. And he's tricky, too. It'll suck if you're a slow learner."

"Think I can handle it."

"If you say so." Other kids came in and I shut up. It was impossible to get a workout done if the Chatty Twins thought you were open to having your ear yapped off.

Five and I were the only recruits to take the gym seriously, maybe because we both had goals. The three girls gossiped while walking on the treadmill unless a Guide was cracking the whip and the boys usually played around and dropped a weight plate on someone's foot or ogled the females in spandex.

Fifteen often made me uncomfortable. If he kept staring at my boobs, one of these days I was going to break his nose.

Wow, all the fight training was getting to me. I finished my miles and went to my room.

Two weeks of this place and it was already getting to me. What would I be like after a month?

Three?

Six?

Grabbing a piece of stationery, I wrote a letter to Mama about school and my grades. I missed her so much. Maybe I could persuade Amelia to let me pick up some postcards so Mom could see bits of London.

Sanctuary was normal in some ways. They had cake in the cafeteria on someone's birthday. People griped about their bosses. Those allowed to date fell in love (for everyone except the Agents set up families and personal ties). There was even a retirement party for the Director's secretary Agnes who was eighty-two years old. She was moving to a drier climate for her rheumatism. I only met her once but the administrative staff seemed sad to see her go.

B2 remained off-limits and secret.

Chapter Four

December

Sensei head-butted me.

"You cheated! You teach me forms and harnessing energy and the honor of a warrior, then you *cheat*." I touched the hurt spot on my forehead and my fingers came away bloody.

"In a fight you use every advantage in order to defeat your opponent. Know the rules so you may break them. Honor is optional. If your enemy is more concerned with honor than living, use it against them. This is how a demon will fight you." Sensei kept circling me.

"Doesn't matter. I'm not sinking to their level."

"Your choice. But one day you might have to choose honor, or death."

"I'll cross that bridge when I get to it, Master."

We started sparring again. He was strong, and fast, but I was faster with more reach. The fight picked up speed and we ramped up the power of our blows. It was something of a shock to me when I managed to pin him to the floor, my fist on his chest from plunging an imaginary stake through his heart.

"I win."

"I'm human. If you end up here with a demon, make sure it's dead. Not every species has their heart in the same place."

"Then what?"

"How's your sword arm?" He rolled us, reversing our positions, and did a dive and tuck to the weapons wall. Show-off.

We were about to go at it again, when there was a knock on the doorframe. Sixteen stood in the doorway, prepared for her lesson.

I bowed to Sensei and went to my room.

There were only a couple days left before I went home for Christmas vacation and I wanted to get some last-minute studying in. If I passed all my tests, I only needed a couple more credits to graduate. Somehow, Amelia convinced the teachers at my school to send materials at the pace I was progressing at, and I would probably take my finals in April around my birthday. I would walk down the aisle at graduation in June, visit with Mama a bit, and leave on my first assignment for The Agency.

"Ah, there you are," Amelia said. "Good news. After holiday, you'll get to go on live exercises."

My eyes widened. "Battle simulation?"

"Indeed. There is little more you'll gain from a classroom, Seven. The agents usually find it fun, like a retreat." She patted my shoulder. "Think of it as a game."

"Yeah..." I'd tackle that thought later.

Right now, all I wanted was home.

"Della, let me look at you!" Mama held me out at arm's length in Baggage Claim. "We need to put some meat on your bones. They're obviously working you too hard."

"I'm fine, Mom, really..." At five-foot-six and lean, I currently resembled a tall gymnast, like those girls on the college teams. They've grown into height and curves, but the power's still there. I never wore make-up when I'd just be sweatin' it off, so I still had the face of a kid.

"Your hair's shorter, too. Who cut it?"

"Ma..." My braid stopped just past that knob on the spine above my shoulder blades. You learned quick that Sensei would use a ponytail or free hair against you, so most of the girls had short hair. I wrapped mine into a tight bun when I sparred. Mama always liked my hair down to my waist, though.

We had dinner and hung out, watching a Christmas movie, then she went to bed. When I lay down, I couldn't fall asleep. My body was used to being exhausted at night and I'd done little more than sit the last twelve hours.

"Screw it." I changed into active gear and snuck out my window, a hood pulled over my auburn hair.

Hunting in Guthrie this time was different. For one, the night was creeping below freezing. For two, I'd just thought of it as *hunting*.

Didn't expect to find anything, really, but the practice made me feel alive. Anticipation, like waiting to blow out the candles, but darker.

Deadlier.

They would fear *me*. If I did find a demon, I *knew* it would be toast tonight.

But no such luck.

When my nose lost feeling, I went home and climbed into my warm bed. Time here was precious.

Chapter Five

January 2006

The Agency loaded us on a small jet. Did they own it? No clue. Only the active Agents knew where we were going. Us recruits were in the dark…all any of us had gathered was they didn't want to run the sim in snow.

I moved to sit next to Thirteen. "Hey."

He smiled. "Hey."

"Been anywhere interesting?"

"Seven, you can't butter me up into spilling the deets." He almost always managed to see through me, dang it.

"I wasn't! I'm genuinely curious."

"Well, then, the surfing in Australia was great."

"You went *surfing*?" I'd been stuck underground for months, and he's having fun in the sun…geesh.

He shrugged. "Nothin' else to do during the daytime. We were watching a clan of wannabe vamp gangsters, see, so all the work was at night."

Lookin' for a good tale, I angled my body in the seat to face him. "What happened?"

"Set fire to the building, picked off the stragglers, and came home."

A fire? There had to be more to the story than that. "Wasn't that dangerous? The fire could spread to innocent properties."

"Nothing was innocent in that neighborhood, believe me. We worked on the Other Side."

"The other side of what?"

"It's a parallel world to ours, the stuff we can't see with the naked eye, and a realm of spirits. In a peaceful, innocent place, the Other Side could look really beautiful, but where demons congregate, they turn it into a nightmare. That feeling of a sudden chill up your spine—that comes from something on the Other Side passing too close to your 'echo', the intangible life energy of all living beings. A summoner can use your echo to bring you to the Other Side and trap you in Hell."

"You mean nasty things we can't even see have access to us *all the time*?"

He shook his head. "Man, what's Thornhill teaching you? It's more complicated than that. It would take a lot of magic juice, and something personal from the target, like hair or blood. Most things don't want to wander in the spirit world."

"Why not?"

"The good is *too* good and the bad is *really* bad. You see the true state of a person or thing. Not something you forget."

"You've been there?"

The look in his eyes became a bit haunted. "A few times, when it was necessary. The Director doesn't ask it of everybody."

"Why you, then?"

"Anybody tell ya you ask too many questions?"

I could take a hint. "So…fight drills. How's that work?"

"We really play Red Rover. Don't tell HQ." He winked.

I elbowed his arm. "Jerk. Fine, don't tell me."

He grinned and my tummy fluttered. I shut off the seventeen-year-old part of me that wanted to crush on him. We weren't the kind of people that got to date, and he was my superior. In another life...well, in another life we wouldn't even meet, with a seven year age difference and comin' from different states. The Order discouraged "entanglements" so we remained "objective".

I went back to sitting with the recruits. Someone had brought a checker board.

The plane landed.

"Recruits — welcome to St. George Island. You won't find it on any published map." The Alpha — Number One — stood at the front of the cabin. He was the oldest active agent and usually worked alone. I'd only seen him once at HQ before. "This exercise will pit you against the Agents." He held up a paintball gun. "If you are marked 'dead', you stay down and play dead because you are out of the game. Those that survive today will get a new objective tomorrow. File out!" The Alpha missed his calling as a D.I.

"I bet he stands at attention in his sleep," Sixteen murmured behind me. I pressed my lips together to keep from laughing.

We exited the plane, backpacks on our shoulders, and formed a line to wait for instruction. It was ten of us against six of them. Jungle was the only scenery around the landing strip. The Alpha started walking and the Agents fell in line. We shrugged and followed. It felt like we'd crossed into the southern hemisphere, summer heat melting me inside my winter clothes. He led us for several minutes down a supply road, until we reached a group of buildings that looked like military barracks.

"Women on the left. Men on the right," he ordered, pointing to the two closest structures. The flat gray was very bland in the midst of the lush greenery.

Bunk beds were inside. We looked to Four, the senior agent in the room, for instruction. "Pick a bed and get changed, ladies. Alpha won't wait long to start."

A set of fatigues was on each mattress. Convenient. I stripped to my sports bra and buttoned the shirt, then hopped into the pants and wrapped the ankle ties around my boots. You didn't want loose pant-legs in a jungle. With my clothes folded neatly on the bed, I took my smaller survival pack out of the big one and slung it over my shoulder. Four and I were the first gals outside.

"Look after your team, Seven," she said in a mild Spanish accent, wearing the custom-made suit all the agents had.

"Huh?"

"The recruits. They look to you as the one of them with most experience." She left me for the Alpha's building and knocked on the door.

The other three girls rushed out behind me. "Did we miss anything?"

"Nope." I turned to them. "We have an even-numbered team, so I think the buddy system would be a good idea. Watch each other's backs."

"I'll be happy to watch your backside, Seven." Ugh...Fifteen. Every group had the annoying person who looked at life as a joke and never shut up. He was ours.

"Get your mind out of the gutter, Fif," Sixteen said. "This is serious."

Fifteen was barely sixteen years old, and strutted around like he was the hottest stuff in town. He acted like being a demon hunter made him a rock star, always arriving late to class, disobeying curfew, sneakin' out of HQ, and generally reckless in training. I didn't want him anywhere near me with live ammo.

"Recruits!" We snapped to attention and formed a line. Alpha analyzed us. "This is not a game, children. This team will be trying to *kill you*." He stopped before us with his hands clasped behind his back. "There are red flags on the trees marking the boundaries of this exercise. Do not cross those boundaries. Work as a team, survive as a team. The Agents will have a two minute head start into the forest. You will follow carrying these dummy rifles. Shoot to kill, children—head and heart. Your opponent will not stop because you discolored his arm. Understood."

"Yes, sir!"

"Collect your weapon, helmet, and goggles." The agents were already fully outfitted and jogged into the jungle minus the Alpha. He had a stopwatch. I didn't know what time to set my watch to, but the sun looked to be at about nine o'clock—just mid-morning and we were already sweating. Good thing I had a water bottle in my pack. "Go!"

We took off for the trees, slowing down to a cautious quickstep when we were close.

"Seven's idea of splitting into pairs is a good one. We're too obvious as a group," Sixteen said. The boys stuck together, and Ten and Twelve disappeared off to my left. "Guess it's you and me," she said.

Two pairs of footsteps started following me into the rainforest. I turned around. "Lev?"

"They left me behind," Eleven admitted. Poor guy.

"Fifteen went off alone, didn't he?" He nodded, and rolled his eyes. I sighed. So typical. "No big. Just stay low. Your height is like a beacon."

Smiling shyly, he nodded again, and fell in behind my right shoulder. We moved into the jungle in wedge formation. The wildlife was noisy at all the commotion, birds calling in every direction. Under the canopy, the light took on a greenish hue, and the ground covering was damp and spongy from the decaying leaves. I had a feeling for Thirteen's tactics, but no experience with the rest. We could expect *anything*.

"Do you think they'll start shooting at us right away?" Sixteen whispered.

I mimed zipping my lips shut.

"I'm just wondering what to expect."

I held my hand up, signaling a pause, and reached in my pocket for a tiny notepad and pencil, scribbled THEY CAN HEAR YOUR VOICE IF I CAN, and showed it to her. She sighed and wrote back I CHATTER WHEN I'M NERVOUS. Eleven sat on a fallen log. I flipped the page and wrote GET OVER IT, showed it to her, and shoved the pad and pencil back in my pocket. If she wanted to give us away, I'd leave her behind, but I'd rather she learned to be quiet.

A twig snapped. We turned our heads to the sound. I dropped into a crouch behind a bush. Eleven showed me a rock and hurled it far into the trees. Heck of an arm. We heard the "pop, pop" of a paint gun firing. I pointed in the opposite direction and jerked my head to the side to signal "let's move". Sixteen took the rear.

We crept along another few minutes, still not hearing any signs of combat.

Sixteen squeaked behind me. I turned, ready to shoot. There was no need. She was pointing at a snake. Eleven rolled his eyes and kept walking.

Pop.

Twenty-one stood out of the bushes. "Ah, crap."

"Same team, idiot," Lev said. He had a blue splat center-torso.

"I heard you coming and—"

"Is he out now?" Sixteen asked.

Pop. Twenty-one got a red paint ball to the side of the head.

"Down!" I yelled. This is why you didn't send kids to war. I crawled among the brush parallel to the boundary, Lev on my heels. Sixteen had run to Twenty-one. I let her go. The agent was sneaky and fast and the only way to survive was to be hard to hit.

More pops behind us, further away. I paused behind an extra-wide tree, rolled onto my butt to sit with my back to it, and took out the pad and pencil. THEY KNOW THE TERRITORY TOO WELL. WE NEED HIGH GROUND.

Lev pointed up.

IN THE CANOPY?

He nodded.

IF YOU'RE GOOD AT CLIMBING GO FOR IT.

He gave me a thumb's up, shouldered his rifle, and took a hold of my tree's trunk. Within seconds he had reached the lower branches. I'd have to start calling him Monkey Man. He mimicked one of the parrot calls, and got an answering cry, then I heard flapping wings to the south. He pointed in that direction and held up two fingers. Two agents. I nodded and gestured for him to head that way. With any luck, they wouldn't be expecting a sniper.

Took a sip from the bottle in my pack and considered how to be proactive about this. I had supplies to set a couple non-lethal traps. That took time, though, and I had no idea how the team was doing. Time to get competitive. Being on the defensive wasn't fun.

When I heard, "Sniper! Sniper! Man down!" I took advantage of the distraction and charged deeper into the forest, looking for agents in head-to-toe black. As the canopy thickened above, less brush grew around the bases of the trees and the light dimmed. The cover was insulator-y, keeping the air humid and hot. Sweat dripped from under my helmet, and down my back. I wanted to leave my fatigue jacket behind, but my white arms would be a dead giveaway against all this green.

Assuming Eleven took out the two, it left four for me and what was left of the team. *If* we had a team left…I hadn't seen the other six since we entered the jungle. Should've asked the Alpha how big the engagement zone was. I could be wandering for hours before finding more red flags.

"*Seven*," someone said in a hissed whisper. I looked up. The twins, Ten and Twelve, were in a tree.

"What are you doing?"

"Three almost got us, and we ran and hid up here. You're the first person we've seen in a long time."

"We shouldn't talk. Get down from there."

These two were too young for this life at fourteen years old, in my opinion. Amelia said anyone with the gift had to be trained, and I agreed with self-defense and warning them about what might come, but I'd been too young to handle it a year ago. How were these two going to survive when they were afraid of a paintball fight?

Ten wasn't carrying a weapon. I held up my rifle and looked at her questioningly. She hung her head. I sighed, pulled a whistle out of my pack, and wrote on the notepad IF YOU SEE THE ENEMY APPROACHING US, BLOW THIS. She read it, nodded, and took the whistle. I shooed her back up the tree. Her sister gestured for me to lead the way.

Guess the Agents were making a point that real hunting could have you wandering, searching for a long time before finding your prey. I'd expected them to be more aggressive, make an example out of our inexperience.

The waiting would've made me paranoid a year ago. Was I more used to this life than I thought? I picked a quick pace weaving through the trees, keeping my eyes and ears open. A body dropped behind me and I spun to land a kick in the intruder's solar plexus.

It was Lev. He doubled over. "Nice reflexes," he groaned.

"Sorry!"

He coughed; tried to stand up straight. "Geeze, Seven, you kick like a mule."

"The hip sled is my friend. Can you move?"

He nodded. I nudged Twelve into walking again and resumed a slower course. Eleven got his wind back after a few minutes.

I passed him a note HOW MANY DID YOU GET? He held up three fingers, then bent one down. ONE INJURED? I wrote. A thumb's up. Cool beans…if we came across the "wounded" agent they'd have to act hurt.

"I'm hungry. Has to be close to midday by now," Twelve said.

"Be quiet!"

"But I'm bored. This is like a *Predator* movie without the Predators."

Lev said, "A Predator would eat *you* for lunch."

"Nuh-uh…they only take trophies."

"Shut up or go back to your sister," I said.

"Who made you the boss? Eleven actually got *kills*."

I walked up to her and stared down the three-inch difference in height. "*Fine*. I don't need tag-a-longs to survive."

"Seven, don't go like that…" Lev said.

"Wouldn't piss her off, Recruit. Might get a right hook to the jaw."

Thirteen.

I took cover and glanced around for him, but I couldn't tell where the voice came from. Lev had his weapon up, his back to a tree. Twelve froze in place. "Been followin' us, Coach, or just get lucky?" I called.

"Can't give away all my secrets, kid."

Lev and I aimed our rifles to my right. "Care to test how much I've learned?" I asked. He liked challenging me to show new ideas. I hoped he couldn't resist a challenge in general.

"Two against one? Odds aren't in your favor." The *other* side. He was circling us.

Wait, two…? *Crap.* Twelve ran off. Coward.

Lev rolled his eyes and crouched with me. "Is he a good shot?" he whispered.

"Even blindfolded."

"Damn."

"Yup. He's playin' with us right now because he doesn't have a clear shot."

"Makes us equal for the moment." An optimist.

I got out my pencil and wrote YOU COULD GO. HE'S NOT A SPRINTER AND YOU HAVE A LONGER STRIDE. He shook his head: an emphatic no.

I smiled my thanks and wondered what to do next. We were saved from deciding by a firefight running between us and where we last heard Thirteen. Five, Nine, and Seventeen were being chased by two agents who'd both been winged by blue paint. Lev and I exchanged a look and shot at the agents. Seventeen went down before we hit one, but Five was able to regroup and shoot the other. That left Thirteen against four of us.

"You two been hiding here all day?" Five teased.

"Fight's not over, hot shot. Thirteen is still nearby."

Nine and Five instantly formed the other two points of the compass so we covered all directions with our backs to each other.

"Why didn't he join the other agents?" Lev asked.

Good question. Territorial respect, probably. And pride. They shouldn't need help against a bunch of kids.

"What's he waiting for?"

"Maybe he left now he's out-numbered."

"He hasn't given up," I said.

"He should. There are easier targets out there."

"Like Ten and Twelve," Lev muttered.

"HELP!" Someone called out from the wilderness.

"Is that Fifteen?"

"SOMEBODY!" Crap…what had he gotten his butt into now?

I took off in the direction of his voice. And almost fell into a sinkhole. The brush nearly disguised the entrance. My foot slipped down the edge. I caught an exposed root and stopped my fall, then scrambled back to my feet. "Fifteen?"

"Down here. Hey, cutie. I heard voices and hoped I wasn't hearing things."

I dug a flashlight out of my pack and shone it down the hole. "Are you hurt?"

"Knocked myself out for a bit when I landed, but otherwise okay. Tell me you have rope or something."

"Give me a minute."

The guys caught up as I took the line out of my pack and started fastening it around a tree. "What's going on?"

"Seven is being a doll and rescuing me," Fifteen said.

I tugged on the knot, making sure it would hold, and dropped the length of rope down the hole. As long as he wasn't too injured to, he could climb up on his own.

"Girl Scout in a past life, Seven?" Nine asked.

"I take this job seriously. My mother needs me to. How ya comin', Fifteen?"

"How many of you are up there? Just pull me up."

I stepped aside for the boys and gestured *be my guest*. Had to be around ninety degrees by now and high humidity, making me grateful I remembered the water bottle.

"Good work. No hesitation to rescue." Thirteen stood behind my left shoulder, whispering in my ear.

I froze. "Gonna shoot me, Coach?"

"Exercise is over. No one left." We watched them pull a dirty Fifteen out of the hole and start ribbing him for not lookin' where he was going.

"Doesn't answer the question."

"No. Extenuating circumstances. He should be looked over by the medic and it's the team's job to get him home."

"Very generous of you."

He didn't reply. I turned around and he was gone. Some day, he'd have to tell me how he did that. Fifteen had a bump on his head and generally felt bruised all over. He started complaining about his ankle hurting on the way back. When we broke into the clearing, the recruits cheered.

Thirteen showed up ten minutes later. "Guess I missed them," he told the Alpha with a shrug.

Supper was cooked over a fire pit. Aside from the barracks, we were roughin' it. There was running water from a well, but we only had five minutes for showers and the water was cold. We sat on hewn logs waiting for the Alpha's next speech. My reward for helping Fifteen out of the hole was getting out of KP.

"You recruits are a bunch of sissies! Could smell the lot of ya across a street with your perfumes and body washes. You know what that screams to a predator? Lunch! Your average vampire has a nose two times more sensitive than a bloodhound. *Gee-zus*—think, children." His face was especially red in the firelight as he dressed us down.

Well, not me personally. Mama had allergies, so I'd grown up on fragrance-free soaps. Couldn't do anything about my shampoo, but I didn't use a strong-smelling version of that, either. If there was means to smell not human, I'd be willing to learn, but Amelia hadn't mentioned one, yet.

I sat staring at the flames and thinking of the fireplace at home, hoping Mama was keeping warm. There'd been snow in Guthrie this winter.

"You look far away from here," my mentor said, joining me on the log.

"Home."

"Ah."

"Ever think of yours, from before?"

He stared into the flames, too. "Sometimes. I'm human. You did a good job today."

"Thanks. What's up?"

"Can't I chat?"

"Sure...but we've never hung out, Coach."

"Alright... A team is going to L.A. soon. I want you on it."

Los Angeles? "But we were warned away. When I told Amelia who the message came from, she was scared and wanted me at HQ right away. Why would they want you to do that?"

"It's undercover work. A rotating schedule of intel gatherers. We're not abandoning innocent citizens just because Juliet thinks she owns the place. She's just as vulnerable to a stake through her heart as any other vamp." He spoke with conviction, the rightness of his cause adding righteous indignation to his voice.

"I'm not going on missions until after graduation. Amelia and I have an agreement. If you still need me in summer, I'm yours."

"Everything has to be on your terms, doesn't it?"

"Don't sigh at me like that. There are much more experienced agents that'd be better for the job and you know it. Look, I promised my mother, okay? It's the last time she'll get to see me do somethin' normal."

"Okay, okay. I know how much she means to you."

"Thanks. So, is the Alpha torturing us tomorrow, or was this it?"

"I don't know. No two years are the same."

"Great."

The Alpha woke us at 5:00AM with an air raid siren. Lord knows how long it'd been on St. George. We scrambled into clothes and hurried outside. I took my pill and vitamins with a gulp of water on the move. We were sent on a run around the perimeter of the island with the condition if we didn't finish, we didn't get breakfast. Back when I trained with Thirteen, he called this *running 'til you puke*. Half the recruits left remnants of supper on the beach trail. Fifteen walked most of the way 'cause of his ankle, but even he made it.

The Agents had cooked while we were away, and served breakfast once we'd hydrated.

The Alpha entered the camp circle. "Who of you can swim?" Everybody raised their hand but me. Uh-oh. "Seven, you're telling me in all the time you've been with The Agency you haven't been in the water?"

"No one asked me to, sir."

"Not a single lesson in your civilian life?"

The recruits stared at me while he fired off his questions. "No, sir. There were more important concerns, sir."

He muttered a few curses. "Well, what am I supposed to do with you, then, Recruit?"

"I-I don't know, sir," I mumbled, and dropped my eyes to my lap, the attention making my cheeks burn.

"Agents — take the recruits to the beach to run water rescue drills. Not you, Thirteen." What did he need Thirteen for? I hated disappointing authority figures. I'd always minded my teachers, been a good student, not talked back at home… "You tested this girl, correct?"

"Yes, sir." No grin present on my trainer's face this time.

"And you didn't put her in the pool."

"There's no pool or nearby lake at the New York base, sir."

More curses from the Alpha I didn't feel old enough to hear.

"Ms. Thornhill is her guide, sir, for almost two years. The oversight lies with her, if anyone," Thirteen added. "You can't fault the kid for lack of instruction."

The Alpha opened his mouth to respond, or argue, then paced a few feet away and back again. "I suppose you're right, Agent. You'll take the girl back to HQ and follow up on any other holes in her repertoire. Seven, you're done on St. George."

"I'm sorry, sir."

He nodded curtly and left us. I bit the inside of my cheek so I wouldn't cry.

"Hey, you're not a failure, so stop thinking it."

I shook my head. "Know why I don't swim? It's not that I haven't been to a lake before."

Thirteen sat next to me. "Okay…"

"I'm afraid to put my head underwater, to be completely engulfed by a substance I can't breathe. Mama told me once that my father tried taking me to a toddler class at the Y before he bailed. I freaked in the pool, she said. Never took me back. Mom had to worry more about puttin' food on the table once she was alone."

"Do you remember the lesson at all?"

"No. Only the fear. I'd wade in the lake a bit when my youth group made trips, but I always conveniently 'forgot' a swimsuit so they wouldn't ask me to play. Pathetic, right?"

"Nah. We all have phobias in here somewhere," he said, tapping his temple.

"What's yours?"

"Oh, no…you'll have to get me drunk first." He stood and started walking to the barracks.

"But I just shared mine."

"And I'll keep your secret, but no."

"Awww…"

I tried to get him to fess up the whole way home, but he wouldn't budge.

Chapter Six

Finding a swimsuit in England in January was impossible, so I ended up borrowing one. Thirteen suggested I start practicing holding my breath underwater in the bath tub, but even that was terrifying. The Agency didn't have a pool in the facility, so he found a gym in the city with one.

When we walked out on the deck, he peeled off his t-shirt and walked into the pool by the steps. Oh, gosh…I hadn't thought about…man, he was pretty. Sinewy muscle head to toe with a nice tan from the recent trip south. Heat bloomed in my face and I averted my eyes.

"Didn't you ever think swimming could be fun?" He did a somersault under water just to show off.

"No."

"You didn't look at all the other kids and wish that could be you?"

Don't look at the hot agent… "You're a lousy teacher."

"Aren't you a little old to pout?" he teased.

"Can you not phrase everything as a question?"

He floated backward toward the deep end. "Fine. Never learn. Maybe you're suited to be an analyst or one of the secretaries."

Wait a minute… "I won't be an agent if I can't swim?"

"It's a liability. You'll be benched until you get over your fear. Ask the Big Boss if you don't believe me."

Uh, no. He already wasn't impressed with me to begin with after I dared to put my mother over "my calling". I'd be sent home with no salary for sure, and I couldn't do that to Mom. I was learning I'd do a heck of a lot for her.

"Fine. But *be nice*. No more dunking me."

"Cross my heart and hope to die." Thirteen swam over to me. Didn't take him long. "Do you trust me?"

"What kind of question is that?"

He eye-rolled. "Do you trust me to teach you or not?"

"When did you learn to swim?"

"Mommy and Me class when I was six months old. I grew up in Malibu—swimming, surfing, and soccer were what you did. You're going to learn to float and hold your breath underwater today."

"What are you gonna do?"

"Stretch out on your back and I'll support you."

"You'll hold me up?"

"Are we going to talk all day or swim?"

"Fine…"

I started down the steps. I was wary of what he might do. Like touch me. No young man had ever touched me that wasn't a relation getting a hug and the thought made my belly cramp. His hands would be under my back if I was floating face up like I was laid out for display. Why couldn't Amelia teach me?

"Does Amelia know how to swim?"

He blinked. "How should I know? Why?"

"Curious."

"Seven."

"It's enough I'm in here up to my waist, okay? Don't rush me."

"You can sit on the steps 'til you find your backbone or start overcoming your fear already. This pool is only private for an hour."

"Don't have to be mean."

"Then start trying!"

"Be *patient*."

He put his face in my face. "You seem to be under the impression this is a conversation, Recruit. It is not. Number One gave us orders. Shut up and do it."

"Yes, sir," I gritted out. He'd never pulled rank on me before. It was embarrassing and pissed me off. I glared at him, then turned around so he could help me lay back, and tensed as soon as he touched me.

"Relax, Seven."

"This is relaxed."

"Maybe I should make Thornhill do this if you're going to be a pain in the ass."

"Language."

"Shut up and float."

This was so awkward. "I would if you'd *tell me how*."

Standing me up, he said, "This isn't working," and waded to the steps. Was he leaving? I watched him walk around the deck in his clingy shorts to a cabinet. Various implements were inside. He picked up a foam rectangle, tossed it in the water, and dove in after it. "This is a kickboard. Name is its function. Hold on to float and start kicking."

"Why?"

"Because I can't make you swim laps yet and I'm hoping you'll get too tired to bitch. Start kicking. All the way across."

"I don't know how." That earned me an *are you stupid?* look. "I'm not trying to be difficult. I don't know how to do any of this."

He sighed. "Seven, you're overcomplicating it. Swimming is pretty natural if you get your head out of the way."

"I'm not ready. This pool is too big."

"Come on, you have the stamina to do a lap, kid."

"Not like that."

"Fine. Let's go home." Shaking his head, he climbed out of the pool and kept walking toward the dressing rooms. Wow. I never thought he'd give up.

Is this what I wanted?

Amelia would assign someone else to teach me or train me herself. She wouldn't let me give up again. The cause was too important to her. And I really doubted the Director would let me put this off or pass without learning, even if I had staked a few vampires.

Standing in the pool, swimming didn't make me nearly as nervous as Thirteen did. I mean, the thought of being under water scared me to death, but my resistance was defensive. I liked him, it was forbidden, and I didn't know how to handle it. Crazy as it sounds for a seventeen year-old, I'd never had a crush before. Not really. Not in the his-smile-makes-me-dizzy kind of way like now. Why couldn't he at least be my own age?

The next day, Thirteen was still in street clothes when I walked out of the dressing room. "You're going in, in jeans?"

"You swim. I'll watch."

"What if—?"

"I won't let you drown, Seven. Just do it."

Okay, Mr. Nike. Seriously, this didn't seem safe. I didn't know how to swim. I could drown. It only took inches of water for that.

"Seven, trust me. Hold your breath and go, or I'll push you in."

"I liked you a lot better two years ago." The water was cold when I started down the steps. Better to get the adjustment over with, I pushed forward to wade in up to my collarbone.

At three feet deep, that put me in a crouch. It was all about moving your arms back and forth, right? Wading. Could I float or would my body sink right away? I didn't have the nerve to find out, yet, so I kept wading a bit deeper, until I was standing straight to have the water below my chin.

"Nothing to be afraid of, kid. You can see the bottom the whole time."

Better than the ponds at home. I didn't know where Dad took me to learn, so maybe that was part of my fear. The unknown black depths. Even so, the white bottom wasn't making me less nervous about feeling the water over my shoulders. If I lifted my feet up, I'd go under.

"Try paddling back to the edge without putting your feet down."

"Not yet."

"Seven, we'll be here forever with 'not yet'. You can swim without putting your head under. It's just more awkward." He sat on a deck chair picking his nails. Jerk. "Want the kickboard to lean on? Don't think they make floaties in your size."

"Bite me."

He laughed. Except for the safety factor, I wished he'd go away. Having an audience wasn't helping.

"Throw the girl in the jungle and she takes charge, but a little clean, sparkly pool and oh no, scary!" For that, I splashed him. Surprised, he let out a good yelp and scrambled out of the chair. "These are *new boots*."

"Now who's running?"

"You're only getting away with that now 'cause you can't swim, Seven. Retribution is coming."

Eye roll. "I'm not lookin' to start a prank war. Don't antagonize me." I walked back to the shallow end and climbed out. "This isn't working. I'll talk to Amelia."

He caught my arm. "I was only playing. I'm sorry. We've always bantered words."

"Yeah, but it doesn't give you license to be a jerk. I'm not going to learn if we keep butting heads." I grabbed my towel. The room was cold. "Are you mad you're saddled with me instead of somewhere else?"

"That's stupid."

"I'm serious. It's been like this since St. George, so—"

"I'm not mad. I blamed Amelia, but I'm annoyed with myself for not thinking to ask when I trained you. We both let it slip by as teachers and The Agency can't afford oversights. Someone could die."

"That's a lot of pressure."

"That's the job. Still want it?"

"Do I have a choice?"

"Of course. Free will is the only thing a hundred percent ours. Seven…"

"How long have you been doing this?"

"Many years."

"Is it worth it?"

"Yes. But that's for me. You have to decide about you."

"No easy answers."

He smiled. "Hardly ever. Let's go before you catch cold."

"No. I want to try again." I dropped the towel on a chair.

"You sure?"

"No, but these lessons can't go on forever. You have places to be."

"Okay." He stripped down to swim trunks and took my hand. "I'm glad you're willing to try overcoming your fear."

"As long as you take a gentle approach this time." We stepped into the water.

"Scout's honor." And I could trust his word.

He started with holding onto my hands and having me follow him around the shallow half of the pool. My being in the water this long was an ultimate show of trust and I think he got that now.

"Will you try floating on your back?"

"If you don't let go."

We'd done trust exercises as recruits before, putting our backs to someone and letting them catch us, and this was similar—only I'd go underwater instead of falling on the ground.

"Lean back with your limbs straight." His hands supported me under my shoulder blades as I did. "Relax. You're too tense."

"I'm trying. This is hard. Don't let the water go over my ears."

"Stop worrying about it. The only important part is breathing, and as long as you can breathe, you're good. Once you get past this, you'll find the backstroke is really easy for a beginner."

"Really."

"Just lay back and kick while alternating arm strokes. Don't even have to be a good floater."

It was weird looking up at his face like this. "If you say so."

"You're a natural athlete, remember?"

"I wouldn't call it 'natural'."

"You know what I mean. Do you argue this much with your parents?"

"It's only my mom, and no, because she doesn't ask me to do crazy things."

"Seven, you've been floating for five minutes while you wouldn't shut up."

"*What?*" My feet struck bottom.

"*Had* been, yes."

"Oh."

"Will you try again?"

"Do we have time?"

He glanced at his waterproof watch. "Yep." I leaned into his hands again. "Stretch out your arms, relax...relax your neck. That's it. Breathe."

"How long are we doing this?"

"The rest of the session."

"Okay." I put my trust in him and focused on making friends with the water. Letting my body get used to its temperature, the way it lapped around my limbs. The hair in my ponytail floating, which was nice.

Before I knew it, Thirteen was standing me up and telling me it was time to go. "Same time tomorrow."

"Yes, sir."

At least these lessons got me outside, even if it was in the cold. He usually wore a dark gray peacoat and always carried an umbrella.

The following day, he put a lifejacket on me he found somewhere. Thank goodness this wasn't a public pool. "There's no way you can drown with that on," he said. "So with your fear out of the way we can work on your strokes. Roll onto your back and imitate what I do."

Fear of the water was a deep-set phobia in me, so learning to swim wasn't a quick process—I guessed, as I had no one's experience to compare it to—but the buoyancy of the lifejacket helped tame my fear enough to follow his instructions. He'd rather I be willing to put my head underwater, but once I started doing what he wanted, he went back to the usual jovial guy I'd come to know.

Baby steps.

I felt more modest in the vest, too, and that helped.

In March, Thirteen was gone again. He told Amelia he was confident I wouldn't drown within five minutes and she could continue my training in the water if she wished.

Chapter Seven

June

Amelia came home with me to see "an American ceremony" and tell my mother about the job offer with their "aid organization". "Della will get to continue her education by correspondence as she travels, of course," she said.

"She better be allowed to. College is important."

"The internet allows a lot more flexibility, Mom."

"You'd know better than I would, honey," she said, patting my knee. I programmed the VCR for her when I was eight.

I hadn't picked a major, yet, especially since I wasn't going to be in the civilian sector anymore—and how wacky is it that I say *civilian sector*—but doing college work felt like a normal thing. I wanted as much normal as I could fit in my life as an agent. They were fitting me for my suit when I got back to London.

My friends and church group thought I'd been part of a foreign exchange program. They were eager to hear about England and welcomed me into the line of graduates like I never left. Popularity really did happen on a whim, didn't it? Worried I was a terrible liar, I kept my answers short and vague and recited anecdotes from a tourist guide of London.

It was a relief to get back to Mom and pose for pictures in my cap and gown.

"You can stay a little while, can't you, Della?" she asked at our celebration dinner.

"Maybe. You'll have to check with Amelia." I twirled the spaghetti on my plate, wrapping a big wad around my fork, then letting it slide off.

"Honey, you don't have to take the first offer presented to you, you know that, right? You're barely eighteen…there's plenty of time to find the right school and the right job. And date! Did you meet any nice boys in London?"

"Just friends, Mom. There wasn't a lot of time for socializing, though."

"And that's not right…this is your first summer as a young woman. You should have some fun. Sensibly, of course, and with your clothes on."

"Of *course*. I'm okay, Mama, really. *Really*. I'm going to get to see things few people ever do. How could I pass that up?" Oh, I wanted what she was talking about—the dates and the parties and seein' movies. I'd give anything to be a normal girl. But for God knows why, it wasn't my path.

"I s'pose you're right. Gosh, you're all grown up, aren't you? You'll write?"

"All the time."

"And visit as much as you can?"

"Wild horses couldn't keep me away, I promise. Guthrie is still home." She took my hand on the table. "*Home* is still home."

Chapter Eight

The next time I walked into HQ, I sensed I was leaving "Della Garvison" behind.

Amelia led me into a room with a central platform surrounded by cameras linked to a computer. I think they were cameras. "Strip down to your undergarments, please?"

"Beg pardon?"

"The suit is custom fit, so the computer needs exact measurements, Seven."

"Ah. Yay." At least it was only the two of us. I got on the platform in my sports bra and undies. Amelia fiddled with the computer, then beams of green light started wandering over my body. "Um, are those lasers?"

"They're harmless. Hold your arms out to the sides, please."

"Are you done, yet? It's cold in here."

"Only another minute. Turn your back to me and widen your stance, please. And stop fidgeting." *Stop fidgeting.* Bet she wouldn't be perfectly still standing like this, either. "You can get dressed now."

Thank God. "Now what?"

"Now the specs go to the seamstresses." She typed on the keyboard.

"How long does the suit take to make?" I pulled my pants up.

"You will get it when it's ready."

"Okay, okay…"

"Go in the next room to get fitted for your boots, please."

"Amelia, are you mad at me?"

She sighed and looked up from the monitor. "No, of course not."

"It's just…you've been a bit brusque since we got back."

"You're not the only one that's been evaluated, Seven. After they learned about your lack of knowing how to swim, the council ruled I'd been too lax with you."

"Oh."

"It's nothing personal. I'm merely trying to maintain a more professional distance in our relationship."

"So you're the boss."

"Well...yes."

"Then I'll go next door, ma'am." Her eyes widened. Guess I surprised her. I left to get my custom boots made.

I expected the work to take at least weeks, but my new gear was ready in a matter of days. When it came to outfitting an agent, The Agency worked with supreme efficiency.

The most surprising part, though, was how many parts and layers were involved.

The outfit started with a cat-suit that zipped down the front. Silver threads glinted in the light, and when I held my arm up I discovered words in Latin and Hebrew. They covered the entire surface of the black material. Pieces of light armor went over the suit — a corset-like torso piece, bracers, and shin guards that fit over my boots. The boots were a classic black combat style, but surprisingly lightweight, and felt like a sneaker inside. I could walk in them without making a sound. The hood-and-mask went on next to reveal only my eyes, and the final part of my wardrobe was the coat.

It was my favorite piece mainly because it looked so darn cool. The coat was cut close to the body, but not constricting movement, the hem falling at mid-calf. It was leather, with more of the silver threads woven in, and heavy from the concealed Kevlar panels. The inner lining had at least a dozen pockets for hiding weapons.

I stepped in front of the full-length mirror in my suite and didn't know who I was looking at, it was so surreal. Eighteen and decked out like a modern-day ninja.

"You forgot these." Amelia walked in carrying a pair of black leather gloves.

"Thanks." It felt weird to talk, the cotton mask buffing my lips. The gloves covered all but my fingertips, with light padding over the knuckles for punching protection. I secured them on my wrists and stood for inspection.

"Black out your eyes for night work and you'll be perfect," she said. "Come. It's time to graduate."

The ceremony wasn't like finishing academics. A minister blessed each of us, then the Director—Alastair Wimbley—handed us a heavy-duty case and our IDs and passport. He was givin' us a lot of power, as that passport granted us no-questions-asked access to almost every country in the world and the ID promised no interference from government employees like law enforcement and medical examiners. I didn't want to know how The Agency had gained such power and would never ask…some things were better left to plausible deniability, and really, we were doing this for a good cause.

Demons didn't respect human boundaries.

Only four of the ten recruits on the island were granted Agent status today, and I was the only girl.

Amelia met me in the hall dressed in traveling clothes. "Ready for our first mission?"

"Long as I can find a burger, I'll take on a hundred vamps."

She shook her head. "Some things are more important than your stomach, Seven."

"Yeah, like sunshine."

I was never so glad to walk out to a hot summer day.

Epilogue

My third mission sent me to Los Angeles.

Of course, I thought it was a mistake when I read the assignment. The Agency officially stayed out of L.A. Unofficially, we spied, but only from a discreet distance and with electronic equipment only. Sure, an Agent would check it out in person on occasion, but we needed to re-grow our numbers before provoking Juliet with contact.

Amelia was just as mystified. And didn't want me to go. She was going to call the Director, but I stopped her.

"Thirteen probably requested me. He wanted me on his team for this months ago. I don't think the situation is that dangerous if they're willing to send a rookie."

"I don't like it, Seven."

"Wanna stay here?"

"Of course not. My duty is to be at your side. But—"

"Amelia, thousands of people fly in and out of L.A. every day without a scratch. I think I can handle a little surveillance mission."

She sighed. "Well, if I can't talk you out of it…"

See, once I became an Agent, she was no longer my boss. We were partners now and I don't think my stubborn streak will ever stop rubbin' her the wrong way, and I liked calling the shots when I was out on the streets. We kept in touch by way of a tiny wireless thing in my ear, but carrying out the missions was my job.

So, we flew to L.A. "Mmm, smell the fresh smog," I said.

The next April, I celebrated my nineteenth birthday getting puked on by a homeless drunk after I saved him from being an easy meal. This suit was relatively new, too.

My first had lasted two months, until I went toe-to-toe with a werewolf in the Cascades.

The second, a little longer. An acid attack from a Khorkhoi demon ate a bunch of holes in the torso armor. My basic cat suit still intact, I got a new torso piece and wore that kit until they came out with a new ensemble for all of us earlier this year.

Mama thought I was in college. It was partly the truth. When I could, I took correspondence courses and traveling had softened my accent.

From Seattle to Sri Lanka, I dusted vampires, put ghosts to rest, captured werewolves, and intervened with victims of black magic.

Could be a worse life.

STRANGE ALLIES

Della discovered she's a paladin at sixteen after a vampire attack, surviving due to her skin burning the undead to ashes. Graduating to Agent at eighteen, she embarks on missions to save the world, or at least as many people as she can.

When the mysterious vampire Adam starts helping Agent Seven's cause, she doesn't trust him. Every vampire is evil, right? But when Adam asks The Agency for her services to rescue children from L.A.'s reigning vampire, Juliet, Seven can't refuse. Will Adam prove her wrong, or be her downfall?

This story is intended for readers over the age of 18 due to adult situations.

Chapter One
Della

I celebrated my nineteenth birthday in April 2007 getting puked on by a homeless drunk after I saved him from being an easy meal.

This suit was relatively new, too. My first lasted two months, until I went toe-to-toe with a werewolf in the Cascades. The second a little longer.

An acid attack from a Khorkhoi demon ate a bunch of holes in the torso armor. My basic cat-suit still intact, I got a new torso piece and wore that kit until they came out with a new ensemble for all of the agents earlier this year. The new material was a lot more durable, most of the armor pieces were part of the suit instead of separate, and it somehow reacted with the wearer's body temp to keep you cool in hot places and warm in cold climates. Our boots and coats also had tiny GPS trackers embedded in them now.

Mama thought I was in college. It was partly the truth. When I could, I took correspondence courses and traveling had softened my accent. Amelia spent the first six months of my training blurting out corrections to my Oklahoma pronunciation.

From Seattle to Sri Lanka, I dusted vampires, put ghosts to rest, captured werewolves, and intervened with victims of black magic.

Could be a worse life.

Dodging the man-turned-werewolf, I tucked into a roll, and—*yuck*—stood with dog poop stuck to my coat. Couldn't people clean up after their mutts in the park? "Note to self: when someone asks you to save the world, say no." I wasn't some dainty girly-girl, but I hated the muck and grime of the job. Three years, and I still couldn't wait to run to a shower when the night was up.

The story of how I got drafted into the world-savin' business wasn't so complicated. Amelia Thornhill directed a vampire at me. A normal girl would probably have been killed, drained of her blood and possibly even turned. Turned out, I hadn't been *normal* since my sixteenth birthday. My touch burned the undead like a cross or holy water. Don't ask how, 'cause I have no clue. Amelia said they're researching it.

I'd been an agent for The Agency nearly a year since right after high school graduation. Amelia was my guide, the book, equipment, and patch-her-up lady. She thought she was my boss. Our latest assignment put us in Southern California, going undercover in the realm of a very old and powerful vampire who thought she owned the city.

Mission: Pose as a volunteer at a church-run shelter for runaways. Assess the current demon-to-human ratio in the city.

Team: Only Amelia and myself.

It was early May and we'd been here a couple weeks.

Amelia couldn't fit in at the shelter with her accent, so she was carrying on a daylight role with businesses rumored to be aiding the bloodsuckers. She was very good playing bureaucracy against itself. This week, she was trying to expose the security leak at the blood bank of one of the hospitals. Juliet ran her nest like organized crime and had been careful about drawing attention with an excess of dead bodies. Shipments of blood would get "lost" here and there, and no one noticed if the homeless disappeared. We couldn't carry out a direct assault, but we could make life harder for her here until opportunity arose.

My personal phone rang. Thinking it was Mom, I leapt out of bed to answer it.

Voice mail? Mama hated talkin' to machines, always hanging up and callin' right back. Dreading that it might be the hospital or her doctor, I listened to the message.

"Hey, Della…your mom said she last knew you were in L.A. and guess where I finally am? Let's catch up, 'kay? I'm staying at the Biltmore."

Charlotte? Talk about a blast from the past. We were cousins on my father's side, Charlotte was four years older than me, and I hadn't seen her since her high school graduation in Oklahoma City. His side of the family all wanted to "make it big". She was the only one that actually did it.

Guess Mom was keepin' in touch…weird that Charlotte would want to connect, though, unless she was merely lonely for a familiar face. I didn't know her well.

I called directory assistance to get the number of the hotel, then dialed the front desk to leave Charlotte a message.

Checking the clock, I'd only been asleep five hours. "Curse these vampire hours…" I grumbled. Vamps were the worst cases. You had to be awake when they were, which meant the complete opposite schedule of any sane human being.

Charlotte called back late afternoon. "Are you free for dinner, Della? I have a night off after rehearsals for my performance Friday."

"Uh, I guess…as long as I'm back by dark."

"By dark?"

"Graveyard shift."

"*Oh.* Well, yeah, I guess we should meet up soon, then. I have a suite. Just have them ring me." She hung up with the assumption I agreed.

Downtown L.A. was way too crowded for my taste, but that's where I'd find my cousin. The Biltmore looked pretty fancy from the inside, but that didn't prepare me for walkin' through the doors, which made me very conscious of the old jeans and tee I was wearing.

"Charlotte Taylor's room, please," I said to the clerk.

"Is she expecting you?"

"Uh, yes, I'm her cousin."

"Ah." He got that look of *oh, the city girl's taking pity on the country bumpkin*. I'd seen it before. "Ms. Taylor is in the Music Suite. Take the elevator over there."

"Thanks." So what if everything I wore amounted to forty dollars?

A man dressed in a black suit answered the door when I knocked. "Yes?"

"I'm Charlotte's cousin."

"Reed, let her in," I heard Charlotte say behind the bodyguard. "Hey, Della!" Reed let me cross the threshold and Charlotte hugged me. She was barely five-feet-tall and fit under my chin. "Welcome to my temporary home. Do you want to eat out or order room service?"

This was no little hotel room—the Music Suite was bigger than my house and included a baby grand piano. I didn't want to think what it cost per night. "Whatever. You called me."

"True. I don't get to spend much time with anyone other than Nicholae and Reed, especially another woman. Your mom said your job makes you travel, too?" The bodyguard went to a chair in the corner and resumed reading a newspaper.

"Uh, yeah. Lots of people in need." The windows looked down on Pershing Square. I didn't like facing people when I talked about work. Someone would inevitably figure out I was a bad liar.

"Well, let me know if you need reimbursement for parking. Should be my treat since I asked you here. So, what are your taste buds in the mood for?"

"I can pay my own way. Just pick your poison, Charlotte."

"Okay, then." She picked up her purse. "Reed, I'll be back in two hours, if Nicholae needs me." She opened the door and I took my cue to follow.

"Who's Nicholae?"

"He's…" She punched the "down" button for the elevator. "My benefactor. He manages my career."

"So he's in the music biz."

"Well, no…" The doors opened and they stepped into the car. "He's not with a record company or anything like that."

"Then how did you start playing professionally?"

"He opened doors. I don't know the intricacies. All I know now is that once word spread, people started asking for me."

"Lucky." My Agency-developed suspicious streak was raising its head, but Charlotte seemed happy, and she was obviously talented if she kept getting offers to do concerts, so I tamped it down. Even if it turned out her start was from shady deals, she'd survive.

"Yeah, it was perfect timing. I didn't know what I'd do for summer work and I was out of my apartment." She stepped out into the lobby. "Where's your car?"

"Out front. Told the valet I was picking someone up."

"*Nice.*"

I shrugged. "A tip goes a long way toward cooperation." So did flashing my very-official-looking ID. The rental was waiting right by the doors. "I live at fast food joints and diners, so if you want somethin' else, you'll have to direct me."

"If you know of somewhere with a taste of home, I'd be grateful." Homesick it was, then.

You wouldn't believe we were related — besides Charlotte being adopted, the family tended toward the cute and wholesome side. She was simply stunning, with a pocket-sized swimsuit model build and a very pretty face. Her dark curls were in striking contrast to her blue eyes and fair skin. I always wondered where her parents found her.

"So, have you been out of the country?" Charlotte asked.

"Some. You?"

"Not yet. Well, the Canada side of Niagara, but, no." She twisted in her seat to face me. "You look different than the last time I saw you."

"That was five years ago. Big difference between fourteen and nineteen."

"I guess. I just didn't expect to see you so…"

"What?"

"Trim."

What did she mean by that? "You thought I'd *look* like I live in a diner?"

"I don't know. You look athletic and I didn't think you were into sports."

"I'm not, except for watchin' football." I pulled into a Norms. "Hope this is what you were lookin' for."

"Della, I'm not trying to insult you. You look great. I'd love the number of your personal trainer."

Oh, good *grief*. I got out of the car and went inside. "Table for two," I told the hostess. Charlotte ran in behind me.

At six o'clock in Los Angeles, most of the diners were still older folk and the restaurant wasn't packed, yet. We were seated right away. I studied the menu, letting time pull my cousin's foot out of her mouth for her.

"So what's it like working all night?" she asked after the waitress brought our salads.

"Dark. Slow. Quiet. Just like anyone else's graveyard shift." Lie ratio—three out of four.

"Okay, I'll shut up."

And now I felt guilty. I never liked answering questions about myself, though, not since the day Amelia found me. The less I said about what I did, the less likely I'd give away a secret. It was safer. "Don't know much about your side of the family, but Guthrie's the same."

"One big, happy Garvison clan?"

"Pretty much."

"I prefer California. Maybe it's in my wiring or something, but I didn't fit back there. Is that why you left, too?"

More like why I was forced away, but I couldn't tell her that. "Nah. I just found somethin' I'm good at."

"Well, good for you, Della."

"Yeah."

With the supper plates we moved on to Charlotte's career and the music she liked to play. I didn't know Brahms from Bach, but I thought I nodded appropriately. Charlotte insisted on picking up the check, and I took her back to the hotel.

Charlotte opened the front door at the same time a man was coming out.

They collided.

Mutual apologies were given.

Then, he looked at her, and his face paled like he'd seen a ghost, and he looked her over again. My cousin was too busy blabbering to notice.

"Sir, are you alright?" I asked.

"Er, yes. Forgive me. I'll get out of your way." His accent was English, less upper-crusty than Amelia's. He stepped aside.

"Thanks," Charlotte said, and continued to the elevator.

I felt him watching us leave, and sure enough when I turned around in the lift before the doors closed, he was staring at Charlotte still. If he didn't know her, he was definitely intent on memorizing her face.

"A fan, you think?" I asked.

"Who?"

"The guy that bumped into you. He was staring."

"He was? Was he cute?"

"Kinda good-looking if you like beards, but that's not the point. You really didn't notice?"

"Nope. If he's staying here, maybe we'll meet again. I haven't had a date in over a year."

I shook my head. Civilians were so clueless. The things people missed from not being observant...

Charlotte said goodbye at her door. "Sorry I can't invite you in, but I have to rehearse before bed. Boss's orders."

"Okay. Well, enjoy your stay, and...break a leg."

She smiled. "Thanks. Goodnight."

The man was still in the lobby when I came down. I walked out of the hotel and so did he. I turned the corner to go to the car, stopped, and pushed him against the wall when he came around.

"Why are you following me?" I asked, pocket dagger held to his throat.

He held his hands out to the sides. "Whoa, steady, friend. I only wanted to inquire about your companion. She looked familiar, see?"

"Saw that on your face. What's it to you?"

"She—" He leaned away from the knife. "She resembles someone I lost, is all. Could you point that somewhere else?"

"Chalk it up to coincidence and leave her alone. She's not stayin' long." I backed off, giving him my best *I'll kick your ass if you hurt my cousin* look.

"Oh? Pity."

The man didn't look dangerous, and I got no supernatural vibes. A pulse, skin color...good signs. "Look, if you're a fan, buy a ticket to the Philharmonic like everyone else, okay? She's just a piano girl." Hopefully sufficiently warned off, I turned my back on him and went to the car.

Real threats were out there and I had twenty minutes to full darkness.

Chapter Two

Adam

Simon raced into the hotel room. "I found her!"

A long-suffering expression took over my face. "Not this again. What caught your eye this time: hair, a scent, a smile?"

We had looked for Simon's lost wife reincarnated for centuries and there had been so many disappointments. Of course I was skeptical.

"*I found her*, Adam. It's my wife."

I muted the television. "No she is not, assuming you have the right young woman. She won't know you."

"I'm perfectly aware of this curse. Lived with it for five-hundred years. I'm telling you! She's in this very hotel, just floors above us."

"How do you know?"

"I ran into her in the lobby. She and a redhead went into the lift and only the redhead came back again."

I sighed. "That is only one reason both women did not leave again."

"You're a right buzz-kill, mate."

"So I've been told. Doesn't mean I'm wrong. Simon, we've been down this road before. A thousand times."

"This is different. I've never been this close before. The redhead told me my wife is a pianist and in town to play a concert. It can't be hard to narrow down the venue."

"No, it won't. Did you get a name, by chance?"

"No."

"Why not?"

"Will you help me find her or not?"

"As your only friend, what else would I do?"

"*Best* friend."

"Potato, po-ta-to, old man."

My skepticism frustrated him, but I had his best interests at heart. He was the most optimistic man I knew, but the centuries wore on him as he failed over and over again. How could I stand back and see his hopes crushed? We'd known each other since 1750.

Chapter Three
Della

"How many so far tonight, Seven?" Amelia asked through my earpiece.

"Four. They're sloppy about who they turn in this town." Per orders, I was only dusting the new ones. Juliet and her minions wouldn't notice the absence of animals.

"With such a huge population, deaths are expected. Humans are doing enough to fill the morgues as it is."

"Homesick?" I set up the scope with thermal optics for my nightly surveillance of Juliet's HQ. The vampire was so "genteel" her clan actually had an office building.

Bloodsuckers were all the same, though. The Bubonic Plague in pretty wrapping paper was still the Black Death.

"My efforts at the hospital were successful," she said. "I also gained some intel from the ER about underground parties. A few adolescents came in for overdose."

"What's new about that?"

"The bite marks."

Oh. Wonderful. The vamps were preying on teens at raves. Shouldn't surprise—a dark, illegal club filled with drug-addled kids was a veritable feast ripe for the taking. If the girl or boy ended up dead, they're just another tragic statistic of teenage rebellion. I couldn't even put a hundred-percent blame on the vamps.

"Did you advise HQ?" I asked.

"Waiting for orders. What is the level of activity at the office?"

I peered through the scope. They were using one of the older buildings, and the windows had fabric shades pulled down except in the lobby. "A few lights on here and there, same as usual. I don't think we're going to learn much about what they do in there without going in."

"Which is strictly forbidden, Seven. We're not ready to start a war."

"I know, I know. I was just sayin'. Hasn't anybody tried to bug the place? We've been watching them for years."

"It doesn't work long. Their ears pick up the electronic noise. We're working on silent technology."

"I never knew vampires could be so boring. Can't believe I had to turn down my cousin for this."

"Seven…"

"Sorry. Didn't mean to say that out loud." I took the earpiece out and set it on the foam lining of my case.

My presence wasn't really required up on this roof. We had cameras on the building twenty-four-seven with a feed straight back to the analysts at HQ, but they liked to have an agent babysitting the equipment. I'd rather be monitoring Juliet's house. That's where the real evil took place.

And I felt naked without my suit on, too. It'd been uncomfortable at first, but now it felt like a second skin. Like Batman was merely Bruce Wayne without the costume and utility belt.

Charlotte left messages again, so I was going to her room for breakfast before I went to bed, and I had a ticket in the cheap seats for her show in the evening. Amelia could chew me out for taking two hours off later. I hadn't had a break since Christmas Day.

Friday

Walking into that hotel was a step into a world that fit as well as a watermelon for a shoe. The wealth implemented intimidated me in my tee and shorts. May in L.A. was pretty warm, after all. I went straight to the elevator and up to my cousin's floor. The bodyguard grunted hello and let me knock.

"Good morning," Charlotte said. She had an elaborate spread already set out in the parlor. "Coffee, tea, juice?"

"O.J., please." The dishes were on the coffee table, so I had a seat on one of the sofas. "Sorry I couldn't drop by yesterday."

"It's okay. I was pretty busy, myself. Had a delightful dinner downstairs, though."

"Food good?"

"It was excellent, but that wasn't the good part." She wore a smile as she served.

"You met someone."

Pink cheeks joined the smile. "The company was pleasant, yes."

"Well, tell me about him. Assuming it's a him?" My plate was piled with scrambled eggs, bacon, sausages, and fresh fruit.

"Yes, it's a *him*. We were both eating alone, he asked to join me, and it was very nice."

"Are you going to see him again?"

"I'm going to be up here except for going to the hall, so I guess not."

"If he's staying in the hotel, Charlotte, look him up."

"I'll see what Nicholae has on my schedule after tonight."

"You always do what this Nick guy tells you to?"

She blinked. "He's my manager."

"Yeah, and I've heard they're supposed to work *for you*. Last I knew, you were an independent woman, cousin."

"The arrangement works, okay?"

I surrendered. "Fine. I'm comin' to see you play tonight. The nosebleed section wasn't sold out, yet."

"I hope you enjoy it."

"Hey, you're family. Of course I'd come."

Breakfast continued, and we compared lists of visited cities. We'd been to a comparable amount of states, though my work usually took me to the rural areas, to towns easily picked on. All of Charlotte's stories had a recurring theme of Nicholae guiding her this way and that, and I couldn't help thinking he was pretty controlling. Why would a gal as capable and independent as Charlotte go along with everything this man said? She didn't love him, so unless it was some kind of daddy complex thing, I didn't understand it.

I feigned a yawn as an excuse to leave.

"You've been up all night and here I am blabbering on and on. Della, it was so sweet of you to come over when you must be ready to drop."

"Think nothin' of it." I hugged her. "Break a leg tonight."

"Thanks. Drive safe."

I nodded and left. Once back in the car, I pulled out my company cell.

"Amelia, run a background check on Nicholae Dragomir." I spelled out the name using the NATO alphabet.

"Who's that, Seven?"

"My cousin's manager. Could be nothin', but I have a bad vibe."

"Supernatural?"

"Haven't met him, so I don't know. Thanks." I hung up and pulled out of the parking garage.

I was yawning for real when I parked in the driveway of the minister's house hosting my stay. It *had* been a long night.

****

Didn't travel with skirts or dresses, so I wore my newest pair of jeans and my best shirt to the concert hall, with my hair in a neat French braid. Several other patrons looked sideways at me, but hey, sittin' way up in the top tier wasn't a dress to impress location, anyway. All eyes would be on the stage.

Fancy my surprise at feeling a vampire walk in just after the curtain rose.

The audience clapped for the orchestra starting to enter and I searched in the dim light for where the tingle down my spine came from.

There.

In the back of the balcony. It was too dark to make out features other than pale skin and a tall frame, but my Spidey sense didn't lie.

Crap.

Charlotte was taking her seat at the piano, too. As soon as the audience went silent, the acoustics would carry any ruckus we made throughout the auditorium.

I darted out of my row and up the aisle. The entry walkway behind his row gave me clear access to sneak up behind him. As the vamp sat down, I touched a fingertip to the skin above his collar. He froze. A puff of smoke started to rise from the contact.

"Outside. Now. Quietly," I whispered, and walked out to the lobby. Oh, please let him follow me.

The figure that walked out of the auditorium was unlike any vampire I'd dusted before, and that was a fair number. He was quite simply *gorgeous*. Dressed in casual business attire of gray and black, he looked like he'd walked out of a catalog. Everything was perfect, from his symmetrical face to the Italian leather loafers on his feet.

"I hope you have a good reason for bringing me out here, miss. The pianist has started to play." He just had to have a nice voice, too.

"Really? You're gonna play the inconvenienced music patron? We both know what you came for."

A faint smile graced his lips. "And what is that?"

I waited for a passing usher to get out of earshot, then said, "I know you're a vampire, and from that burn mark on your neck, you know what I am, too. Let's leave the nice innocents be and take this outside."

He stepped a bit closer, hands at his sides. "You have me all wrong, paladin. I came for the music by recommendation of a friend, and that's all. I'm Adam. And you are?"

"Not givin' you my name. You really want me to believe you didn't come for a snack."

He shrugged. "It's the truth. Do you think I want blood on this shirt? It's expensive."

Okay, I didn't have a comeback for that one.

"Look, sit next to me and babysit if you wish, but I'd rather not miss more of the performance than I have, so—" He turned to go back inside. I grabbed his arm—and ended up with my back to the wall. Couldn't tell ya how, it was *that fast*. He held me pinned there by the shoulders. "Listen carefully, paladin. I will say this once. I am not your enemy unless you force me to be."

With his face this close, I discovered his eyes were gray framed by enviably-long black lashes. "You're *all* the enemy. Swear on a Bible you've never killed a human for food and I might believe you."

Try for a comeback to that one, bub. He'd be left with a stump by the time he finished the oath, which is why what he did next shocked the hell out of me.

He gripped my cross pendant, his skin instantly sizzling. "I have *never* willingly killed a human for blood." He let go and went back in the auditorium, quick and silent.

White smoke wafted off my necklace.

He had me.

He had me dead to rights, and didn't kill me. Didn't compel me.

Didn't blink when he made his profession.

He was a really good liar if it wasn't the truth. I'd been trained to recognize tells.

This was crazy…"good" vampires were products of fiction.

Weren't they?

One thing I did know, he was old and he was strong. I doubted I could take him with only the stake hidden in my boot. I found a quiet place to use my phone.

"Amelia. Yes, I'm at the concert hall. Hush a second. Do you know of a vampire named Adam?"

"Adam what?"

"I don't know. Black hair, gray eyes, six-foot-one, no accent at all, and old. Definitely felt powerful."

"My God, are you alright?"

"I'm fine. Everyone seems to be fine. Very brief encounter. Do you know of him or not?"

"I'd have to check the archive. Sorry, but I don't have every vampire in existence in memory."

"Don't have to get snooty, just figure it out. I have to go. I've already missed some of the concert." I hung up and put the phone back in my pocket.

Should I sit by Mr. Undead? Stand in the back to observe him? Pull the fire alarm and clear the building? I wished Thirteen, my trainer, was here. His judgment was impeccable.

Sitting with two empty seats between us was as close as I could stand. The feeling of a newborn vamp nearby was irritating. The sense of an old and powerful one was enough to set your teeth on edge and make your ears ring. I'd been near a creature like that once before and been lucky to get away alive. Thank goodness the balcony was mostly empty tonight.

So, I watched him, while all eyes were on Charlotte and her beautiful playing...including the man next to the vamp.

The guy from the hotel? Sitting next to the vampire...that *couldn't* be coincidence.

"It's impolite to stare, paladin."

"It's unnatural to still walk the Earth, vampire."

"Would you two shut up?" the Englishman said.

"Make me," we said in unison, then looked at each other. The vampire winked at me.

The audacity!

An usher appeared at the end of the row. "Please be quiet or you will be asked to leave."

I mimed zipping my lips shut. Getting thrown out wouldn't help me protect anyone.

It was a relief when the lights came on for intermission.

The human stood. "Can we get through one more hour like adults, please? I came to watch a pretty lady play and you two are a right buzz-kill."

"Your *friend* runs the risk when he comes out of his coffin," I said.

"Please, that's so two hundred years ago."

The human moved between us and offered his hand to me. "Hi, I'm Simon. And you are?"

"Not giving that information."

He dropped the hand. "As is your right. For the sake of peace and my sanity, I propose this site be accorded neutral status for the duration of the evening."

"Boundaries?" I asked.

"The parking lots."

"Deal," the vampire said.

I nodded. "I agree to your terms."

"Thank God. You may resume your original seat, paladin. Adam, here, will be frightfully boring the rest of the night. *Won't you?*"

"Hey, she started it."

"And I told you I didn't need company, but you insisted, anyway."

"You bicker like old marrieds," I said. The lights flashed on and off to warn everyone back to their seats. The human smiled at me. The vampire glared.

Della—1, Vampire—0.

When Charlotte's concert ended, I followed the vampire when he left. Just because we'd agreed to a truce, didn't mean I trusted him out of my sight. And letting him be out of my sight wasn't part of the deal.

I guessed he felt confident I couldn't do much to him. He walked through the crowd at the same pace as everyone else and never bothered looking over his shoulder until he was outside, where he turned around and waited for me to come through the door.

Just standing there with his hands in his pants pockets. "Got trust issues, don't you, girl."

"Why are you waiting out here?"

"Figured you won't be satisfied until you see me get in my car and drive off."

"Where's your friend? Or should I say minion?"

"Simon is a *friend*, and he's off trying to congratulate the pianist. He's a fan."

"She doesn't need fans like you."

"Every artist needs a ticket buyer." He turned and started for the parking lot, just as casual.

It stuck in my craw that he didn't respect me. I was his mortal enemy! One of the best women The Agency had with an excellent success rate in my first year solo. So what if I was in street clothes?

"You are the most irritating creature I've ever met," I yelled, running ahead of him.

"Thank you." He grinned and kept walking past me.

"Why can't you act like a normal vampire?"

"Never been one. Besides, this is more fun."

"And 'fun' is what you're about?"

"Fighting boredom is what I'm about, paladin. I don't fancy a sun-soaked suicide, so I live."

"And not on people."

"Yup. No biting humans."

"Why are you in L.A.?"

"Why are you?"

"You can't answer a question with a question!"

"Just did. You want to play Twenty Questions. I don't."

Don't hit him in public. Don't hit him in public. "Where did you park, the back?"

"It's right there." He took out a key fob. The alarm chirped and the lights flashed. A Lincoln Towncar. "It's a rental, so don't get any funny ideas, please."

"Me? Your kind are the ones known for *destruction*."

"You know nothing of 'my kind', child. I happen to be undead and require blood to survive, but that's where the similarity ends. I won't say it again." He opened the car door.

"Why should I believe anything you say?"

"Read my file. I'm sure your Agency has one." He started the engine, closed the door, and drove away.

Round 2: Vampire—1. Della—0.

I called Amelia when I was in the car. "Any luck?"

"Not on your first request, but there is an Adam in the archives."

"Hit me."

"A vampire with that name popped up around 1730, following the razing of a monastery in Northern Italy. But I doubt the one here would have let you leave unscathed."

"Why not?"

"He's said to be in Juliet's family."

"Oh." Yeah, that would be a bad run-in. "But how can an old vamp with the name of Adam be in Los Angeles by coincidence?"

"I...can't answer that. Perhaps this can be included in your surveillance. *Carefully*."

"Yeah. I'll sleep on it. I'll check in later. Seven out." I ended the call and started the car, pondering the mystery that was Adam.

It would've been nice to find my cousin to congratulate her, but duty had called, as always. Sitting on that rooftop, I went over the conversations with Adam again and again, looking for some clue I'd missed the first time. Nothin'. A perfectly outstanding citizen outside the lack of a heartbeat. He hadn't even sped in the parking lot.

I headed home from another bland night of watching the vamps, left a report for Amelia, and went to bed.

But I couldn't sleep that morning. I called Charlotte.

"Della? I'm surprised to hear from you at this hour. Are you okay?"

"I'm fine. I forgot to ask you how long you're staying in L.A."

"Oh! We're leaving for Portland today." Thank God.

"Oh, do you play there tonight?"

"Yes. Hey, I'd love to chat, but I have to go. It was great catching up. Keep in touch."

"Sure. Safe travels, Charlotte."

"You, too. Bye!"

Thank the Lord for small miracles. My cousin would be safely out of town and away from all these vampires. With any luck, my time in L.A. was up, too.

Chapter Four
Adam

While Simon could find his own way home, I didn't want the earful I'd receive if I ditched him, so I circled the parking lot until I was sure the paladin was gone, then parked in a different spot and waited.

Didn't take long. He came out with hurried steps. Opening the passenger-side door, he said, "Hotel."

"Struck out, eh?"

"They don't allow audience members backstage and she didn't come out the front."

"It was a long-shot."

"I can still run into her at the hotel. The night is early."

I sighed. "Maybe you do. Maybe you have dinner and charm her socks off. Then what? This concert was one-night-only, so she'll be off to another town."

"So? We'll follow her."

"What if she doesn't like you?"

"That only happened once."

"Which doesn't rule out a second time. If you stalk the girl she'll only call the police on you. Again."

"Bloody hell, Adam, it's like you don't want me to be happy!"

"That's absurd and you know it. I'm counseling you to take it slow. A modern girl in her twenties knows to be wary of strange men. Exchange numbers or e-mail or something. Court her properly, or she'll never fall in love with you and we'll be doing this all over again twenty-five years from now."

He went silent. An acknowledgement I was right.

I parked the car at the hotel. Simon was out and heading inside as soon as I turned the engine off. I wouldn't see him again until he got his answer.

Upstairs in our room, I checked in on Darius by phone, then searched through the TV channels until I found something palatable. L.A. wasn't a city I could wander around in if I valued my hide, so I'd be glad to move on. Staying cooped up wasn't my style. With any luck, the next city would be cloudy and wet. I didn't understand why any vampire would choose to live in Southern California with all this sunshine threatening to reduce them to ash.

Shortly after ten, Simon came in. By the droop of his shoulders, he had bad news.

"What happened? Did you see her?"

"No."

"Maybe you haven't waited long enough."

He shook his head. "I had the front desk clerk ring her room. She turned in for the night." He took off his boots. "Must've entered a different way. I was sure she'd come down to eat..."

"Tomorrow is another day."

"The clerk said she's scheduled to check out tomorrow."

"Oh. Let me guess, during daylight?"

"Got it in one."

"Look, now you have her name, we can call Darius and have him search the Web for her concert schedule. The hunt has just begun."

"What happened to your cautionary speeches?"

"I want you to be careful, not give up."

"Now you tell me."

"Go on, then. You don't need me to find the woman." Plenty of his searches before and after we met had been carried out alone.

"At least I have a woman to look forward to, mate."

Not this tune again. "Oh, no. I have no interest in a wife. Don't even start."

"Darius won't be around forever, eventually I'll be free of this curse, and then you'll be alone again. And that wasn't a pleasant Adam."

"I can fill my time without the company of females, mortal or otherwise."

"Just think on it? Immortality is a lot of years to fill. Believe me."

Of course I knew that. But he spoke from the heart of a man in love and couldn't understand my comfort with solitude.

Vampires were good at it. As a species, we rarely got along with anyone — not that I had much in common with them beyond physical requirements — and generally couldn't be trusted. I despised my kind for good reason. Other supernatural beings? There were allies, acquaintances, even a couple I would call friends, but no one I would enter into a relationship with. And mortals were out of the question.

Simon had snatched the remote. I groaned at his selection. He had a penchant for obnoxious reality shows. I took the remote back and turned the TV off.

"Call Darius. Faster I unload you on your reincarnated wife, the better."

He laughed.

Chapter Five

Della

Seven months later…

I finished writing the note inside my Christmas card to Mom, hoping it'd make up for missing Thanksgiving. Amelia came back in the room and put her phone in her bag. "Let me guess — the evil biz is so slow, they're sending us home early for the holidays?"

"Nice try. We have a new assignment. Germany. Something's harassing a village."

"Okay…what does that have to do with me?"

"Intelligence in the area thinks it's likely someone summoned a hellhound."

"Aw, crap." Never a good sign. Not only would I have to kill the beast, but find the summoner that wanted his-or-her neighbor's soul carried off to the Underworld, too. "Who celebrates Christmas with a *hellhound*?"

Amelia gave me her *I'm-not-dignifying-that-with-an-answer* look. I stuck my tongue out at her and sealed the envelope on the card.

This sucked.

One week to Christmas. Instead of traipsing through a German forest after a hellhound, I should be shopping and sipping wassail from my Frosty the Snowman mug. Thirteen was in the Caribbean right now on a simple vamp case, but I got stuck tracking a demon dog.

In the dark.

With a possibility of snow.

"Here, doggy…"

I heard a howl nearby and took off in the direction of the sound. The cry of a hellhound was similar to a wolf's, if the wolf was dead and trying to scare the crap out of you. That sound still sent a chill up my spine. The forest broke ahead to reveal a small clearing. I took a plastic Ziploc bag out of my coat pocket and opened it, dumping the fresh bloody steak in the center of the field.

"Hope you're hungry," I muttered, and backed into the trees and shadows.

"Be quiet, Seven, or the dog will hear you," Amelia scolded through my earpiece.

A dry twig snapped on the other side of the clearing. Birds flew out of the trees above, disturbed out of their slumber. My Spidey-sense started tingling, alerting me to the nearby presence of a supernatural being.

The hellhound padded into the clearing, sniffing for the raw meat, the full moon above making it visible. It was a big one, the size of a small bear. To say it was black would be incorrect—the dog was cloaked in shadows and darkness, like its body swallowed the light around it as it moved. The demon stopped at the steak, smelled it, and snatched the meat up in its massive jaws, tossing its head back to chomp down on the steak with one gulp. The action exposed its breast to me.

I drew back the string on my compound bow and fired an arrow. It was a steel-shafted arrow with a titanium tip, one of the few substances hard and sharp enough to pierce a hellhound's hide. The beast moved at the last second and the arrow struck its shoulder. It snarled and narrowed its orange eyes in the direction the shot came from.

"Great, Della, you made it mad." I drew my sword and charged the beast.

An earthly animal would likely run away. Demons try to take your head off. The hellhound angled its wounded side away from me, bared its teeth, and growled loud enough to echo.

"Come on, Ugly. You gonna yell at me all night, or do somethin'?"

"Seven, what are you doing? Report!"

"Little busy, Amelia." I watched the hellhound tense its body to pounce, knowing I had to time this right or I'd be a snack.

The beast leapt for me. I ducked under the attack at the last second and plunged my sword up into its soft underbelly, pushing my weight into the dog at the same time in hope he wouldn't land on me. The hellhound crashed to the ground at my side with an enraged howl. I withdrew my sword from its flesh, the dog trying to scramble to its feet, and swung my blade down on its neck.

Blood spurted out beneath the severed head and I skipped back to avoid getting my boots soaked.

"Yuck! I thought their *breath* smelled bad."

"It's dead?"

"As a doornail."

I cleaned my blade off in the dead grass and watched the body smoke and shrivel away. The chill breeze blew past from behind me. Feeling eyes on me, I turned to glance up at the ridge above, and spotted a figure in black. Nodding my head to the voyeur, I sheathed the sword and headed home. It was too late to deal with anyone who got their jollies from watching me kill a demon. A hot bath and warm bed awaited me, then we'd move on from the Black Forest.

"Excellent, Seven. Return to base."

"Amelia, it's a hotel for tourists."

"*Protocol*, Agent Seven."

"It's past midnight and I still have a long walk back. Protocol can wait 'til tomorrow."

"I'll be glad to send you home for the holiday," she said. "You've been most difficult this month."

Difficult was Amelia-speak for me speakin' plainly. I hadn't seen my mother in a year and I was homesick for baked ham, apple cobbler, and high-school football games. It was easy for Amelia to make duty and protocol all she was — she chose this life.

I didn't. Well, not the first day.

Don't get me wrong. Saving humanity one soul at a time was rewarding, and The Agency took care of all of my expenses. I loved reuniting families and getting rid of the bad guys, and seeing the world was pretty cool, too. But…some days I wondered what it'd be like to be a normal young woman in college with a boyfriend and a job that didn't include washing guts out of my hair.

Mostly, it killed me to lie to Mama about what I did.

Chapter Six

Adam

Visiting a friend in Eastern Europe, I learned my sire had been through the region picking up treats for her solstice party. "Treats" being another term for children fourteen and under. I picked up her trail, even learned her plans, but couldn't catch up to her in time to attempt a strike on this continent.

I couldn't attack Juliet and her guards alone, so I tracked a female paladin from the Black Forest region of Germany to The Agency's European headquarters in London.

They put the "secret" in the term "Secret Organization". Some said their paladins (an antiquated term used by the supernatural types of the world) got their power from God. Others said it was some kind of magic The Agency had created. No one knew exactly how they came into their ability to burn the unholy with their bare hands.

Heavy rain pelted the December day. I stood across the street from a fairly commonplace building, two stories high and not very long, with a matching door I assumed only *looked* like wood.

She and her companion had entered overnight.

They would least expect a creature like me at midday. I felt the enchantment around the building, a ward compelling others to keep walking and ignore the place, but didn't sense any anti-demon magic. Perhaps it was only cloaked.

"Father, are you sure this is a good idea?" my adopted son asked.

"You worry too much, Darius. Besides, where else will I find a trustworthy warrior capable of facing Juliet's minions?" I stumbled upon him as a teenager, homeless and dirty, but bright.

"You can take her on anytime. I just don't see why it's so urgent."

"Juliet is outside her compound. That doesn't happen often anymore. I could wait decades before there's a chance at her again. And don't forget the victims."

Darius nodded. "Right. You know best, sir, of course."

Not on everything, but the boy was merely seventeen. I would hardly disavow him of the notion of my all-mighty wisdom. Leaving him sitting in the coffee shop, I crossed the street. With any luck, I wouldn't have to pick the lock on the door.

The knob turned freely in my hand.

No alarms sounded when I stepped inside their headquarters. The warm interior felt pleasant to my chilled body. The long hall, perhaps the whole length of the building, had doors on both sides. Didn't know where to find whom I sought, so forward I went, trusting my nose.

I neared a room with several voices talking in casual tones and paused before passing the doorway. The paladin wasn't in there, as everyone in the room was a native Brit. She had the cutest hint of a Midwestern accent. A burst of speed carried me past the entry without alerting them. Her scent continued to the stairs.

I crept silently past the second floor offices. It would figure my target was in the last. If I needed a fast escape, I'd have better luck diving out a window than running out of the building. Oh, well…time to have my fun.

The paladin's companion answered the door when I knocked. She was blonde, wearing a tweed ladies suit that hugged her curves in a polite fashion. "Yes?" she greeted me. Another English native.

I stepped forward and nodded respectfully to those in the room. "Good afternoon. I was wondering if I might engage the services of one of your warriors." Figured making a formal request would score brownie points. Politeness was worth a shot until they brought out the stakes.

The aged gentleman behind the desk rose from his seat. "How did you get in here, young man?"

"With this." I held up a very old, simple silver cross by the chain. The center had two Greek letters stamped into it: alpha and omega.

The old man and the woman gasped. "You have two seconds to explain yourself, sir," the Englishwoman said.

"Miss Thornhill, stand down," the old man ordered.

"Sir?" She didn't take her eyes off me to ask the question. Good girl.

"It is a valid key past the wards. I would inquire, though, how you managed to obtain it, young man."

"Had it nearly all my life. Nearly three hundred years, as it were. Had to take it off when it started to burn me."

"Adam," the paladin said behind me.

Turning halfway, I smiled at her. "In the flesh. Now, can I share my proposal, or do I need to take it to another office?"

She narrowed her eyes at me and took a defensive stance. On the cute side of pretty, she was dressed in specialized armor fitted close to the body. One hand was behind her back, no doubt reaching for a knife hidden in a sheath under her coat.

The other two looked curious. *Baited and hooked.* The old man gestured for me to take a seat.

I preferred standing, but did let the paladin into the office. "You know of the vampire Juliet." They nodded. "There is an opportunity to end her if taken now."

"She's left her mansion?" the old man asked.

"Gone 'shopping' and on her way home. She always travels cross-country by train, so if one were to fly ahead to one of the scheduled stops, she can be intercepted."

"Shoppin' for what?" the girl asked.

"Rare treats, dear paladin. Children from foreign lands she and her guests rarely get to sample." I doubted she'd included me in her report since the other two hadn't recognized me.

"The blood of innocents…" the woman said with horror.

"You know her itinerary?" the old man asked me.

"I do. I'd feel better leaving as soon as possible."

"We can handle it, vampire," he argued. "Just give us the information and we will save the children."

"Sorry. Not how it's going to work. You try to storm in there, and she's going to catch wind of it before you have a chance." I grinned. "*I* only need one partner."

"Excuse me, sir, but who the hell is this man?" the Englishwoman asked.

"I am Adam, born the first son to my parents in 1700. An eye disease was taking my sight, so my mother sent me to a monastery to be taken care of. In 1730, Juliet and her minions raided the monastery a week before I was to take my vows."

"The very order that started our organization, Miss Thornhill," the old man added. "As far as we have on record, Adam has never willingly taken a human life."

"*Willingly?*" she asked.

I shrugged. "A couple accidents happened when I was young. I'm not fond of my kind. Never have been. Juliet is one of the worst of us the Earth has ever seen." I pointed at the paladin. "I want the best."

"We have others more experienced, Adam," the old man said.

"But not better. I've seen what you have to offer on this continent. She's the one I want."

I watched her kill a *hollenhund* — a hellhound — alone in Germany. Took balls to face a demon dog with eyes glowing orange in the dark and breath smelling like sulfur.

Her face turned red from being discussed like she wasn't in the room. Red stood out more intensely for me than any other color. "Sir, are you going to order me to go into battle with a *vampire*? We don't even know if he's tellin' the truth!"

She still didn't trust me. After Los Angeles, that hurt a bit.

The old man met my eyes. "He is." Perhaps I'd met this one in his youth. Humans all looked alike to me as they aged.

"Sir, perhaps…" Seemed the guide shared her paladin's misgivings.

"We can't afford to miss this opportunity, Miss Thornhill. Juliet's horde murders too many civilians every year. Agent Seven, you will accompany Adam on this mission and aid him however he best needs it."

I winked at the paladin. She frowned. "Cheer up, kid. I promise not to bite."

She rolled her eyes. "Like you could." She sighed, resigned. "Very well, sir. Where are we going?"

"Los Angeles. She has to be intercepted before she gets there," I said.

"How am I gettin' *him* across the Atlantic?" she asked her boss.

"Arrangements have been made, Agent Seven. Sunlight won't be a problem."

"Very well," the old man said. "Adam, if you don't mind, I'd like a minute with my colleagues."

I nodded. "Of course." I could hear just fine outside the door, too. They probably knew that, but appearances were to be kept.

"…*Sir, I was going to see my mother for Christmas!*" Seven argued.

Aww, now I felt bad.

"The duties of our calling outweigh our personal needs, dear. I'm sorry. Perhaps you can see this as motivation to get the job done quickly."

"Yes. What of the vampire once I'm finished?"

"Use your discretion. I have faith in your abilities, Agent."

"Thank you, sir. I guess I should go pack."

Hearing her step to the door, I backed away to lean on the wall.

"I guess I'm with you," she said. "Try anything funny, and you're dust." She said it just as evenly as stating the sky was blue today. Gutsy, now she knew my exact age. I followed her down the hallway to the stairs and onto the first floor. When I didn't turn for the exit, she whirled around and stopped, hands on her hips. "Stop followin' me."

"How else can I make sure you don't sneak out the back way?" I teased.

She crossed her arms under her breasts. "I'm not showin' a vampire my living quarters."

"I wish you no harm, paladin. We're on the same side."

"I'll believe that when I see it." Tough cookie. I loved redheads. So feisty, like Rita Hayworth in the movies.

"Very well…and what would make you more comfortable, oh *young, noble* paladin?"

"Stop calling me that, for one. My name is Agent Seven and you know it."

I grinned. "I doubt your mother gave you that nomenclature at birth."

"True, but I'm not tellin' you the real one. Second, you can wait outside. Assuming you're a…*man* of your word, you won't run off."

"As you wish. I'll be in the coffee shop across the street."

That seemed acceptable to her. She turned on her heel and headed deeper into the building, leather trench coat billowing around her legs. The cut of the coat reminded me of the one Kate Beckinsale wore in *Underworld*. Yeah, I know…cliché for a vampire to watch a vampire movie, but I spent a lot of time indoors. Beggars couldn't be entertainment choosers.

Darius paced outside the shop across the street. He visibly sighed with relief upon seeing me exit Agency headquarters. I waited for a car to pass, then joined him.

"You weren't worried, were you, Darius?"

He attempted indifference. "Of course not. Got bored."

"Right. Well, better or worse, they accepted. She's packing to come with us as we speak."

He whistled appreciatively. "You sure have a way with people, sir. Hope she doesn't dust you in your sleep."

I clapped a hand on his shoulder. "That's why I have you, Darius." He looked nervous. I laughed. "Ah, there she is."

Agent Seven spotted us and waited for her turn to cross the street. She carried a large duffle bag and had changed into street clothes, the hood of her coat pulled over her auburn hair to shield against the rain. Out of the specialized gear the paladins wore, I was reminded how young she was. I'd do my best to not get her killed.

The woman in the suit, Miss Thornhill, came out and joined her. They crossed the street together. Uh-oh.

"The invitation is only for one, Agent Seven."

"Where I go, she goes. You know how we work, vampire. One warrior, one guide with the book know-how." She peered around me to Darius. "Who's he?"

"My son, Darius. Darius, meet Agent Seven."

He stuck out his hand to greet her. "Hi."

She hesitated before she shook it. I saw the surprise in her eyes when she realized he was human. The expression turned to contempt as she leveled her gaze back on me. "What exactly are you doing with him?"

Darius spoke up for both of us. "I've gotten a classical education, ma'am, and a bit of defensive training against the supernatural. Adam saved my life and put a roof over my head."

"I'm practically a saint." She glared at me. It was cute. "As I was saying before, passage is only booked for three, so your guide will regrettably have to stay behind."

"I can meet you there, Seven," the guide said. "You know how to keep in touch."

Agent Seven sighed. "Fine. We're flying out, correct?"

"Yes. We should hail a cab. Our plane is waiting."

Darius took the front, so Agent Seven, Miss Thornhill, and I ended up in back, Seven in the middle. The paladin put herself between me and the human, though she was clearly just as uncomfortable sitting next to me. I appreciated that she wore gloves. One accidental touch could sear a chunk of my flesh, if not dust me altogether.

At the airport, the guide parted with us to obtain her own transport. I led my companions to where the chartered planes board passengers. Seven looked surprised.

"You didn't expect me to fly commercial, did you?"

"Euro trash."

Darius laughed. See, I said this would be fun. I liked doing what she didn't expect, like opening doors and taking her bag out of the cabby's trunk. It wasn't surprising she expected so little of my kind. Her experience was with fledges, little more than rabid animals. At my advanced age, I required little blood unless I was injured, and my mother *had* raised me to be a gentleman.

I trusted Darius to see to the details once we were on the plane and attempted to be a good host. "Beverage? We have a wide variety of sodas, sparkling and regular water, a couple ales…"

"No thank you," Seven replied. "No offense."

"The food is safe. Darius stocks his preferences."

"I'm fine."

"Alright. Agent Seven, if this mission is to be successful, you're going to have to exercise a little faith."

"I have plenty of faith. I just don't trust monsters."

"Simple as that?"

"Just as. Where I come from, we don't like to complicate things. I do my job, I'm good at it, and I go home. It's nothin' personal. Your people try to eat my people, and I try to stop that."

"Clinical detachment."

"Yep."

"Interesting. Your kind is usually quick to judgment. No offense."

She shrugged. "Life is too short for resentment and hatred. I leave the judgment of souls to the Almighty."

"Your prickly stance in L.A. and at HQ your version of not judging?"

She sighed. "It's only business. If I walked into your home uninvited, wouldn't you be suspicious?"

"Fair enough. Then I hope you won't refuse to eat or drink on this trip again, or you're no good to me."

She blushed. Ask Darius some time how often he won an argument with me. Yeah, I might've been a bit hard on the girl, but she needed to get past any prejudices The Agency had drilled into her head pretty quick if we were going to make this work.

Darius came back from the cockpit. "We're ready, sir, so they'd like us to take our seats. Can I get you anything, Miss...uh?"

"You can call me Seven, Darius. Not right now. Maybe later." She smiled at my apprentice.

I frowned. He was sort of attractive, I guess, in a human way. Perhaps my charm was a little rusty... Or maybe it was merely because he was human. I settled into a reclining chair in the back corner to rest. It never felt natural to be awake at this hour, and it would take us six hours to fly to New York.

The kids were talking when I awoke.

Scratch that. It sounded like they were *flirting*.

It bothered me, but I didn't know why.

"How soon do we land?" The question might have come out a bit grumpy based on the way I made them jump.

"T-twenty minutes?" Darius said. "I'll go check."

"Not a morning person?"

I grunted. My schedule was off and I was hungry. Plus, I was preparing to face my she-devil of a sire I hadn't seen in decades, and before that, centuries. Made a vamp cranky. I got up, grabbed a bag of blood from the refrigerator and locked myself in the bathroom to eat it.

Fanging out in front of Darius, I was used to. But not for her. Never liked strangers seeing me like that. After making sure my face was clean, I retook my seat.

The "fasten seatbelts" light came on as we made our descent to New York City. I considered letting the kids take a walk while the plane refueled. Early afternoon time kept me inside. "Don't leave the airport, but I suppose you can get some supper."

"Is there anything you need, sir?"

"I'm fine, Darius. Take the young lady to get a souvenir or something."

"We should be discussing strategy. I don't know your plan," Seven argued.

"There's plenty of time between here and California. Go, eat. Might not have a chance later."

She frowned, then followed Darius out of the plane. I tried to calm my mind and get some more rest.

Chapter Seven
Della

Adam's entrance into HQ exposed a weakness in our security. I insisted it be fixed while I was away. A vampire never should've been able to enter without alarms going off, even if he did have a way past the wards.

This could be an elaborate trap, of course. We had no assurances of his intentions. With age, vampires could be very patient, so he could be playing a long game.

And I was on a plane with him and his minion.

Mama would be telling me to be polite and respect my elders. She didn't know what it felt like to be in the proximity of a demon or vampire, especially an old one like Adam. I didn't like going into a deadly scenario without a plan, and I certainly didn't like taking orders from a vampire. Honestly, he could've given me more time to prepare, but I could see the strategy in that. Present a dire situation with an immediate deadline to The Agency and they were going to react.

We saved the day or died trying.

My life changed at sixteen when Amelia directed my first vampire to me while I was walking home from Mom's diner. I flipped out at the fangs and red eyes, screaming my fool head off, and ran. He caught me, I pushed back, and no more vamp.

Dust.

Ashes.

I screamed again.

Amelia told me about my destiny, then convinced my mother I had an invitation to a "good school for gifted kids". Before that night, I was on track to be the first woman to go to college in my family, so Mama was eager to send me off to a "good opportunity".

That was hundreds of dead monsters ago. Adam was right. I prob'ly was one of the best The Agency had. Didn't scare easy anymore.

"So, what's your story, Darius?" I asked as we looked for a restaurant.

"Huh? Oh, not much to tell. I ended up on the street a few years ago. Don't have parents anymore. Bounced around the foster system for a while, then ran away from the last one because the guy tried to hit me for mouthin' off. Adam saved my life on the street, offered me a meal and clean clothes, and decided to finish my education. How long have you been in the hero racket?"

"Three years. I'm nineteen."

He pointed to himself with his thumb. "Seventeen. Adam's not so bad once you get to know him, you know. He can't help what he is, but he means well."

Sighing, I said, "Maybe. I'd just prefer to know what I'm gettin' into ahead of time. I'm sure he's used to doing things a certain way, but so am I."

"McDonald's okay?"

"Yeah."

Darius was a little too nice. I didn't know what to do with that. Hadn't had a date since I joined The Agency. Well, I never actually dated, but not the point. Even among agents, we were discouraged to make friendships and dating was strictly forbidden. Anyone in our lives could be used against us; part of why we worked in secret. No one wanted "I got my family killed" on their conscience.

We ate quickly and checked out the shopping mall before heading back to the plane. Darius was a pleaser. He *really* didn't want to be late. I picked up a card for my mom and a set of earplugs.

Adam was reclined in the corner seat again when we got back. His chest slowly rose and fell. A set of ear-buds were in his ears and his eyes were closed. I touched his knee with my gloved hand. He opened his eyes and tilted his head like dogs do when they're curious. I handed him the package of earplugs and shoved my hands in my pockets.

"Peace offering," I said. "You have really sensitive ears, right?"

He glanced down at the package in his hand. "Yeah." Then he looked up and smiled at me, the real genuine kind. "Thank you."

I nodded and fled to my seat. *Wow.* The man could sell toothpaste to dentists with that smile. I'd forgotten how beautiful he was. Holy heck, I shouldn't be thinking a vampire was hot. *Mercy,* he was, though…even though I didn't go for the scruffy type. His hair was a bit too long and a couple days' stubble grew out of his face. Nice clothes, too. Didn't know much about fashion, but I could tell expensive when I saw it. He might look pretty good with a shave and his hair combed back out of his eyes.

Should be thinking about the mission, dummy. I picked up my bag.

"Going somewhere?"

"I'm waiting for my partner."

He sat up. "You agreed to come on the mission."

"And I'll be there, but she is my partner. I'm not leavin' the airport without her."

"You don't know what plane she managed to get. You could be waiting for hours."

I shook my head. "I do know. She was on the soonest flight after our take-off. Trust me." I stood at the door. "You want me with you, you take both of us."

A couple things went through my head:

I'm facing off with a vampire in close quarters.

A vampire I might have to kill if I've pissed him off.

A vampire that is still sitting and hasn't blinked.

He slowly rose, all fluid grace, and stood before me. Darius fidgeted nervously out of the corner of my eye.

Adam suddenly smiled. "I like you. Go get your friend."

I nodded, set my bag on the floor, and turned to leave.

"Seven... Thirty minutes, or we leave without you."

Great. Amelia, I hope you weren't delayed...

We were back in fifteen.

"I told you she'd be here," I said to Adam.

"Now, Seven, don't be rude to our host. We have much still to learn from each other."

Amelia rarely approved of my speaking plainly in front of others. It was how she was raised. Even insults had to sound polite. We didn't agree about much outside the job, but I respected and trusted her. She knew her stuff.

"Please take your seats, ladies. We don't need to be further behind schedule." Adam wasn't pleased, though he was very quiet in his anger.

He talked to the pilot, then sat in his corner staring out the window. Vampires didn't need to blink or breathe, so they could go very still. It was a scary thing, seeing a living statue.

Darius got up to whisper to his master, so I moved as far front as I could to read a chick mag I picked up at the airport. Yeah, I had a secret girly side, so sue me.

When Darius came back to his seat, he handed me a Coke. "Hungry? I have snacks."

"I'm okay. Em, do you need anything?"

"I brought my own, thank you." She buckled up for take-off, then settled her headphones in place.

"Do you know the plan?" I asked Darius.

He shook his head. "He shares when he feels it's necessary. Don't take it personally."

Lord save us from cranky undead Europeans. But as long as we saved those kids, nothing else mattered. Still, I wanted him to know who he was dealing with. "Look…Adam. I'm sure you're used to doin' things your own way and all, being the dark, brooding hero or whatever, but I'm not some lackey to be kept in the dark and fed bull-crap. Full disclosure or I go home as soon as we touch the ground."

"When we land, it will still be light, so nothing can be done until dark. I suggest you relax."

"You are the most irritating *creature* I've ever met."

He smiled. "Thank you, Agent Seven."

I crossed one leg over the other and swiveled the chair so I could give him the evil eye. We'd see whose patience won out.

Chapter Eight
Adam

Poor girl worked up a fine temper, then fell asleep before midnight London time. I signaled to Darius to get a blanket. The other woman's eyes were closed as well.

I studied Seven while she slumbered. Humans were so rarely still enough for me to see the tiny details. I had clear vision now at my age, but in muted color like faded photographs. Reds stood out the strongest. Her hair was auburn, tightly woven in a French braid down her back. Up close, I could see the freckles across her nose and cheeks. I don't think I have any freckles. She was young enough to still have lineless skin and fullness to her cheeks. That word came to me again: cute. I hadn't paid attention to her eye color—could rarely tell besides light and dark without being right on top of the subject, anyway. The clothes she wore were ordinary: a plain blue sweater, blue jeans, and a black winter coat. Black combat boots were on her feet.

I gently laid the blanket on her and retreated to my corner. Darius ignored me, his nose buried in a text.

When we landed in Los Angeles, I needed to send him on an errand.

It was time to wake up the paladin. I touched her shoulder. A hand shot up and grabbed me by the throat. "Seven…" I rasped.

She blinked, her eyes widened, and she loosed her grip. "I-I'm sorry."

I rubbed my throat. "It's alright. I should have said something first."

She blushed. "Reflex. You need somethin'?"

"We're landing soon."

"Oh. Okay."

I hadn't been that close to death since my first one. Ah, but for the existence of one glove... I went up to the cockpit to check with the pilot. I didn't want her or Darius to see me shaken, so I stayed until we were on the ground.

You know what was truly embarrassing? Running to the terminal under a heavy blanket. I almost preferred the old method of traveling in a pine box. "Stop snickering at me, boy, and go rent a van," I snapped. Darius saluted me and did as I asked. Kid was getting cheeky in adulthood.

"Do you miss the sun?" Seven asked while we waited.

I shook my head. "I barely remember being out in it. I don't like being restricted by it, though."

"Makes sense." She paused. "Why is this important to you?"

That was personal. "Curiosity killed the cat, paladin."

She let out one of those sighs women were so good at. The "men are such a pain" sigh. "Not tryin' to be rude, *vampire*. Knowing the emotional attachment of my team just makes good sense."

"Trained to be a good little soldier, aren't you?"

She narrowed her eyes, glaring at me. "Hey, *you* needed *me*. I'm fine with booking the nearest commercial flight home."

I felt the energy crackling around her from her emotions. I doubted she was aware of her strength. Most Creatures had an otherworldly sixth sense for magic, life energy, and the like that humans rarely achieved. Humans were entirely too wrapped up in themselves to be aware of much of anything around them. If they ever learned to stop and listen as a species, we'd have nothing to prey on.

"My past with Juliet is personal," I finally said. "All you need to know is that I want her dead."

"Dead enough to be reckless?"

I looked straight into her eyes. "Never."

"Good."

Darius came back with a set of keys. "Van's out front, sir."

"Thank you, Darius."

I picked up my two stacked trunks with ease and gestured for him to lead the way. Seven shouldered her bag and maybe looked impressed. Her partner looked bored. I flexed my arms a little as I adjusted my grip. Hey, I'm dead, but still a man.

"Where to, sir?"

"Raven's."

"Ohhh…"

"What's that?" Seven asked as we piled into the van.

"Not a 'that'. Who. She's a seer," I said. Darius merged into traffic once it was clear.

"Oh." She didn't look comfortable with the notion.

Raven was the most reliable seer in the Western U.S. Didn't know if that was her real name, but it was how everyone knew her. She looked to be in her late twenties, with blue-black hair down to her waist and modelesque cheekbones.

We parked in the drive under an arch of bougainvillea. Seven stayed in her seat.

"What?" I asked.

"We'd rather stay out here, if you don't mind."

"Suit yourself." Just as well.

A silver-haired woman answered the door, hunched with age. Raven referred to her as Grandmother. No one knew if they were actually related.

Raven sat in her living room with coffee waiting on the table. "Adam." She rose to her feet. "I've been expecting you."

"I've come to expect that. This is Darius. I took him as an apprentice since last we met."

Raven showed him a warm smile, then sat down again. We took the chairs opposite. My son stared at the beautiful seer. I kicked his foot.

"You have other traveling companions…" she said.

"Yes."

"She fears the source of my information. Don't apologize. I sometimes fear it, also." She pushed two steaming mugs across the table. "What is it you seek, friend?"

"I need to know how far Juliet is behind us." I sipped the coffee out of politeness. I preferred cocoa.

Raven closed her eyes and focused. Her heartbeat slowed a fraction. "Several hours…almost a day," she said. "She is most displeased by the delay."

A delay was most advantageous. "I'll bet. Where would be best to attack?"

She focused, then frowned. "Hmm…unclear. Too many still have decisions to make. The future is fluid."

I sighed. "I figured you would say that. Anything else?"

She shook her head. "I'm sorry. But there is time to rest."

"Thank you. Darius, there's a small box in my top trunk. Would you retrieve it, please?"

"Yeah."

Once we were alone, I asked her if there was more to hear.

"Nothing specific." I offered her my hand. She declined. "Be careful. That girl out there is important."

"Important how?"

Raven shrugged. "Just important."

Darius came back with the box. I presented it to her. Swiss chocolates usually kept me in a woman's good graces.

"You haven't lost your touch, Adam. Thank you. It was nice meeting you, Darius."

"And you, ma'am."

I kissed her on the cheek when she walked us to the door. "Lovely to see you again, Raven."

"Quite a lady," Darius said outside. He opened the driver-side door of the van.

"Yes, she is. One of these days, you're going to have to stop staring when a pretty woman says hello."

"I didn't stare."

"You were seconds from drooling."

"What did she have to say?" Seven asked.

I climbed into the windowless back of the vehicle. "Juliet was delayed almost a day, so we have time to grab some sleep. Darius—"

"Find a good hotel. I'm on it."

Thankfully, sundown was approaching, daylight short so close to the solstice. The entrance to the hotel was in shadow, so I could walk in with dignity. I glanced at Seven. She looked ill-at-ease with our selection. "Problem?"

"Bit extravagant, isn't it?"

"I need a room with a refrigerator."

"*Oh*. For the, uh…"

"Yes." I stopped Darius before he approached the front desk. "Two rooms."

"Thanks," she mumbled. "It's crowded in here."

"Must be the holiday influence." Hmm, two whole minutes and we hadn't annoyed each other, yet. I liked that.

"Here are your passkeys," Darius said, handing them over. "But there's a glitch."

"What kind of glitch?" I asked.

"They're booked solid, so I could only get one room with two beds and a rollaway." He shrugged. "It's Christmas."

Seven sighed. "It's the thought that counts."

If she could be gracious, then I'd keep my whining to myself. At least we wouldn't be here long. While Seven used the bathroom in our quarters, I took Darius aside. "Best behavior, understand? Don't try peeking when they're not paying attention."

"I wasn't thinking about it!"

Right. "You're not that innocent, kid, so let's not pretend. It's going to be crowded enough in here without giving her a reason to slay us."

"I *got* it. Man, I'll be glad when this is over and you're back to normal," he groused.

She opened the door. "All yours, guys." She claimed the bed farthest back in the room to share with Miss Thornhill. Guess she didn't want to turn her back on us, the correct choice for survival every time. She kept proving me right in my selection.

"Don't say it. I know which bed is mine," Darius said.

I stretched back against the headboard. "One day you'll have your own apprentice to boss around and you'll miss times like this."

"Yeah, yeah…"

I hoped he lived that long. I was pretty fond of him most of the time. Being a mentor gave me a glimpse at real fatherhood, in a way. I'd never considered that possible.

"Should I make a supply run?" he asked.

"Might as well. I'm almost out of fresh blood, and we don't know what condition we'll find the captives in. Grab some blankets and first aid supplies."

"On it. Seven, wanna come?"

"I could stretch my legs."

"I'll go, as well," her partner said. She hadn't spoken much since getting on the plane.

I should have been happy to be alone, so I could sleep. Instead, I felt disappointed.

Chapter Nine
Della

I still didn't know what Adam had in mind tactically and that bothered me. "So, what's the story on this vamp we're after?" I asked Darius. He'd been pretty open with me so far.

"She's really old, and Adam's maker. She's supposed to be smart, and beautiful, and totally cold. He doesn't share about his past much, the time with her, but it's obvious there's a grudge there. The kids she grabbed are the meal for some big party she holds on the solstice. All the demon muckity-mucks show up."

"Why hasn't anyone taken her out if she hardly leaves home?"

"Couldn't tell ya for sure, but L.A. has a large demon community. We only pass through."

A shudder passed through me. "He warned me not to go into her compound."

"Nope."

His info chimed with what I knew. The Agency refused to attack Juliet at home. Any agent in L.A. was under strict orders to observe only and never engage. I didn't know why everyone was so afraid of her other than her age. We suspected she was behind the attacks dwindling our numbers, but there was no concrete evidence so far.

"How about dinner? I'm starving."

"Yeah, I guess…" I'd need the fuel if we attacked before dawn.

It surprised me how easy it was to get blood from a hospital. I'd have to include that in my report to Headquarters. Darius only bought a couple bags, but who knew how many Creatures might be doing the same thing? I'd feel a lot better if they were getting animal blood, instead. Perhaps that was why the Red Cross constantly asked for more donors.

I called Mom while Darius and Amelia were in Wal-Mart. Christmas was in five days. With the nature of this mission, I'd either be home or dead in that time, so I told her I'd see her soon. What with her Lupus diagnosis, I worried about her workin' at the diner too much. The Agency was paying her health insurance in exchange for my services, but she didn't know that. If she knew what I really did...

"Earth to Seven..." Darius waved his hand in front of my face.

I blinked. "Huh?"

"You spaced. Where did you go?"

A blush warmed my cheeks. "Thinkin' about Christmas."

"You have a place to go?"

"Yeah...home, in Oklahoma. Mama decorates every surface of our house. Most of it's cheap junk, but I love it."

He nodded in understanding. "I had that when I was really little. Adam's not much for holidays, but we have a nice meal if we can."

"He eats human food?"

He grinned. "Weird, huh? Doesn't hurt him or anything. He'd probably kill me for telling you, but he has a thing for chocolate."

"Serious?" I couldn't see it.

He nodded. "The really dark stuff. Any bitter food, actually." He leaned forward. "I think it's about an opposite of the blood," he whispered.

Huh. "Why would he want an opposite?"

Darius looked at me like I was stupid. "He's a good man. He lives on it because he has to, not because he wants to."

"You really believe that."

"Of course I do. I've lived with him for years. If he was planning something evil, I think I'd have noticed by now."

"I'm sorry. It's just hard to grasp after all I've seen. But I'm here, aren't I?"

"Yeah. Just don't think about staking my friend."

"I hope I won't have to." I really did, at least for Darius' sake.

We'd taken our time, so Adam was awake and in the shower when we got back. Darius turned on the TV and plopped down on Adam's bed with a bag of Cheetos. I figured I might as well study while there was time to kill and opened my school text. Amelia was downstairs making an update call to Headquarters.

Steam billowed forth when the bathroom door opened. Adam came out with a towel wrapped around his waist and his wet hair slicked back. Yup, I was right about the hair. *Oh, golly...* His chest and abs were chiseled, black hair outlining the definition. Not in a Sasquatch way, merely a sprinkling of fuzz. A drop of water trickled down the center of his torso, and I felt warm.

This wouldn't do.

"You're back," Adam said. He just stood there in that towel.

"Yep," Darius said. "Got everything we were looking for."

"Didn't expect you, yet." He finally moved to his smaller trunk for some clothes.

Adam's back was as yummy as his front, and why couldn't I stop *staring*? This one-room thing really wasn't gonna work! The curtains were hiding a sliding glass door, so I escaped to the tiny balcony. Must've been forty degrees by now, but I welcomed the cold to clear my head. I'd been a good girl all my life. I didn't lust after men, especially not *vampires*. That must be it, a supernatural mojo. Weren't my fault if he was putting the whammy on me. Clinical detachment, Della. You're good at it, remember?

I stayed out there until my nose got numb and Adam would have to be dressed.

Inside, all business: "What's the plan? I'm losin' patience."

Chapter Ten
Adam

One moment, friendly; the next, she was back to treating me like the enemy. I began to feel rather offended. "You could say *please*, paladin."

"That's it. I've had enough of your stalling." She picked up her duffle and stomped toward the door.

I shot in front of her and blocked her exit. "Don't."

She pulled a sword halfway out of the bag. Sneaky. "Get out of my way, or lose your head." I had seven inches on her, so she had to tilt her head back to glare at me.

"Uncouple the train car with the prisoners."

She blinked. "That's it?"

"Well, the first part. Are you going to play nice and retract the claws?"

She had the katana pressed against my neck with a flick of her wrist. "Why should I? You've been jerkin' my chain since this mornin', and I don't need you to find the train."

"Hey, guys…" Darius pleaded.

Seven took her eyes off me to tell him not to move. It was all the distraction I needed to take the sword from her hand. She put her hands up and backed away slowly from the blade.

I shouldn't have trusted the retreat.

She kicked the sword away with one foot and connected with my chin with the other. I slammed into the door and heard a crack. Thankfully, the wood, and not me. I tasted blood.

"Nice kick."

"Thank you," she said. "Gonna move?"

"You're on the same team, dammit. Stop this," Darius said. He stepped in between us. "Please," he said to Seven. She sighed and relaxed her stance. I rubbed my jaw. I'd seen stars from that kick. "I'm gonna see if a room has opened up," he said. "Can you keep from killing each other for five minutes?" He picked up the phone and called the front desk.

I used the bathroom to spit out a tooth. Yeah, it would grow back, but the hole was going to drive me nuts for now. Rinsed it off, dropped it in a glass, then rinsed my mouth. Took the glass out there and set it on the dresser. "Last trophy you'll get off of me," I promised her.

She looked in the glass; snorted. "I'll treasure it always."

"Uh-huh…thank you." Darius hung up. "Down one floor. Someone will meet you at the elevator with the passkey," he told Seven.

She took the slip of paper with the room number. "Thanks." I let her go this time. Didn't know what she might do now, but things had just gotten interesting.

"Guess you aren't meant to coexist," Darius said when she was gone.

"Yeah…"

A half-hour later, I knocked on her door.

"Who is it?" she called

"It's me. Adam."

The latch turned, then she opened the door. "Yeah?" I held out a folded piece of hotel stationary. She took it, opened it. "Nice handwriting."

"Juliet's address. In case Darius and I fail."

"Thanks." She started to shut the door.

I stuck my foot in the gap. "I'm sorry for being a jerk. Darius doesn't take it personally. I don't socialize with other humans much."

"I accept your apology. Um, g'night."

"Good night, Seven." See? I could admit when I was wrong.

I took the van to scope out the territory, but the evening's events kept nagging me. After an hour, I turned around and went back up to Seven's room. I could hear the TV, so she hadn't skipped town. I knocked.

Amelia opened the door. "Oh, it's you." Seven came up behind her.

"I don't know why, but it's bothering me we have this tension. May I come in?"

"No tricks?" she asked.

"Swear on my mother's grave."

Seven sighed and let me inside, shaking her head. I could practically see the thought bubble of *Why am I doing this?* floating above her head. She turned off the TV.

"I don't know what I did to upset you, but I'd still like your help." Preferred it. This would be a hell of a lot harder to accomplish alone, especially with the children involved.

She sighed and sat on the bed. "Bein' around you puts me on edge. I don't know if you sense we're different from other humans, but we sense Creatures. The older or more powerful, the stronger it is. Close proximity makes that danger voice scream in my head to get rid of it."

Interesting. "So you can't relax around me."

She shook her head. "No. Not yet. Usually don't let one of you live long enough to find out if that changes." She shrugged; an apology for the mistrust.

"And you never should," Amelia said. The guide stood with her hand on the doorknob, waiting to throw me out. Seven gave her a look. I hadn't figured out who was the boss between them, yet. Even in partnerships, one led, one usually followed.

"I'm sorry I make you uncomfortable," I told her.

"I shouldn't have pulled a sword on you…it wasn't fair. You've been a decent host."

Good enough. "Well, goodnight, again. We move out at sunset tomorrow."

Amelia opened the door to let me out. No dawdling, then. One prickly female. If I was going to reach some common ground with Seven, I'd have to do it when she was alone.

Chapter Eleven
Della

The Agency and I knew where Juliet lived, but Adam didn't know that. He didn't have to apologize twice or offer the address. Confused over how he could be so different, I didn't sleep well. All the traveling this year — Los Angeles, to Germany, to London, back to L.A. — didn't help, and if Amelia asked, I'd blame it on that, but man...he was one confounding vampire.

There were at least three families of vampires — the Red Eyes, the Gold Eyes, and the Green Eyes. The history on Juliet described her with red eyes when she vamped, so Adam would have them, too. Most vampires I dusted did.

After six years, I still wasn't used to seeing irises change color before my eyes. The fangs growing disturbed me less. The Agency studied specimens from all three families in the depths of HQ, along with all the other monsters out there, leading to the discovery that each family line shared at least a little DNA — the infection. Hopefully, we'd one day cure the virus that created new vampires.

So the scientists believed, anyway. Others weren't convinced the vampire plague on humanity was solely biological.

First day of winter
The solstice

The Southern California night was cold and breezy. We'd need to approach from downwind to avoid alerting Juliet and her men too soon. Adam went back to his seer for an update. We picked him up after he called and were now on our way to the railroad tracks. Juliet's train was stopping on a secluded stretch with little human traffic. The children would be transferred to a truck to take them to her compound.

I almost felt more "me" in my armor than regular clothes nowadays. Think less medieval and more ninja, then add inscriptions of protection in Latin and Hebrew sewn into the material with genuine silver thread. Over the full-body suit I wore bracers, shin guards, and steel-reinforced boots. Sections similar to Kevlar protected my torso. A mask and hood completed my disguise. I tucked weapons into the pockets and loops in my coat while Darius drove to the site. Amelia had seen this process a thousand times, but Adam seemed fascinated.

"Got enough on you to start a war," he said.

I shook my head. "Nah. No room for the rocket launcher." He laughed.

Amelia rolled her eyes. She thought battle should be entered into with seriousness and meditation. Eh, hers was the easy job, hanging back on the sidelines. She prepared me with info, restocked my supplies, and patched me up when I came back injured. Oh, she could handle herself with a blade or rifle…it's just she rarely had to. Tonight, she and Darius would be getting the children out of the train car while Adam and I kept Juliet and her guards occupied.

"Find a place to stop out of sight near the marker, Darius," Adam said.

"Yes, sir."

"What then?" Amelia asked.

"We wait for the train to get near."

"You'll know when to go for the kids, Amelia," I said.

Adam and I left them in the van and got into place at opposite sides of the track. We could see the light from the train in the distance. I hoped he'd done the math correctly. If the train was going too fast when it reached us, I wouldn't be able to do my part.

The engine neared and I ran for it, timed my steps, and jumped for a handle on the side. I swung myself inside behind the engineer and pulled one of my pistols. "Don't touch that brake, sir."

He startled, turned to look at me, and his eyes widened in fright. Human, by all appearances. My gun was only loaded with tranq darts, but he didn't need to know that. "I-I'm not carrying any money. Don't shoot."

"I won't have to unless you can't follow directions. Clear?" He rapidly nodded his head. "Good..." I glanced at his name tag. "Edgar." I checked the speed of the engine—twelve miles per hour. Also good. "Come with me, Edgar, nice and slow." I nudged him ahead of me toward the next car, pistol raised. "Open the door to the passenger car." Once he did, I shoved him inside.

Juliet's guards stood at once. I waved, then shut the door and found the ladder to climb on the roof. Only had to buy time for Adam to disengage the second car where the children were kept. Like we planned, the minions followed me. A couple ran into the engine, followed by Edgar.

I heard Juliet order someone to stop the train and the rest to go after me. Crouched on the roof, I waited for the first minion to show his face and fired a dart into his neck. He slumped down the ladder out of sight. I glanced behind me. Adam had been successful—the other car was left behind.

Minion Number Two decided not to go the way of his buddy and started shooting through the roof of the car—with real bullets.

"Crap!"

Edgar was slowing the train, so having nowhere else to go, I jumped off the side, rolling upon impact to allow the momentum to keep me from breaking anything. It still hurt. Looked up and saw Adam open the rear door of Juliet's passenger car. Got to my feet and ran to help, trusting Amelia and Darius to do their jobs with the kids.

The train screeched to a halt.

We didn't have much time before Juliet's truck arrived with who-knew-how-many reinforcements. I climbed into the car to see Adam and Juliet facing off. Wow, she was gorgeous. I couldn't help thinking it. The woman—vampire—was stunning. Long ebony hair, brilliant blue eyes, and creamy skin. She wore a perfectly tailored business suit in ruby red that looked really expensive. Probably a designer I couldn't pronounce. She spotted me and smiled at Adam like he'd surprised her in a special way.

"A paladin, Adamo? Well, you are serious. I'd love to hear how you convinced her to come." She glanced around his shoulder at me again. "Come in, dear. Introduce yourself." Her voice was as lovely as the rest of her, a sexy bedroom tone men would pay to listen to on the phone.

"See to the others," Adam told me.

"Sure?"

"Go." Well, if he was sure...

I left to handle the minions from the other side and tossed a mini smoke bomb in the front door of the car. The minions came out coughing, and it would flush Juliet out where Adam wanted her. The minions were easy pickings, coming out one by one.

I used the tranq gun pfft, pfft, pfft.

Never heard the person who crept up behind me and bonked me on the head.

Probably Edgar.

Chapter Twelve

Adam

When the smoke started filling the train car, I gestured "come get me" with my hands and hopped out the rear door. I knew Juliet would follow me, loving a good chase. She laughed as she did, deftly dancing over the railroad tracks despite wearing four-inch heels. That contralto laugh had once stirred my blood three hundred years ago.

Now I only wanted the sound to stop.

Her face went cold when she spotted the empty disconnected car. "Oh, you'll pay for that, boy." She picked up a rock and pitched it at my head. Like dodging a hundred-mile-per-hour fast ball. It narrowly missed my ear. "Always wrecking my parties!" she screeched. "Do you see me stopping the mortals from celebrating Christmas? No! So why can't I have one little party for my friends?"

"You try serving children for dinner; you're going to make enemies."

She darted around the car, playing games. "Oh, who cares about orphans? Really, I'm doing them a favor, Adam. They lost their potential the moment society abandoned them."

Every time I got near her with my blade, she dodged away, refusing to engage. It was pissing me off. I swung wildly and missed, embedding the sword in the railcar. *Dammit.*

"Temper, temper, boy. You can do better than that."

She danced out of my reach again and ran through the car. I ran along the outside to cut her off, only for her to double back and speed out toward the street side of the tracks. Right to the expected truck. She hopped into the back with a helping hand from a minion and waved goodbye.

Laughing.

I shouldn't have let her goad me into a game of Tag. Well, the important thing was the children were alive and safe. I could find Juliet again later. Wasn't getting any older.

Darius drove the van up. I got some rope out of the back once he stopped and tied up the unconscious minions. The night was quiet again, save for the wind.

"Where's Seven?" he asked.

"I...I don't know. Seven?" No response. "SEVEN!"

Darius looked in the passenger car, then the engine. "Sir, she's not in there."

"Look around. Maybe she's hurt."

The children were whispering and crying inside the van. Miss Thornhill came out to look with us. "Here," she said, and picked something up. The tranq pistol.

Seven was gone. I was such a fool. I'd fallen for a trap and led an innocent woman to die in my quest for revenge, letting my desire to kill Juliet get the best of me. As I ran after her, I knew deep down she drew me away from the others on purpose. Even in defeat, my sire didn't escape without causing damage.

Somehow she knew. She knew Seven meant something to me.

No time to mope about it, idiot. Seven's on borrowed time.

For now, the girl was bait, but that wouldn't keep Juliet from killing her even if she couldn't sink her fangs into the paladin's throat. The holy mojo didn't protect the agents from...so many things. Humans were infinitely fragile. Damn the creator that made them that way!

I loaded up every weapon still in the case that would fit in my pockets, my belt, my boots... I was angry enough to go at this with fists and fangs, but I had to be rational. Surgical. Storming Juliet's fortress wasn't the best idea, but I could do it. I felt it, knew it...just had to get there before her guests arrived. We were screwed if she had the backing of the Elders.

At least the children were safe. Even though I'd known Seven mere hours, I knew she wouldn't forgive me if the mission failed. Nothing mattered more to her than saving innocent lives. Should have been enough for me, too, but I wasn't the one with assured salvation.

I stole an old car in under a minute and drove up into the hills.

Juliet's mansion was secluded in two ways: the private drive setting it back from the humans, and the magic that actually put the property on the Other Side. Your Average Joes couldn't see what really went on around them without help. They'd freak, think they're in Hell, and start trying to kill every Creature in sight. Leaving their belief in us behind was the best and worst thing a human could do for their survival.

The moonless night gave me one advantage, at least. She couldn't have any were-dogs guarding the perimeter. I crouched beside the fence and listened. Several heartbeats...humans? I grinned. My sire had grown cocky in her old age. Sure, you wanted a few beings around to protect you during daylight, but a whole crew of mortals?

Sloppy.

It meant she and Vittore had parted ways.

I easily vaulted over the fence into a California pepper tree for a better look. Whispered, "Forare il velo." *Pierce the veil.* Simple magic, really, allowing me to pass through any barriers Juliet might have created, and see what she wanted to hide.

I jumped out of the tree, landing silently, and crept toward the house. She was expecting me, but I didn't think she knew how I would come for her.

Chapter Thirteen

Della

Ow... Someone had conked me on the head. I slowly opened my eyes, feeling like I was two feet behind my own body. Must have a concussion.

"There she is."

Oh, crap. That melodic alto belonged to Juliet. She stood before me dressed to the nines. That dress probably cost more than Mama made in a month.

"You can't touch me." But someone had, since I was tied up.

She smiled, fangs showing. "You're right. I can't. Oh, boys..." Three henchmen stepped into the room. They must've been standing right outside the door. Juliet stroked a long red fingernail down the neck of the one closest to her. He shuddered and looked at her with obvious lust. Her initial was branded on his throat. "You see, I have billions of servants to choose from on this planet, paladin. Lots of eager Happy Meals begging for my favor." She snapped her fingers and a lackey handed her a syringe.

Uh-oh... There was nowhere to go, restrained as I was, when she approached me with that needle. I *hated* needles. The bitch plunged it into my bicep and depressed whatever that liquid was into my body. I felt my head start to swim and my legs turn to jelly.

Gave her my best glare.

She laughed. "That's so...cute. Strip her, boys." She walked to the doorway. "And she better be untouched when I send for her. Can't be spoiling her blood so soon."

The lackeys untied me and started stripping off my armor. I tried to struggle, but my body was so slow to respond I wasn't getting anywhere.

Juliet tossed a spool of red ribbon three inches wide to one of her servants. "Make sure she's wrapped up nice with a pretty bow. My childe will be along soon to collect his Christmas present."

"I'll have your head!" I yelled before she shut the door. She laughed.

I wanted to cry when they'd removed enough layers to unzip my suit. *Don't give them the satisfaction* Mama's voice rang in my head. I did my best not to make their job of rendering me nude any easier, but I wasn't going to flinch at their liberties. Juliet ordered them not to rape me, but that didn't stop them from grabbing and pinching any bit of flesh they felt like.

Later, I would cry. Mourn my lost innocence.

If I survived.

Naked now, one of them held me standing while the other two wrapped the ribbon tightly around my body from ankles to arm pits. A red Christmas mummy. My arms were pinned down so I wouldn't be able to help myself when the drug wore off. They tied a big bow around my shoulders, then let me fall to the floor.

Ow, again.

"You think she'll turn you when you've earned enough favor?" I asked them. Taunting. I had nothin' to lose.

"That's the deal. The boss rewards loyalty."

I rolled my eyes. "Oh, please. She'll drain you dry the second she's bored. That's how vampires work."

"Awfully mouthy for a girl that can't move."

"Death doesn't scare me. But you might wanna worry. With Juliet's treats gone—courtesy of me and my friends—who's she gonna serve for supper?"

They shared looks with each other and left the room, locking me in. I closed my eyes and willed away the sobs that threatened to overtake me. And then I prayed. I believed everything happened for a reason under Heaven, so I had to hold on to that thought about this as well. If I died tonight, The Agency would avenge me. If Adam somehow managed to rescue me, I'd continue my work. But I hoped whatever was coming, it would be soon. The waiting was the worst.

The door finally opened again and a bigger minion than the others I'd seen came in and hoisted me over his shoulder like a sack of potatoes. I thought about biting him as I dangled upside down, but he'd probably drop me on my head. My stomach still felt queasy from the concussion, so bad idea. The minion carried me into…a room for an indoor pool?

"You may put her down," Juliet ordered.

Big Minion put me on my feet, resting his meaty hands on my shoulders to keep me upright. My body still resembled a wet noodle. The cement chilled my bare soles. Juliet had a lot of henchmen in here.

"Nice place," I said.

She smiled. "Thank you. I suppose you're wondering why you were brought to me."

I shrugged, much as I was able. "Not really. You're going to rattle on 'bout some evil plot and I'm supposed to look suitably impressed. And then Adam will kill you."

"So sure of him, when you've just met?"

"He was very serious about killing you. Pretty convincing."

Juliet dismissed my words with a wave of her hand. "He'll have to get through my guards first. Even vampires are subject to nasty odds." She walked to me and met my eyes. "But, he will make it far enough to watch you die."

"I think he's smart enough not to storm the front door."

Glass fell out of a skylight above. It crashed to the cement just ahead of Adam's landing, a gun in each hand. He'd snatched my extra pistols. I had to admit, the vamp knew how to make an entrance. He took the first four minions down by headshot. They dissolved to ash from my wood bullets.

Show-off.

More minions ran into the room upon hearing the shots. Adam dropped the guns and pulled a katana from a scabbard strapped to his back and made beautiful violence.

Quick.

Graceful.

Efficient.

He sliced through our enemies like butter. Hope welled up from my gut.

"Adam!" Juliet barked. The action froze.

I'd been so busy watching him; I didn't notice her move to my side. She gripped my right arm, the silk ribbon protecting her from burning.

Adam growled, his eyes red with bloodlust. The first time I'd seen him look like a demon. "Hurt one hair on her head and I'll—"

"You'll *what*, boy? I had your gift wrapped so prettily… Tell you what…" She pushed me hard from behind.

I hadn't noticed we were so close to the edge of the pool, either.

Adam sprung into motion right before I hit the water.

One deep lungful was all I had to work with.

I tried to dolphin kick to the surface, but the ribbon was wrapped so tight…

I got my eyes above the waterline, then sunk like a rock. I'd never been all that buoyant.

Two minutes.

After that, I'd need a breath or CPR.

I started counting.

Chapter Fourteen

Adam

I lunged for Juliet and she super-jumped to the beams high above. Tracking her movements on the rafters, I shot bullets in a pattern to drive her to the chandelier, then severed the cord. She and it came crashing down on more minions. The scent of her blood filled the air from several cuts by the shattered crystal and my rage welled anew. Unarmed, she could only dodge my strikes until her fancy shoe slid on a puddle of blood and water.

I brought the blade down to sever her head from her neck and—

She wasn't there anymore. What—

Seven.

After throwing off my coat, I swam to her as fast as my body was capable. She wasn't struggling anymore. *Oh God…* I wrapped my arm around her waist and pushed off the bottom of the deep end with all my strength. The momentum propelled us out of the water and onto the deck. I laid her on her back. She wasn't breathing.

Screw it. She needed air more than I needed skin. I tilted her head back, pulled her jaw down, and forced my breath into her lungs. No pain…I felt my lips. My skin was intact. She wasn't burning me. What…? She couldn't be clinically dead. *Not yet. Please.* I breathed again into her mouth and there was too much resistance.

The silk. The knife in my boot made quick work of the layers binding her chest and her ribcage expanded. Again I gave her air.

Putting my hands on her chest, I started CPR.

One. Two. Three. Four.

No response.

One. Two. Three. Four.

"Breathe, dammit!"

Another four compressions and a breath.

She gasped.

Finally! I rolled her onto her side so she could cough out the water. "Easy…" She hacked and wheezed until her lungs were clear.

"Took long enough." She rolled onto her back.

"That's the thanks I get?"

She started shivering, her body reacting to the cold water and room, and she attempted to curl into a ball. "Juliet?"

"Gone."

"Escaped or dead?"

"I don't know. She vanished."

"Knife?" I gave it to her. She created a sort of mini-dress by cutting and knotting the ribbon so she could walk. The soaked ribbon clung to her skin, making us both aware of how little she wore.

"Let's find you some clothes."

"W-where did all the minions go?" She lifted her head and looked around the room. "Oh."

I retrieved the guns and stuck them in my belt, then handed her my coat. "Any idea where they put your outfit?"

"I d-don't know. The cell is d-down th-that way." Getting to her feet was awkward business, but she wouldn't let me help.

She walked with baby steps, trying not to dislodge the ribbon wrapped around her hips. Part of me wouldn't mind if it all fell away. She had a lovely body, feminine, yet strong. It'd been a long time since I stopped to admire a woman.

She paused at a doorway and started coughing again, then swayed on her feet. My first instinct was to gather her up into my arms, but she'd probably be offended.

"Does Juliet keep trophies?" she asked.

"In her bedroom."

She nodded. "Any c-clue where that is? This place seems kinda big."

"Enormous mansion. Could never fault her taste. We need to find the stairs."

At least we were walking on carpet now, warmer to Seven's bare feet. She stayed in step with me with her arms folded over her breasts. The coat rest on her shoulders like a shawl.

"If you let your arms swing, it'll help with circulation."

"I'm fine."

She started walking again. Stars above, what was with me? I didn't entangle my life with relationships. Sources, contacts, a couple safe havens, but that was it. Getting involved with humans highlighted my immortality. I only allowed Darius to stay because he was happy being a nomad right now and that would change one day as he matured.

I admired her, for certain, her tenacity and conviction to her calling. The sweetness not crushed by all the ugliness she had to face. Perhaps that's all it was—admiration. A little crush on a fellow warrior.

She wasn't next to me anymore. "Seven?" I spun and discovered I'd passed a staircase. "Ah. Mind on the mission, moron," I muttered.

She waited at the top of the stairs, tapping her foot. "Looks better that way."

"Huh?"

She pointed. "Your hair, off your face. It's better."

"Oh. Thank you." And thank you I was no longer capable of blushing. When had someone last paid me a genuine compliment? Had they ever?

"Well, come on!" She started down the hall.

"Yeah, yeah…"

I heard voices ahead at the junction and handed Seven my sword.

"...Ya think this stuff is real antique?" Mercenaries. With their employer who knows where, they were looting the place. Seven rolled her eyes and gestured me ahead. I poked my head into the room.

"Hi. Which room belonged to your boss?"

They jumped and reached for their weapons. I smiled. Still enjoyed a good fright. "Who wants to know?"

I let the demon show. "The guy that killed her. Don't want anything from you but directions."

"That way. Top floor."

I grinned around my fangs. "Smart decision." I stepped out of the way of the door. "Move along." The mortals scurried away like I expected. Seven rolled her eyes at me. Was that a generational thing? "What?"

"Nothin'," she said. "Let's get my armor so I can go home."

Juliet's boudoir was downright palatial. Several hundred years of her most precious treasures were in this suite. It'd be a waste to abandon them.

"Wow..." Seven said. "I could set Mama up for twenty years with this stuff, huh?"

"Longer, with wise spending. Take anything you like. You could say I'm her heir."

She snorted; a boyish sound. "Thanks for the permission."

I sighed. "I remember a time when young people didn't sass their elders..."

She found a closet. "I don't 'sass my elders'. Just vampires. And demons. Werewolves..."

"Oh, so it's a species-ist thing."

"A what? No."

I found a suitcase I could put loot in. She could find her suit. It was most likely in Juliet's bedroom, anyway.

Took what I wanted from the sitting area and looked in the bedroom. The red brocade décor took me back. My sire's preferences hadn't changed in three-hundred years. Favorite color red, favorite fabric silk…the four-poster bed and dressing table despite her lack of need for the mirror. I knew if I looked under the bed skirts I'd find chains anchored to the floor. She liked to play with her food if she thought them pretty. An involuntary shudder of revulsion welled up within me. Her chest of jewels from the dresser joined the case.

The closet had one of those modern designs with the rods and shelves built in. It was full of designer clothes. "Feel like upgrading your wardrobe?" I called out.

Seven came in carrying a towel, squeezing the water out of her hair. "Whoa, bordello style."

"Found the bathroom?"

She shook her head. "A wet bar. The bathroom should be in here. Have you found any of my things?"

"Haven't checked the drawers."

She rolled her eyes at me again. Maybe it was a female thing. "Look for a safe or something. I'll check the drawers."

She had to be feeling better if she was chastising me. I smiled once she turned her back to me. A safe… Could be hidden behind a painting, or perhaps in the closet. I started with the paintings.

Chapter Fifteen
Della

I pulled drawers out of the dressing table. "A silver hairbrush!"

"Keep it."

"I only noticed because my mother always wanted one." Felt like real boar bristles, too.

"Seven, I don't care. Loot what you like. You don't have to justify it to me," Adam said.

"I'm not. I don't care about fancy things." I'd like a bit of comfort when I was ready to retire, but that's all.

Nothing in the dressing table I was looking for. I stood tall and glanced in the mirror. Eww. My hair didn't react well to gettin' wet. It frizzed like I'd been rubbing a balloon on it.

"Not even this." A tiara appeared on my head in the mirror. Gold filigree style, with pearls and diamonds.

"I…"

"Picks up the highlights in your hair."

I took it off and turned so I could see him. "Not my style."

He accepted it back and shrugged. "Too bad."

"Stop playin' around." Maybe the closet had something of mine.

Talk about excess. A lot of the clothes still had the tags on them. There was a leather coat in my size… I shouldn't. Everyone would ask where I got it. I could say it was a trophy, couldn't I? Especially if I didn't find my stupid boots. I loved those boots.

"I found something," Adam called.

Thank heaven. "What is it?"

He thumbed through a stack of papers. "Records of where she bought the kids, plans for the party… Pretty sure we don't have to worry about her guests showing up."

"How come?"

"A pre-arranged signal was supposed to be sent at midnight if she was ready to receive them. It's 11:30 now." *That late already?* "Then they would portal travel."

"Good. I'm really not up to another fight."

He grinned. "I don't know…one high kick would have a pretty nice stun effect right now."

"Adam! You perv!"

Way to remind me I'm not wearing underwear. It was so embarrassing that he knew. He laughed and dodged my attempt to swat his arm. *Ooops, no gloves.*

His eyes crinkled up nice at the corners. *I shouldn't notice his eyes…that led to seeing his perfect teeth, pretty collarbones, the pecs and abs carved like sculpture…no, I shouldn't be seeing those things at all. He was a vampire even if he was on our side right now.*

"Found something you like?" he asked, pointing to the coat in my hand.

"Maybe…"

He smiled. "I'll keep looking for a safe."

"Okay." I went back to ransacking the closet, feeling a blush warm my cheeks. *Ridiculous. What would Amelia say? A Creature's appearance was only relevant to the archivists.* I found accessories and — ack — lingerie, but none of my gear. *If that harlot threw my armor in the trash, I was going to dust her twice!* "Where could it be?"

"Found the safe!"

"Thank God!" I found Adam in the bathroom.

"There's another closet here, see, and it's set into the back wall."

"Okay, so, open it."

He shook his head. "She upgraded the unit. It requires a thumb scan."

"So. Can't we bust it open?"

"With tools."

"And you didn't bring any with you?"

"I didn't anticipate safe cracking."

"Some vampire you are… Shoot it." Yeah, I was being a bit of a brat, but I was wet, cold, and just wanted my bed. And I couldn't leave without my gear.

Adam clenched his jaw in an effort to control his temper. "I'll call Darius."

I nodded. He left the bathroom to find a phone. Boy, it was a nice bathroom. The tub was huge and so tempting. I imagined it filled with steaming water and overflowing with bubbles, and sighed. Closing the door, I wanted to at least shed the ribbon digging into my skin. I unbuttoned Adam's coat and placed it on the counter. Silk was very strong wet, but now it was drying, I had a chance of ripping it and unraveling my bindings.

They'd wrapped two layers around my body, so it took a while to see skin. When I could, I found bruises. Bruises from the edges of the ribbon — purple lines created when I moved — and greenish-blue marks from the pinching and grabbing. Seeing my body in the mirror was not a good idea right then.

"You will not fall apart," I told my mirror image.

I stared at my reflection until my lip stopped trembling, then put Adam's coat back on and left the room, looking for something in Juliet's closet I could wear out of here in case we couldn't find my gear. A sweater, skirt—the woman didn't own pants—and a pair of boots a half-size too big, later; I was dry, at least.

"Hey."

"On his way?" I asked.

"Yeah. Your partner is taking care of the children. Aside from being drugged into complacency, they're in perfect health."

At least one thing went right tonight. "Good. Job well done."

"Couldn't pass up the closet, after all?"

I handed his coat back. "Something like that."

He did the head tilt scrutiny thing. "You alright?"

"Tired. Warming up now."

"Seven—"

"Do you think she's coming back?"

"No. Not tonight."

"Good. Thanks…for the rescue. I should've thanked you already."

He smiled, a sweet one. "I knew you would eventually," he teased. "I'm glad I pulled you out of the water in time."

"Uh, yeah, a little easier on the chest compressions next time." My ribs were tender.

He chuckled. "I'll remember that."

"Not that there will be a next time."

"Seven…I know the depths of Juliet's—"

"I'm fine, really. Only need some aspirin and a goodnight's sleep." I plucked the leather jacket off the bed, tore the price tag off, and slipped it on.

"You look nice," he said.

I frowned. "It's a bit Goth."

"Maybe, but you wear it well." Was he flirting? Okay, this was getting too weird.

"We should wait for Darius near the front door, don't you think?" I didn't wait for a reply, leaving the bedroom in a direction I hoped was the right way.

I turned a corner down a corridor ahead of Adam and came face-to-face with one of my gropers. Didn't think, just brought my knee up into his privates. He sunk to the floor with a groan, holding his groin.

"That's for grabbing my ass."

I kept walking.

Chapter Sixteen

Adam

My coat smelled like her now, the scent enveloping me. I hurried to catch up with Seven and found a downed human cradling his nuts. Her scent was on him and I knew in an instant he'd been part of wrapping her up like that. Rage welled up within me, a feeling more possessive than I'd ever had in my existence. *Take revenge,* that dark part of me whispered.

I could make it quick. Snap his neck like a twig. I could already feel the bones crunch between my hands.

She wouldn't want that, my conscience whispered. Shaking off the blood rage, I spat on him instead.

Stars above…I'd do anything for that bright, brave young woman. I caught up with her. "Nice groin shot back there."

"He deserved it."

"Deserved more, in my opinion."

She glanced at me then. "Not for me to decide."

"Are you alright?"

"Why wouldn't I be?" she countered, her voice even.

I grabbed her arm and turned her to face me. "Seven—"

"Darius will be here soon, and I'd like to find my gear before Amelia finds out I lost it." She broke my grip on her elbow and sped up down the hallway.

We finally found the front stairs and the front door. The breeze outside was cold. Seven pulled her coat closed and hid her hands in the pockets. Leaving her on the front steps, I went to see about the gate, wrenched it open, and turned back to the house.

"You have pensive face."

"Beg pardon?" I asked.

"Thinkin' heavily. What's up?"

"Nothing." I sat on the porch. "So, what comes after the mission?"

"Christmas at home, I hope." She stayed standing.

"They let you do that?"

"I'm an adult, you know. I can go where I wish between jobs."

"Huh. Where's home?"

She smiled. "Oklahoma. My family's been there since the Land Rush. Mama has a diner. I worked there after school, before this."

"Quite a career change."

"Heh, yeah. But, it's what I was meant for. What about you? Any descendants?"

"I never married. I suppose I could have distant nieces or nephews, but I never looked. We either walk away from family, or eat them."

"You really didn't choose it?" Curiosity shone in her eyes.

"No." That came out harsher than I intended.

"I'm sorry."

I shook my head. "You didn't offend. Tell me about Christmas."

She sat on the step. "Well, we start with the tree—"

A vehicle honked. Darius drove the van up the driveway. I waved and he cut the lights.

"Finally," Seven said and hopped down the steps to meet my son.

"Got what you asked for, boss." He handed me a metal toolbox.

"Good work tonight, kid." I started back to the house, the youngsters chatting behind me.

She preferred talking to a human. I wasn't surprised, but it did sting. I saved the woman from drowning, but she still didn't trust me. While I was complaining, the wet squish of my feet inside my boots was really setting my teeth on edge.

By the time we reached the master suite, I wanted to do this the quick way.

"You're going to blow it open?" Seven exclaimed when she saw the "tool" I reached for.

"You want your property or not."

She backed off, hands raised in surrender. It only took a tiny bit of contact explosive to open a safe door like this. People were too touchy about explosives nowadays, in my opinion. Sometimes they were handy.

"Voila, mademoiselle."

"Thanks. Out of the way." She knelt on the floor and reached her hand into the safe. "Dammit!"

She stormed out.

I spotted a folded piece of paper in the safe and recognized the handwriting immediately.

Better luck next time, Adam – J.

I tucked the note into my back pocket.

"Quite a place, boss. Might be nice to stay now it's empty."

"Not empty, kid. Besides, it wouldn't be right, Darius. I doubt Juliet had the house legally. Take that case down to the van. I'll wait for Seven."

"Yes, sir. Father...?"

"What, Darius?"

"Why would her uniform be in a safe?"

"It's none of your business, kid." He nodded and left. What happened tonight was Seven's story to tell, and I doubted she'd be sharing all the details any time soon. Physically, she was fine. Emotionally...well, you noticed things when you'd lived my years. I searched for her. "Seven?"

"Dining room," she called.

"I was only going to say we're ready to leave when you are."

"Okay." She was undressing a dummy. The table was set with gold-rimmed china and jeweled cups. Juliet showing off her wealth.

"I'm sorry."

"You just don't quit, do you?"

"Is all of it there?"

"My weapons are missing."

"Will you be in trouble?"

She sighed. "Not much. I need to go change."

"Take any reparations you like. Please. Don't forget the silver hairbrush."

She smiled and took it from my hand. The world would be alright as long as I could preserve that smile.

Chapter Seventeen

Della

I talked with Darius about the kids we saved so I wouldn't have to talk to Adam. I was starting to think he could read me, and it was unnerving he wanted to chat. What part of "mortal enemies" didn't he understand? Saving my life didn't make us instant best friends.

The children were sheltered at one of our ally churches. Darius and I left Adam outside. Amelia smiled when she saw me walk into the rec. room. We would've hugged if we'd been alone, but the look of relief on her face was enough for me.

Most of the kids were asleep on cots. "How are they?"

"Scared, tired, missing their families. We handed out cookies and juice to any that were hungry. I sent the list you found into Headquarters, so they're running them against recent abduction reports."

"Good. I hope they can go home soon. What are our orders?"

"Standby. Provided no emergency call comes in the next twelve hours, we're on holiday leave."

Thank God. "I'll include that in my prayers, then."

Amelia touched my shoulder. "I know you're looking forward to going home, Seven."

Mom needed me to show up. "Yeah. Anywhere I can get a shower and sleep?"

She handed me a motel key. "It's around the corner."

"Thanks." I exited the hall and went in the direction Amelia pointed me to. Outside, I sensed I wasn't alone. "Don't need a chaperone," I said, still walking, knowing he could hear me.

Standard chain motel, clean and nothin' fancy. I found my duffle and got out my bathroom kit, grateful to strip out of my suit since I'd been left with no undies at the mansion. Did a rare thing and ran a bubble bath. Mama gave me this scented stuff for my last birthday that was s'posed to be soothing. I sure hoped so.

Avoiding the mirror this time, I coiled my hair into a knot. The water was just on this side of too hot. Once I'd sunk in to my shoulders it felt fine. Purifying. I wanted to close my eyes, but I was afraid to let my mind wander. Acknowledging the fear brought tears, and I wept.

Wanted to scrub my skin raw, 'til there wasn't a single cell left they'd touched. Yeah, it could've been a lot worse, but that didn't comfort me. To think that being molested should comfort me...

I wanted to kill something.

Needed it, for the first time ever.

What had they done to me?

A gym. With a punching bag or hit pads. That's what I needed. One thing for sure, I couldn't sleep, yet. I let the water drain, turned the shower on, and rinsed the bubbles away. Then I dressed in a pair of sweats, made sure I had the key, and went for a run.

Adam appeared in my path just as I found my pace. He wore fresh clothes.

"Leave me alone."

"Look like you could use a friend."

"Not unless you have a gym open at midnight."

He blocked my way. "I can find one, and I have wheels. Unless you want to spar with a real target?"

"Just go away."

He stepped closer. "Don't think so. Not tonight."

I pushed him away hard enough to give me room to go around him. He caught up, passed me, and turned to jog backward in front of me. I stopped and glared at him. "That's rude."

He grinned, shrugged. "It's a perk."

"Fine." I turned to run the other way. I had energy to burn, dangit!

"You can't outrun me, Seven. Let's get in the van and find a gym. Or if you'd rather talk—"

"No." I whirled on him, my hands landing on my hips. "Can't you take no for an answer and leave me alone?"

"I may be a vampire, but I haven't forgotten empathy. I know the cruelty Juliet is capable of. I want you to know I understand." Looking at his face, earnest and compassionate, I wanted to believe him. He'd saved my life, been nothing but kind, if a bit annoying. I already knew I couldn't talk about it with Amelia.

It was bad enough I'd been kidnapped. She didn't need to know how helpless I was tonight. The extent of my failure as an agent. No one should've been able to sneak up on my six and conk me on the head.

Adam persisted. "What would you like to do?

What did I want? To go home, see my mom, have a normal life, maybe meet a nice guy, have a family…the big things. Little things? Time to read a book in one sitting. See a movie. Find out what's on current radio. Learn what other people my age were in to.

What I said out loud was simpler. "I'm hungry."

He smiled. "Easily remedied. Come on."

Don't know why I went with him to the rental van. Thought I wanted to be alone. I could find some place to eat late at night, a fast food joint or somethin'. But I let him open the door for me, and I stayed quiet as he looked for a restaurant.

"How about here?"

I couldn't help giggling. "Bob's Big Boy?"

"What, it's open. Is it not good?"

"No…no, it's fine. It's…never mind." I didn't feel like explaining my sense of humor.

He shrugged and parked the van. We tried opening my door at the same time. Gosh, he was fast. "You don't have to open my door, Adam. I'm a big girl."

He huffed, and scowled. "It's only polite. Am I not allowed to be undead and polite at the same time?"

I didn't want to argue, not tonight. "Of course you are. I'm just not used to it."

"Alright."

I let him get the door of the restaurant. He requested a table in the back. There weren't many people here, so we were seated right away. The corner booth was perfect—neither of us had to sit with our back to the room.

A waitress came to take our drink orders and give us the specials. She dropped her pen when she glanced at Adam. He leaned over, picked it up, and handed it to her with a charming grin. I expected her to fan herself any moment and kicked his foot under the table.

"Quit it," I said once the waitress left.

"Quit what?"

"Puttin' the whammy on innocents when I'm around."

He rolled his eyes. "Really, Seven, all I did was smile. I can't be nice, either?"

"You can be nice…just…"

"What?"

"Nothing." I studied my menu like it held the secrets of the universe.

"I've never used thrall and I don't feed from people. Since I'm buying you dinner, can you give me the benefit of the doubt for one hour?"

"You don't have to pay," I mumbled.

"I owe you. I shouldn't have left you alone at the tracks."

"I can take care of myself! I only—got surprised. Learned my lesson." The hard way.

Pity party for two, please. Guess misery did love company. I understood the difference between us and the bad guys now—the guilt.

Since it was his dime, I indulged in a double cheeseburger and chocolate milkshake. The aroma made my stomach gurgle and I was suddenly famished. He watched me eat with an amused twinkle in his eye, nibbling at his piece of French Silk pie.

"Smell good on the way down?" he teased.

"Shuddup," I said around a mouthful of beef. Only a quarter of my burger still rest in my hands. I swallowed. "How can you eat regular food?"

"Well, I place a bite in my mouth, chew it, then swallow. Repeat as necessary."

"I know that, smarty pants. I mean, how does it not make you sick or somethin'?"

"It does not make me sick."

"Then you can still process it?" I didn't know why this fascinated me so much, but think about it…no one knew if vampires had to poop.

Adam squirmed in his seat. "You are a very strange girl."

"You don't have to talk about it…"

"Really, Seven, some things should be left a mystery!"

I slurped my milkshake. Hee! I'd embarrassed him. "If you say so."

Gray eyes narrowed on me. "You're deliberately picking at me."

"Would I?" I gave him the same innocent look I gave my mom.

He chuckled, shaking his head. "Definitely. But I don't mind."

"Cool." Yesterday morning, if someone told me I'd be sitting down to a friendly meal with a vampire, I would've said they were out of their gourd. Plum crazy to seriously suggest it.

Life was full of surprises.

Even more surprising—I enjoyed his company. Maybe because he was new, different. I'd spent the past years with Amelia as the primary source of conversation.

Maybe because he seemed interested in me-the-girl as much as my skills. Sure been persistent about being friends. Don't judge a book by its cover, Mama taught me. Judge a man by his actions. Well, Adam's actions said he was on the up-'n'-up.

So far.

"So, you'll be home for Christmas, evil permitting," he said

"Huh? Yeah…home for a few days. Maybe a week, if I'm lucky. It'll be nice."

"You mentioned a tree before."

"Did I? Yeah, we have this ancient thing that belonged to my grandparents. It's artificial, white, and probably really cheesy, but—"

"It's your tradition."

I smiled. "Yeah." He got it. "Did they do Christmas when you were a boy?"

"Yes…but not like here, or how it is today. It was a holy time. Nativity scenes were very popular, for instance. No tree."

No tree? "Wow…how old are you again?"

"Born in 1700. I look good for my age, yes?" He winked. Funny guy.

"I guess so, since you'd be a rotting corpse otherwise."

Adam picked up on my teasing. "Indeed. The preservation aspect is handy."

I dumped the extra milkshake out of the metal cup into my glass and started dipping the smaller fries left on my plate in the ice cream. My high school friend got me to try it, and now I always had fries with a chocolate shake or malt. It was just yummy. He finished his last bite of pie and slid the plate to the end of the table for the waitress. Now he had to wait for me to finish. I needed to hurry up.

"You'll give yourself a headache sucking it in that fast," he said.

Caught. "Darius get a brain freeze before?" I switched to using a spoon. "Better?"

"No need to rush on my account, Seven."

"Della."

He froze. "Beg pardon?"

Shocked me to hear it come out of my mouth, too, but I elaborated. "My name. Della. You saved my life tonight. That makes us a little less formal." He wanted a show of trust, right? Anyway, going by a number never felt right to me. I understood it, but it wasn't me.

"I...I don't know what to say. Thank you."

I'd made the vampire speechless. Wow. Stop the presses, folks.

Chapter Eighteen
Adam

Her name.

I knew instantly she hadn't made it up, her cheeks turning pink as she explained what she gave me. Anyone living in our world knew you did not give a Creature your Name. Names were connected to the very identity of a person, their essence, and they held great power in the wrong hands.

She trusted me with her first name...

I didn't know how to react. It was different with Darius. I asked the boy what to call him and he told me, but I had nothing to gain from him besides his blood and I didn't want that. I held a place of authority over him merely by taking him in.

Seven...*Della*...was making us equals. I never expected...

Special, this girl.

I needed to know if being able to touch her was a fluke, a moment of allowance because she was technically dead. If it was something more permanent, I couldn't keep my knowledge from her, not now.

Stars above, what did I get myself in to?

She didn't press for conversation after I thanked her. Maybe we were both surprised. The waitress brought the check, Seven gulped down the last of her shake, and we headed for the exit.

She paused at the van. "Could you still use my code name in front of Amelia? I don't think she'll understand why I told you."

"Of course." I put the key in the door and unlocked it. "Back to your lodging?"

She stared into the distance for a moment. "Yeah..."

"Are you sure?"

"Stop trying to read me." She climbed into the passenger seat. "Drive."

I shut her door and sighed. One step forward, two steps back.

After around ten minutes, "Was this a one time deal for you?"

"Dinner?" I asked.

"Fighting evil."

"It wasn't my first time."

"Duh. I mean saving people. Killing monsters." She shifted in her seat to face me. "What do you and Darius normally do?"

"Ah." I got it now. She was fishing for a place to put me in her world view. "We travel, I educate him, and I take out the occasional local threat. A little violence helps me sleep. Is that what you wanted to know, Della?"

She frowned. "Why are you always evasive?"

"'Always'? We've only known each other for a few days." I turned into the motel parking lot.

"Forget it." She opened her door before the van rolled to a complete stop and stomped off to her room.

I put the van in park, killed the engine, and followed her. "Seven!"

She stopped and turned to me, looking annoyed. "What?"

"Were you trying to recruit me?"

"Maybe…" She stood with her chin lifted, arms crossed over her chest, one hip cocked to the left—daring me to poke fun and reject her offer.

I smiled. "Then I wouldn't mind working with you again." Hoped it would happen, actually.

She nodded once, quickly covering her surprise. "Okay."

"I'd offer to shake on it, but…"

"Wait." She pulled the sleeve of her sweatshirt over her right hand. "Here."

I met her hand with mine, then lifted it to my lips and kissed it through the cotton fleece. She blushed. "Goodnight, Della."

"Bye, Adam." She quietly unlocked the door and slipped inside the dark room.

Darius stepped out from behind a tree.

"What are you doing over here?"

"Came looking for you. Wondered if Seven had seen you." He grinned. "Guess she did. How was your date?"

I started for the van. "What date? I took her to find food."

"Did you pay for hers?"

"I don't see how that matters—"

"Oh, definitely a date. Man, you really have a taste for the unattainable!"

"Get in the van and quit talking nonsense. Seven is a temporary colleague. She had a rough night and I owed her, so I drove her to a restaurant where she had a good meal. Subject. Closed."

"Whatever you say, boss."

Chapter Nineteen
Della

Amelia wasn't in our room, so I guessed she was staying with the children tonight. Fine with me. I'd rather try to fall asleep alone right now. If I could just get home, I'd be okay. No Adam, gropey minions, or psychopathic vampires. A few days of normal would put me right.

Only one nightmare while I slept, and it was short.

Amelia woke me up at 8:00 with a bag of donut holes. I dressed in street clothes and walked to the church to work with the kids.

They were all between eleven and fourteen. I thanked God we got to them before anything really terrible happened. Two of them were already going home. Luckily, the church had a good size youth group, so we had games and a couple basketballs to keep them entertained. Playing a game of Horse outside with the boys was good therapy for me, too. Last night slipped to the back of my mind, until the tallest boy accidentally bumped one of my bruises. I assured him I was fine, then went inside to see how Amelia was faring with the girls.

"Switch?" I asked.

"Might as well," she said. "I'm getting killed in Monopoly." The little girls giggled.

I plopped down on the carpet and studied the board. "So, who's winning?"

By dusk, our replacements arrived and took the children to the airport. Only two of the kids were from the US. Headquarters determined us officially off duty, so Amelia and I were parting ways.

I had a ticket for tomorrow morning to Oklahoma.

December 23rd…

Home. *Finally.*

Home at Christmastime, with the big old light strand around the roof and the white fake tree over-loaded with vintage ornaments passed down generations. The sticky Santa scenes on the windows. Every surface decorated with some kind of holiday knick-knack.

The tension finally uncoiled in my belly. I patted the three-foot light-up Frosty the Snowman on the head as I neared the front door. I was going to ring the bell, just to see her face, when she opened the door.

"Della!"

"Merry Christmas, Mom." I dropped my bag and hugged her. "How are you feeling?"

"Fine. It's been a good month."

"You look a little tired."

"Oh, I just stayed up too late watchin' a movie. Look at how long your hair is!" We moved inside and she shut the door.

"Yeah, I was hoping you could trim it while I'm here."

"Sure, sure. So, how's college?"

The living room smelled like pine and cinnamon. Mom had been in the scented candles again. "Oh, you know. Busy. Academic. Amelia says hello."

"I wish you could study full time, honey. You'd be halfway to your degree by now."

I put my duffle in my room. "Maybe, but I like my job. How's the diner? You lettin' your managers help out?"

"Yes, Della. I follow doctor's orders. You hungry?"

I'd been looking forward to her cooking for weeks. "I could eat."

She grinned. "I'm sure I've got somethin' quick... Any special people in your life?" she asked, her head in the refrigerator. Everybody's heard about small town gossip. The queen of it stood right in this kitchen. Mama heard everybody's stories in the diner.

"Quit fishin'. You know I'm in no hurry to add a man to my life."

She put a ham steak in the microwave to reheat. "Sweetie, you're almost twenty. I'd already had you by that age. Would it really hurt to bring home a boyfriend before I'm old and gray?"

"Mommmm..."

"Della, I just don't want you to be alone. Travelin' everywhere... I worry."

I squeezed her hand. It was cold. "I know. But I'm fine, really. I'm doin' good, helpin' the world."

"That reminds me — we took another collection at church for your organization for Christmas."

"Aww, you didn't have to do that..."

She pressed an envelope into my hand. "Aid organizations always need funds. Don't argue with your mother."

I smiled. "Yes, ma'am." It would go right back into the fund that paid her medical bills.

Mom used a Santa oven mitt to remove the hot plate. "Cider?"

"Please."

"After your snack, we'll head over to the diner to show folks you're home."

"I just got home, Mom. Can't it wait until tomorrow?"

She pouted. "Well, I s'pose so, but they'd be so happy to see you, Della! The gals live for your stories of far-off places. Most of us don't get further than Oklahoma City, you know."

"Yes, I know, Mama, and I will share. But not today. I wanna sit on the couch and do nothin' but watch movies and eat your famous cookies."

She sighed. "Very well...go sit, eat."

"Thanks, Mom."

"Just glad you're home, baby."

My bedroom hadn't changed since I was sixteen due to me not being home much, so it felt kinda juvenile to me now. Time to take down the Britney Spears poster on the back of my door. It was obvious Mom kept the room spotless, and I felt another pang of guilt for not being here. The room existed as a shrine to an innocent girl that no longer existed.

I couldn't tell her that, of course. If I'd merely grown up and moved out, she could turn the room into a guest room, but I didn't. Hadn't. Keeping my room as it was probably held both of us in the past.

Gee, gloomy enough, Della? Get a grip. It's Christmas, for goodness sake.

The next day, Christmas Eve, we visited our friends, Mom with plates of cookies. She must've been baking for a whole week. We'd be at my cousins' tomorrow for supper, so tonight was only us. After fried chicken and apple pie, we sat in front of the tree to open one present each. I wrapped the silver brush before she got up this morning and she'd be getting it tomorrow. Tonight, I gave her a pair of earrings from Greece. I'd had them in my bag for two months.

"They're gorgeous, Della! Tell me you didn't spend a lot on these."

"Mom, you shouldn't ask how much your presents are!"

"I only want you to be wise with your money."

"I know, but trust me, okay?"

"Of course, dear."

I knew before I opened mine that it'd be a sweater. My Christmas Eve gift was always a sweater. Mom was the type to suggest a sweater at seventy degrees. "Thanks, Mom."

"You're welcome, sweetheart. Don't stay up late, now, or Santa won't come."

I grinned. "Okay."

Christmas Day kept me so busy, I felt normal again. Mom loved the antique brush. There were even a few tears.

I went out with a couple high school friends two days later. Walking back home in the evening, I felt a supernatural presence. I crouched under the pretense of re-tying my shoe and reached for the stake tucked into my sock. The feeling faded and I wondered if I imagined it. Could've been the cold giving me goose bumps.

Headquarters called me to the Boston area on the twenty-ninth to check out a possible werewolf sighting. Imagine my surprise when Adam met me at the airport.

"What are you doin' here?"

"Same as you," he said. "Dog catching."

"I don't need help." I'd dealt with dozens of wolves.

"Far as I'm concerned, I got here first. It's my hunt."

I stopped walking to Baggage Claim. "I was sent to do a job. You're not going to kill this person."

He looked confused. "How else do you deal with a werewolf?"

"They're human the other twenty-seven days of the month, okay? You can't kill them, Adam. We sedate them and get them help."

"A noble effort, but it doesn't always work that way. You can't disable an opponent a hundred percent of the time, Della."

"I've been able to so far." I retrieved my checked bag and headed for the exit. He followed me, of course. Beginning to think that man-vamp would never leave me alone.

"Well, I'm happy for your record, but you should be careful and prepared for the possibility."

"Thanks, *Dad*. Can I go now?"

He held his hands up in surrender and faded into the crowd. I had a feeling this was only the first time I'd see him in town.

****

January 2008

It'd been two weeks since I last saw Adam. I didn't tell Amelia I saw him in Boston, though I included his involvement in the mission in my report to Headquarters. There wasn't much to tell, really: we made the bet, I got to the werewolf first, and we settled the debt at Baskin Robbins. I left the ice cream out of the report. My superiors tended to frown on human pleasures. All work, no play, for them.

I missed my mom even more after the week at home and had sent her a postcard from every location change since I left.

Tonight was a standard hunt for some kind of demon. I beheaded the beast with a flick of my sword and knelt beside the body to whisper a few words, bowing my head in prayer. Standing, I wiped the blade clean, slid it back into the sheath, and left.

Entered home base and peeled off my mask and hood. Unbuckled my sword belt and set the weapon on the table. Next went the bracers, the shin guards, then I unzipped my suit down to my breastbone. I grabbed a bottled soda out of the refrigerator and plopped down in a chair with a sigh.

"Good hunting?" Amelia asked, thumbing through a tome.

"It's dead, if that's what you're asking."

"It's what I always ask, Seven. I do have reports to send."

"I've always wondered if they have a board up somewhere, keeping track of our kills. Betting on the best hunter?"

"Don't be gauche. Our mandate is sacred. We take ridding the world of demons very seriously!"

"Amelia, I was raised around truckers. Gauche is what I know."

She made that little noise of disgust she always did when thinking of where I came from. Not that there was anything wrong with my upbringing—small town middle-class in Middle America—but it differed greatly from Amelia's. She was born with a silver spoon in her mouth. My job was to wash them.

"What is going on with you? You've been moody for weeks," she asked.

"Nothin'…gettin' tired of it, I guess. I'd rather be home."

"You want to quit?" Disbelief colored her voice.

"I don't know…but I want more from life than hunting demons."

"I…I don't know what to say." Amelia was raised to be a guide. She knew no other life but to serve.

Loneliness was probably the easiest description for my discomfort. You didn't make friends or boyfriends in this line of work, never staying in one place for more than a few days. The only agents living at Headquarters were those put out to pasture, too old or injured to continue fighting. Every one of 'em would bend your ear about their "glory days" if you let them. And none of us actives wanted to be in their place.

It was so selfish of me, but right now, I needed variety or excitement. Thinking about it brought me back to Adam. Never dull, that vampire. I wondered where he could be on the globe right now.

Epilogue
Adam

    Della won the bet about the werewolf. She bagged it the first night out. Poor soul was off to some Agency installation to learn how to deal with his inner canine or something. Loser had to buy the winner their favorite treat, so I took her for ice cream before we parted ways.

    Her favorite flavor was Mississippi Mud. I tried Fudge Brownie, which was quite good.

    A familiar scent wafted to me when we left the shop, but I couldn't place it. I saw Della to her room for the night and left.

    My first impulse was to follow her to her next destination. Darius said that made me a stalker, so I contacted The Agency instead, and offered my services. Perhaps with two successful missions carried out with both of us in the same town, they'd be likely to pair us up another time.

    Because now that it was only me and my son again, I missed her. It didn't make sense, I knew that, but I couldn't explain it in any other way.

    I missed my redheaded paladin.

SAVING CHARLOTTE
Strange Allies #3

Charlotte was a high-school music teacher when Nicholae Dragomir found her and charmed his way into managing her career. She's happy with her new life of minor fame until she meets Simon, a mysterious Englishman she's irresistibly drawn to. He's sweet, funny, handsome…everything she could want in a potential boyfriend—except he's keeping a huge secret, and he's not the only one.

Nicholae is a vampire in Lady Juliet's clan and has taken control of Charlotte's life, molding her for his sinister purposes. When Simon refuses to divulge his past, it sends Charlotte straight into Nicholae's arms—and a path of destruction. If Simon, Adam, and Agent Seven can't find her in time, she'll be lost forever.

CLASSIFIED

Sacra Aedes Archive: Ref. No. 4302.

Contents: dated May 2006 — 2008

References: See Biography — Agent Seven; Biography — Thornhill, Amelia; Biography — Vampires, Adam; Vampires, Juliet.

Prologue
May 2007

To my eyes, Caroline was the most beautiful woman in the village, of fair countenance and even fairer heart. Kind, virtuous, quick to laugh…I'd loved her since I was a boy.

Elevator or stairs—neither way was fast enough.

Simon raced into the hotel room. "I found her!"

A long-suffering expression filled his friend's perfect face. "Not this again. What caught your eye this time: hair, a scent, a smile?"

Since 1750, they had looked for Simon's lost wife reincarnated and there had been so many disappointments. Of course the man was skeptical.

"*I found her*, Adam. It's my wife."

He muted the television. "No she is not, assuming you have the right young woman. She won't know you."

"I'm perfectly aware of this curse. Lived with it for five-hundred years. I'm telling you! She's in this very hotel, mere floors above us."

"How do you know?"

"I ran into her in the lobby. She and a redhead went into the lift and only the redhead came back again."

Adam sighed. "That is only one reason both women did not leave again."

"You're a right buzz-kill, mate."

"So I've been told. Doesn't mean I'm wrong. Simon, we've been down this road before. A thousand times."

"This is different. I've never been this close before. The redhead told me my wife is a pianist and in town to play a concert. It can't be hard to narrow down the venue."

"No, it won't. Did you get a name, by chance?"

"No."

"Why not?"

"Will you help me find her or not?"

"As your only friend, what else would I do?"

"*Best* friend."

"Potato, po-ta-to, old man."

Adam's skepticism was frustrating, but he couldn't blame him. His friend was only looking after him. Looking out for his battered heart.

It was her, though. *Finally.* And with a little Providence, they'd break this curse once and for all.

PART ONE

Charlotte goes from teacher to performer.

Chapter One
Charlotte
2006

The hotel was really too nice for Charlotte, but it was the closest to the school while she waited for rental insurance to pay up. They had an old but well-maintained Steinway grand in the lounge. With Nicholae coaxing her to sit at the bench, she tested it out.

"What do you want me to play?" she asked.

"Your choice. Your favorite, perhaps."

She'd had a full-size keyboard at home growing up. Knowing how to play was a requirement for a music major, of course, but she only played what she loved when she was alone. Mother was pushy enough about her "exploring her gifts", really missing her calling as a stage mom.

Sitting in the lounge with Nicholae standing next to her, she closed her eyes and tapped into her teenage passion. When she finished and looked up at him, his eyes were gleaming like he'd just discovered the treasure of El Dorado.

"I haven't performed in a while, so—"

He touched his finger to her lips. "Stop. You're wonderful."

"Thanks." Heat bloomed in her cheeks again.

He walked her to her door.

"Well, this is me. Thanks for lunch. Perhaps we'll even talk about more than music next time," she said.

He stepped closer. "Mmm, I like that…'next time'. You've made my time in this city much less lonely, Charlotte." He slowly raised a hand to caress her cheek. "When can I see you again?"

"I-I don't know… This is the last week of school, so…"

He smiled gently, his voice soft, like he was dealing with a skittish animal. "I understand. I will call you in a couple days and see how you are doing, yes? We need to discuss your future."

"Okay." She was *not* admitting his voice turned her to jelly.

Nicholae pressed a soft, slow kiss to her cheek. "Until then. Goodbye, Charlotte."

Leaning against the door, she watched him walk away, then shook her head and went inside.

With school over, Charlotte had no pay until classes began again in the fall. The next time he offered to sponsor her, she said yes.

Nicholae was…like no one she'd ever met, not that she had extensive experience with men. He got her into concert halls all over the place, the seats always at least three-quarter filled. Sometimes she sat in with orchestras, sometimes performed on stage alone. She played, they applauded, and flowers and champagne came to her dressing rooms. She didn't know how he did it, but she was having the time of her life, if feeling a bit uprooted on occasion.

By August, she was prepared to turn in her resignation at the high school.

He doted on her, yet never asked for something in return. Flirted with her, but didn't try any moves. She would've thought he was gay, if not for the fact she noticed him admiring women too many times to count. They never talked about anything personal. It was always about art, or music, or culture, or history. Even so, she felt drawn to him in a way she couldn't explain.

The only thing marring her new semi-stardom was during her sleep.

I'm positive I'm being watched. I get out of bed and shut and latch the window, drawing the curtains, too. My neck throbs and there's a trickle of blood from two holes. I feel I wasn't alone in the room while I slept. A hand covers my mouth before I can scream and I'm pushed back on the bed.

"Usually, I like a screamer, but I'm not keen on you drawing the attention of the entire hotel," he says.

He bites my throat and I reach blindly for the lamp. I crash it over his head and he moans, rolling off me. I run for the door and the hallway.

And she woke up.

Sometimes, it wasn't that dream. There was another that passed in flashes — a small town, people screaming and running around, children hiding or calling for their parents, and always the glimpses of monstrous faces. She always awoke the instant before she died. It felt very real, almost like a memory.

Weird dreams had been with her all her life — well, as far back as she could remember. *It's normal for dreams to be weird*, her ever-practical, ever-logical mother would say. She gave up telling Mom they were the same images over and over by age nine. At nearly twenty-three, she was so bored with them being a part of her nightly mental repertoire she blocked them out and rarely remembered dreaming them when she woke anymore.

One dream in particular had come back since her birthday. She was in a small stone church, standing up at the altar, and feeling the happiest she'd ever been in life. She felt a wreath of flowers on her head and knew she wore her best dress, like you do in dreams. It was obvious she was standing up there to get married, but she could never see the groom's face or hear his voice—only feel his hand holding hers, thinking they made a good fit. Pretty innocuous, huh…except the style of their clothes was from hundreds of years ago. Was it a memory of a past life (ha!) or merely a yearning for Ren Faire?

She felt juvenile for not wanting to sleep alone, but it'd always been a guard against troubled sleep. From her mother's arms, to a bed full of stuffed animals, she'd always taken comfort from sharing a bed. These hotel beds were unfamiliar and too big.

Lonely.

So how did a high school teacher become a concert musician? That was where Nicholae came in.

Charlotte brought her student orchestra to a festival in May. They performed Mozart's Symphony No. 40. The top school would receive a trophy and donation from the Philharmonic Society. She was about to go into the room storing their belongings when someone called her name.

"Ms. Taylor?"

"Yes?"

"I wanted to meet you. I became a fan today. For someone so young, you understand Mozart very well."

"Thank you, Mr.—"

"Nicholae Dragomir. I'm an…aficionado of Old World culture, so this is a frequent haunt of mine. I would love to discuss Mozart, and the others, further with you…perhaps, over dinner?" His slight accent added a charming lilt to his voice.

"Perhaps." She tried not to blush and dug around in her purse for a business card. "My office number. You know, I don't often accept dinner invitations from strange men, but I'd be willing to discuss the classics with you on an academic basis."

He bowed his tall frame to kiss her hand, meeting her gaze with grey-green eyes. "I look forward to it. Until we meet again, Ms. Taylor." He nodded courteously, then left, disappearing into the corridors.

"Oh my god, Ms. Taylor, he was majorly hot!"

"And that accent!"

She turned around, adopting her teacher's voice. "Alright, girls. That's enough. Everybody to the bus! We have to get you back to the school by two-thirty."

Her apartment building had suffered a mysterious collapse recently, waking her in the middle of the night to evacuate. Luckily, she had a unit at the opposite corner from the damage so it was still stable enough to go inside, but the fire department made all tenants move out in a day before they red-tagged the building.

The apartment was drafty in winter, the hot water usually ran out, and the next-door neighbors fought all the time, but it was home. All the furniture had been bought at thrift stores or yard sales except her bed and the only appliance she owned was a microwave, but it was the first place she'd lived in and paid for alone after college.

Thankfully, her boss gave her time off with pay. She was finishing her first year as an orchestra teacher at a high school in L.A. and barely able to afford the tiny apartment, but she really didn't want to move back home to Oklahoma. She boxed up all the sentimental things fast as she could, took her clothes from the closet, and stuffed it all in the car.

Her phone rang the next morning. She sat at her desk grading reports when the switchboard put the call through.

"Room 203, Ms. Taylor speaking."

"Ms. Taylor, this is Nicholae Dragomir. We met yesterday. Is this a good time?"

"Well, I was grading semester reports… I have a free period at twelve-forty-five, if it's important."

"No rush. I must confess I am not used to seeing female conductors. They are not common in Europe, you see. You've been well taught. Forgive me if this is too forward, but I have two tickets to the opera for Friday night. I was going to take my mother, but she cannot attend. I would be deeply honored if you would join me?"

"Mr. Dragomir…"

"Nicholae, please. I understand the hesitation of a single woman in a large city. We could meet at the theater, if you would be more comfortable. I would greatly enjoy the company of one educated such as you. Will you consider it?" His genuine charm couldn't be denied.

"I…call me back this afternoon, and I will have your answer." She twisted the phone cord around her finger. Why was she even considering this?

He chuckled. "Very well. I look forward to it. Good day, Charlotte." He hung up the phone.

Shaking her head, she picked up where she left off reading, but the invitation mulled about the back of her mind all morning.

A 12:45PM on the dot, Nicholae walked into her classroom. Her eyes widened in surprise as she hurried the last two girls out the door. "What are you doing here?"

"Calling on you. You said you would have your answer at this time. These are for you." Smiling, he held out a bouquet of pink daisies.

"As in call back on the *phone*! I can't have male visitors unannounced! I'll get in trouble with my boss." She took the bouquet and tossed it on the desk, putting hands on her hips and scowling at him.

"I was discreet coming in, I assure you. I would not want to cause you trouble, Miss Charlotte." Nicholae stepped forward, tilting his head. "I meant no offense."

She huffed out a breath, weighing options. "If I agree to go, will you leave now?"

"You have my word."

"Fine. Leave the details, and I'll meet you on Friday."

He smiled. "Excellent!" Nicholae moved toward the door adjacent to the parking lot, stopping to lean close to her ear. "It will be a pleasure, Ms. Taylor." His breath tickled her neck. She suppressed a shiver.

"Good day, Mr. Dragomir."

He nodded and left. She sighed in relief once she was alone and turned to the desk. Had to make sure to bring the daisies home.

Attending the opera with a mysterious European...wouldn't Mom have a field day with this?

****

Nicholae stood by the door to the concert hall dressed in a very sharp suit. Charlotte looked over her date as she ascended the stairs. If you liked the tall, dark, and handsome type, he was very attractive—and she did. His grey eyes lit up upon spotting her, sweeping over her from head to toe and back again. He reached for her free hand and kissed it.

"I am a lucky man to have such a lovely companion tonight. Shall we?" he asked, offering his arm.

She placed her hand on his bicep. "Indeed. I'm looking forward to the performance."

"Are you familiar with this opera?"

"Only with a couple of the arias. I used to participate in singing competitions in high school. I've been meaning to ask you — where are you from?"

"Eastern Europe, originally, and a bit of everywhere. My family, they like to roam. I have seen much in my life."

She held her skirt up a couple inches to walk the stairs to their section. He had box seats. "We did something similar, though only in summer, starting out seeing the rest of the U.S. when I was five. I enjoy traveling, though a teacher's salary doesn't afford me much of it nowadays. Do you prefer living here, or back across the Atlantic?"

He held open the door to the box, then allowed her to pick a seat first. "It depends on my mood, I guess you could say. There are many opportunities available here, of course, but this country is still also so young. There are times I miss the feel of…history. Can you see well enough?"

She turned to him and smiled. "Oh, yes. I'm fine. It's really all in the hearing, though, yes? Music is just as able to reach the blind, or the deaf…because you can *feel* it."

He hummed in agreement. "Never let passion fade from you, sweet Charlotte. It will serve your work well, just as life."

The lights flashed off and on, indicating everyone should take their seats, and the orchestra started to play the introduction…

She clapped as the final curtain closed. He touched her arm. "Perhaps we could go for coffee or dessert, and discuss the performance?"

She hedged. "I…"

"Tomorrow is Saturday, so you do not have work, yes? It is not so very late, yet."

"You're right, it's not…but not tonight. I actually have someone waiting for a call."

"I see. Well, permit me to walk you to your car, then, and we will say goodnight. I hope you enjoyed the opera?" They moved out of the box into the crowded hallway.

"I did, very much. Thank you for inviting me, Nicholae. I hope your mother feels better soon."

"I'm sure it is merely a cold or something. You know, I have tickets for the summer concert season…perhaps tonight will not be our only outing?"

She smiled enigmatically. "Perhaps…"

It took a while to escape the crowded theater, but they made it to the parking lot. Charlotte managed to find a close spot, so it wasn't a far walk. "Well, this is me."

"Of course. It was a lovely evening, Charlotte. I hope to see you again soon." Nicholae took her hand to kiss it; only this time, he placed the kiss on the inside of her wrist in a manner that could only be described as sensual. She dropped her eyes, blushing.

He smiled and backed away a few steps before turning and leaving.

She exhaled to release the tension, then unlocked her car.

Nicholae made lunch plans with her the next day. She had a hard time saying no where he was concerned.

"You mentioned longing to travel. What if I could help make that happen?" he asked.

"What do you mean?"

"Let me ask you this: do you prefer teaching, or would you rather perform? Guide someone else's talent, or make the world adore yours?"

"How would you do that?"

"I'm a patron of the arts, Charlotte. There's a piano in the lobby of your hotel, yes?"

"I think so…"

"Play for me when we get back. Then we'll talk more. Now, where was I before?" He continued his dissertation on Russian musical influences.

Chapter Two
Della
May 2007

Agent Seven's latest assignment put her and Amelia in Southern California, going undercover in the realm of a very old and powerful vampire who thought she owned the city.

Mission: Pose as a volunteer at a church-run shelter for runaways. Assess the current demon-to-human ratio in the city.

Team: Only the two of them.

It was early May and they'd been there a couple weeks.

Amelia couldn't fit in at the shelter with her accent, so she was carrying on a daylight role with businesses rumored to be aiding the bloodsuckers. She was very good playing bureaucracy against itself.

This week, she was trying to expose the security leak at the blood bank of one of the hospitals. Juliet ran her nest like organized crime and had been careful about drawing attention with an excess of dead bodies. Shipments of blood would get "lost" here and there, and no one noticed if the homeless disappeared. They couldn't carry out a direct assault, but they could make life harder for her here until opportunity arose.

Seven's personal phone rang. Thinking it was Mom, she leapt out of bed to answer it.

Voice mail? Mama hated talkin' to machines, always hanging up and callin' right back. Dreading that it might be the hospital or her doctor, she listened to the message.

"Hey, Della…your mom said she last knew you were in L.A. and guess where I finally am? Let's catch up, 'kay? I'm staying at the Biltmore."

Charlotte? Talk about a blast from the past.

They were cousins on Della's father's side, Charlotte was four years older, and Della hadn't seen her since Charlotte's high school graduation in Oklahoma City. His side of the family all wanted to "make it big". She was the only one that actually did it.

Guess Mama was keepin' in touch…weird that Charlotte would want to connect, though, unless she was merely lonely for a familiar face. Della didn't know her well.

Called directory assistance to get the number of the hotel, then dialed the front desk to leave a message. Checking the clock, she'd only been asleep five hours. "Curse these vampire hours…" she grumbled.

Vamps were the worst cases. You had to be awake when they were, which meant the complete opposite schedule of any sane human being.

Charlotte called back late afternoon. "Are you free for dinner, Della? I have a night off after rehearsals for my performance Friday."

"Uh, I guess…as long as I'm back by dark."

"By dark?"

"Graveyard shift."

"*Oh*. Well, yeah, I guess we should meet up soon, then. I have a suite. Just have them ring me." She hung up with the assumption Della agreed.

Downtown L.A. was way too crowded for her taste, but that's where she'd find her cousin. The Biltmore looked pretty fancy from the inside, but that didn't prepare her for walkin' through the doors, which made her very conscious of the old jeans and tee she was wearing.

"Charlotte Taylor's room, please," she said to the clerk.

"Is she expecting you?"

"Uh, yes, I'm her cousin."

"Ah." He got that look of *oh, the city girl's taking pity on the country bumpkin*. She'd seen it before. "Ms. Taylor is in the Music Suite. Take the elevator over there."

"Thanks." So what if everything she wore amounted to forty dollars?

A man dressed in a black suit answered the door when Della knocked. "Yes?"

"I'm Charlotte's cousin."

"Reed, let her in," she heard Charlotte say behind the bodyguard. "Hey, Della!"

Reed let her cross the threshold and Charlotte hugged her. She was barely over five-feet-tall and fit under Della's chin.

"Welcome to my temporary home. Do you want to eat out or order room service?"

This was no little hotel room—the Music Suite was bigger than Della's house and included a baby grand piano. She didn't want to think what it cost per night. "Whatever. You called me."

"True. I don't get to spend much time with anyone other than Nicholae and Reed, especially another woman. Your mom said your job makes you travel, too?" The bodyguard went to a chair in the corner and resumed reading a newspaper.

"Uh, yeah. Lots of people in need." The windows looked down on Pershing Square. Della didn't like facing people when she talked about work. Someone would inevitably figure out she was a bad liar.

"Well, let me know if you need reimbursement for parking. Should be my treat since I asked you here. So, what are your taste buds in the mood for?"

"I can pay my own way. Just pick your poison, Charlotte."

"Okay, then." Charlotte picked up her purse. "Reed, I'll be back in two hours, if Nicholae needs me." She opened the door and Della took her cue to follow.

"Who's Nicholae?"

"He's..." She punched the "down" button for the elevator. "My benefactor. He manages my career."

"So he's in the music biz."

"Well, no..." The doors opened and they stepped into the car. "He's not with a record company or anything like that."

"Then how did you start playing professionally?"

"He opened doors. I don't know the intricacies. All I know now is that once word spread, people started asking *me*."

"Lucky." Della's Agency-developed suspicious streak was raising its head, but Charlotte seemed happy, and she was obviously talented if she kept getting offers to do concerts, so Della tamped it down. Even if it turned out Charlotte's start was from shady deals, she'd survive.

"Yeah, it was perfect timing. I didn't know what I'd do for summer work and I was out of my apartment." She stepped out into the lobby. "Where's your car?"

"Out front. Told the valet I was picking someone up."

"*Nice.*"

Della shrugged. "A tip goes a long way toward cooperation." So did flashing her very-official-looking ID. The rental was waiting right by the doors. "I live at fast food joints and diners, so if you want somethin' else, you'll have to direct me."

"If you know of somewhere with a taste of home, I'd be grateful." Homesick it was, then.

You wouldn't believe they were related — besides Charlotte being adopted, the family tended toward the cute and wholesome side. She was simply stunning, with a pocket-sized swimsuit model build and a very pretty face. Her dark curls were in striking contrast to her blue eyes and fair skin. Della always wondered where her parents found her.

"So, have you been out of the country?" Charlotte asked.

"Some. You?"

"Not yet. Well, the Canada side of Niagara, but, no." Charlotte twisted in her seat to face her. "You look different than the last time I saw you."

"That was five years ago. Big difference between fourteen and nineteen."

"I guess. I just didn't expect to see you so…"

"What?"

"Trim."

What did she mean by that? "You thought I'd *look* like I live in a diner?"

"I don't know. You look athletic and I didn't think you were into sports."

"I'm not, except for watchin' football." Della pulled into a Norms. "Hope this is what you were lookin' for."

"Della, I'm not trying to insult you. You look great. I'd love the number of your personal trainer."

Oh, good *grief*. She got out of the car and went inside. "Table for two," she told the hostess. Charlotte ran in behind her.

At six o'clock in Los Angeles, most of the diners were still older folk and the restaurant wasn't packed, yet. They were seated right away. Della studied the menu, letting time pull her cousin's foot out of her mouth for her.

"So what's it like working all night?" Charlotte asked after the waitress brought their salads.

"Dark. Slow. Quiet. Just like anyone else's graveyard shift." Lie ratio—three out of four.

"Okay, I'll shut up."

And now Della felt guilty. She never liked answering questions about herself, though, not since the day Amelia found her. The less she said about what she did, the less likely she'd give away a secret. It was safer. "Don't know much about your side of the family, but Guthrie's the same."

"One big, happy Garvison clan?"

"Pretty much."

"I prefer California. Maybe it's in my wiring or something, but I didn't fit back there. Is that why you left, too?"

More like why she was forced away, but she couldn't tell Charlotte that. "Nah. I just found somethin' I'm good at."

"Well, good for you, Della."

"Yeah."

With the supper plates they moved on to Charlotte's career and the music she liked to play. Della didn't know Brahms from Bach, but she thought she nodded appropriately. Charlotte insisted on picking up the check, and Della took her back to the hotel.

She opened the front door at the same time a man was coming out.

They collided.

Mutual apologies were given.

Then, he looked at her, and his face paled like he'd seen a ghost, and he looked her over again. Della's cousin was too busy blabbering to notice.

"Sir, are you alright?" Della asked.

"Er, yes. Forgive me. I'll get out of your way." His accent was English, less upper-crusty than Amelia's. He stepped aside.

"Thanks," Charlotte said, and continued to the elevator.

Della felt him watching them leave, and sure enough when she turned around in the lift before the doors closed, he was staring at Charlotte still. If he didn't know her, he was definitely intent on memorizing her face.

"A fan, you think?" she asked.

"Who?"

"The guy that bumped into you. He was staring."

"He was? Was he cute?"

"Kinda good-looking if you like beards, but that's not the point. You really didn't notice?"

"Nope. If he's staying here, maybe we'll meet again. I haven't had a date in over a year."

Della shook her head. Civilians were so clueless. The things people missed from not being observant…

Charlotte said goodbye at her door. "Sorry I can't invite you in, but I have to rehearse before bed. Boss's orders."

"Okay. Well, enjoy your stay, and…break a leg."

She smiled. "Thanks. Goodnight."

The man was still in the lobby when Della came down. She walked out of the hotel and so did he. She turned the corner to go to the car, stopped, and pushed him against the wall when he came around.

"Why are you following me?" she asked, pocket dagger held to his throat.

He held his hands out to the sides. "Whoa, steady, friend. I only wanted to inquire about your companion. She looked familiar, see?"

"Saw that on your face. What's it to you?"

"She—" He leaned away from the knife. "She resembles someone I lost, is all. Could you point that somewhere else?"

"Chalk it up to coincidence and leave her alone. She's not stayin' long." She backed off, giving him her best *I'll kick your ass if you hurt my cousin* look.

"Oh? Pity."

The man didn't look dangerous, and she got no supernatural vibes. A pulse, skin color…good signs. "Look, if you're a fan, just buy a ticket to the Philharmonic like everyone else, okay? She's only a piano girl." Hopefully sufficiently warned off, she turned her back on him and went to the car.

Real threats were out there and she had twenty minutes to full darkness.

Chapter Three
Charlotte

Nicholae was sitting in Charlotte's parlor when she returned from dinner with Della. "Where have you been?"

"Dinner. I told Reed to tell you I'd be back within two hours and I am."

"You shouldn't leave the hotel alone."

"I didn't. Besides, it's not my first time in California. I used to live here, you know." She went in the bedroom to change from shoes to slippers. "Nothing happened."

"Who were you with?" He stood in the doorway.

"Family, okay? Nicholae, we've talked about this mother hen thing."

"Your family came all the way here to visit you?"

"No, we happened to be in the same place. Now, if you don't mind, I'm going to practice."

He turned to the side and let her by, back into the parlor to the baby grand. She flexed her hands, cracking knuckles, and started a warm-up exercise before going into the piece she was performing Friday.

"Would you like to extend our stay?" he asked, and leaned against the piano, resting one elbow on the top.

Her fingers froze on the keys. "Why?"

"To spend time with your relative, of course."

"What about the schedule?"

"There is a bit of time, if you wish it. If you'd rather not spend more time with this person, then the discussion is moot."

"No…today was fine. I'll, um, see what she says. Thank you."

He smiled. "My dear, I enjoy seeing you happy." He pushed off the piano and took a seat on one of the sofas.

Nicholae takes such good care of me. "Are you sure it won't be an inconvenience?" She went to him.

He took her hands in his. "Charlotte, do you think I would bring it up if it wouldn't work?"

Well, when he put it that way… "No. I guess not. I'm being silly, aren't I?"

"A bit. Would you like some of that tea you like before bed?"

"No, I think I'll sleep alright. Goodnight, gentlemen."

Reed nodded. Nicholae kissed her hand and let her go. She went in the bedroom and closed the door. They'd come from back east this morning and her internal clock was still two hours later than L.A. time.

She would leave a message for Della tomorrow.

The marriage dream came to me again. I still didn't get to see the groom's face, but I heard him say his vows with an accent. The voice was completely normal to hear to my dream-self though I couldn't place it as familiar. By morning, the details faded like usual and there was little I recalled – merely the same feelings that'd always been there.

My subconscious needed a new hobby.

Charlotte took breakfast at the hotel restaurant Smeraldi's. The food was such an enjoyment. She came back for dinner at La Bistecca in the upper level when Nicholae begged off for "business concerns".

"No lady as lovely as you should dine alone." The statement came from a man at a table adjacent to hers.

"Beg pardon?"

"That was probably a bit forward, wasn't it? If you wouldn't mind some company, I'd be happy to join you, unless you're expecting someone," he said.

"Do I know you, sir?" She didn't feel particularly in danger in a populated restaurant, but the request wasn't something she was used to — men had certainly paid her attention before, when she had the time to date, but... "You know what? Pull up a chair."

"You're most kind, Miss..." The man moved his plate and glass to the seat across from her.

"Charlotte. Mr. —"

"Simon Cole." He extended a hand, which she shook. "So, Miss Charlotte, what brings you to the City of Angels: business or pleasure?"

The first thing that came to mind about him was *pleasant*. His voice, his smile, the twinkle in his eyes...she suddenly didn't mind the intrusion at all.

"Business. And you, Mr. Cole?"

"It's Simon, please. A bit of both, really... I'm searching for something."

"Ooo, a treasure hunt?"

"The very dearest of treasures." He said it with such reverence. Wow.

The waiter came to take her order. She hadn't looked at the menu yet and picked something at random to make him go away. "Now you've peaked my interest. Are you some kind of collector?"

"No...the item in question was stolen from me many years ago. I live in hope of reclaiming it."

"It's that precious to you."

He met her eyes. "More than I can describe." The depth of feeling in his voice...whatever he'd lost must be very personal, a family heirloom or gift of significance, perhaps.

"I hope you find it," she said, and meant it.

"Thank you. So, what kind of business are you in?"

"I play the piano."

"I imagine you play quite well to stay in such elegant surroundings," he said, nodding to the opulence around them.

"I do alright." It was Nicholae that always chose the posh accommodations.

"Modest *and* beautiful. My lucky night."

She blushed and reached for water. How long did it take to make a plate of pasta? Simon's eyes twinkled over the rim of his wine glass. All men were rascals, looking for any opportunity to turn a woman pink. She'd wished for dark skin in high school just so it wouldn't show when she was embarrassed.

Clearing her throat, she said, "You're obviously not from around here, so where is home?"

"England."

"Well, duh." Even she could tell that.

"Touché. But true. I've lived in many places."

"London?"

He nodded. "The longest, I think. And you're not a native of California."

"Raised in Oklahoma. Don't know where I was born."

"Oh?"

She shrugged. "Never seen my birth certificate. My parents adopted me as a baby. I left to go to college."

"Did they approve?"

"Mom did. She calls me a star now. She was always that mother that was too involved, wanting the best solos, the best costume, coaching my performances…"

"Sounds charming," he said, laughing. "Yet you still play."

"Only recently. I started out as a teacher." The waiter finally brought her plate. "Thank you." He nodded and left.

"An educator. Do you miss the children?"

"Sometimes. This started as a summer gig, but the paychecks kept coming in. Nicholae has been good to me."

"Oh. Boyfriend?"

"My manager." He smiled, looking relieved. His hope she was unattached gave her more confidence to flirt. "I'm single. It's been a busy year."

"But not too busy for a lovely supper. My luck strikes again. How are you at cards?"

"Funny."

"People don't often appreciate that. I have a friend who thinks I was put on Earth specifically to annoy him."

"That's rather self-involved," she teased.

"You don't know the half of it. I'd be in your debt if you could tell him you found me quite charming."

"Night's not over, yet, Simon."

"Oh, and the lady doth wound," he said, clutching his chest.

"Drama queen." And yes, very charming.

One elbow on the table, he propped his cheek on his fist. "You have the prettiest smile." From anyone else, it'd sound like a line, but he was completely sincere, saying it as a statement of fact.

She swooned. "Are you always so sweet to women?"

"There was only one."

Was? "I'm sorry."

"No need to be, Charlotte. The piano—are you here to perform or record?"

She told him all about the concert with the Philharmonic and what she was working on. He was a good listener, only interrupting to ask for clarification. They ordered dessert, then coffee, and before she knew it, the staff was warning them about closing time at ten.

"Oh, my gosh, I didn't realize how late it was."

"Early start tomorrow?"

Standing for the first time, she got to see how tall he was. Average, about five-foot-nine or ten. It was nice to not have to crane her neck up so much to look a man in the face. He wasn't large in build, either.

"No, but Nicholae doesn't like me out at night. I told my bodyguard he could stay upstairs since I wasn't leaving the building, but I'm surprised they haven't come looking for me."

They walked out to the lobby.

"Are you allowed to have any fun?" Simon asked.

"*Yes*. Sometimes."

"The bar is still open."

"I don't drink."

"Not what I asked." He winked.

"I'd love to talk some more, but…"

"You're expected."

"Yeah."

"I've heard of this amazing device for exchanging information. They call it the telephone."

She shook her head. "You don't do subtle at all, do you?"

"Rarely."

Upgrading opinion from pleasant to cheeky. "Fine. I'll check in."

Simon stayed where he was, hands in his pockets, while she walked to the front desk and asked them to call her room. Reed answered.

"Hey, just letting you know I'm not lost or dead. I'm still downstairs." She hung up before he or Nicholae started asking questions. A part of her wanted to keep this date to herself and she went with that feeling.

Simon offered his arm when she returned and they strolled to the bar. The hotel had been here since the '20s and displayed the pinnacle of Art Deco elegance. The Gallery Bar was heavily detailed, with oak paneling and carved angels floating above the granite bar. Every seat was leather. It was classy and romantic.

"The Cognac Room is a bit quieter," he said, and led her to the smaller lounge filled with Biltmore memorabilia and soft couches. "They have a live band on the weekends."

"You've been here before?"

"Read the brochure."

"Ah. What did it say they play?"

"A mix of jazz, blues, and rock. Shame this is a Thursday night."

"Why, would you ask me to dance?"

"Hypothetically."

"Ohh, *hypothetically*. Well, if you hypothetically asked, I might hypothetically agree."

He smiled, and she felt warm. "I'll remember that."

"I don't know how long I'm staying after the concert tomorrow. We normally leave the next morning, but I have a cousin in town and Nicholae said there could be room in the schedule. We could meet for breakfast?"

"I can't."

"Oh."

"I want to. I'd love to. I'll just be otherwise engaged."

"Bummer."

He chuckled. "You're adorable. And I'm keeping you past your bedtime, aren't I?"

She stifled a yawn. "I'm sorry. You're not boring me, I promise."

"May I see you to your door?"

"Thank you."

The evening had been so nice, but she was already pushing her luck, and it had been an early morning. Their leisurely goodbye ended when she saw Nicholae get out of the elevator.

"I have to go." She hurried away before he saw Simon.

"Charlotte—"

"I'm sorry, I have to go," she called over her shoulder.

Nicholae didn't look happy. She pushed the "up" button and showed her most innocent smile.

"Why have you been down here so long? You should keep Reed informed of your whereabouts. You know I don't like when you go off alone after dark."

"Can we talk about this in the room?" She stepped into the elevator. "Voices carry in this big hall."

He pushed the button for their floor and the car ascended. "What were you up to, Charlotte?"

"Merely enjoying my meal, talking with some people…a normal night."

"What people?"

"Other guests. Does this really require a third degree? I never left the building."

He turned her face to gain eye contact. "Charlotte, you may see your cousin, but stay in the room except for your performance. Understand?"

She did. He made perfect sense. "Yes, Nicholae."

He caressed her cheek. "Good girl. I have your tea waiting."

"That's very thoughtful. Thank you."

Chapter Four

Della

"How many so far tonight, Seven?" Amelia asked through Della's earpiece.

"Four. They're sloppy about who they turn in this town." Per orders, she was only dusting the new ones. Juliet and her minions wouldn't notice the absence of animals.

"With such a huge population, deaths are expected. Humans are doing enough to fill the morgues as it is."

"Homesick?" She set up the scope with thermal optics for the nightly surveillance of Juliet's HQ. The vampire was so "genteel" her clan actually had an office building.

Bloodsuckers were all the same, though. The Bubonic Plague in pretty wrapping paper was still the Black Death.

"My efforts at the hospital were successful," Amelia said. "I also gained some intel from the ER about underground parties. A few adolescents came in for overdose."

"What's new about that?"

"The bite marks."

Oh. Wonderful. The vamps were preying on teens at raves. Shouldn't surprise—a dark, illegal club filled with drug-addled kids was a veritable feast ripe for the taking. If the girl or boy ended up dead, they're just another tragic statistic of teenage rebellion. Della couldn't even put a hundred-percent blame on the vamps.

"Did you advise HQ?" she asked.

"Waiting for orders. What is the level of activity at the office?"

She peered through the scope. They were using one of the older buildings, and the windows had fabric shades pulled down except in the lobby. "A few lights on here and there, same as usual. I don't think we're going to learn much about what they do in there without going in."

"Which is strictly forbidden, Seven. We're not ready to start a war."

"I know, I know. I was just sayin'. Hasn't anybody tried to bug the place? We've been watching them for years."

"It doesn't work long. Their ears pick up the electronic noise. We're working on silent technology."

"I never knew vampires could be so boring. Can't believe I had to turn down my cousin for this."

"Seven…"

"Sorry. Didn't mean to say that out loud." She took the earpiece out and set it on the foam lining of my case.

Her presence wasn't really required up on this roof. They had cameras on the building twenty-four-seven with a feed straight back to the analysts at HQ, but the Council liked to have an agent babysitting the equipment.

She'd rather be monitoring Juliet's house. That's where the real evil took place.

And she felt naked without her suit on, too. It'd been uncomfortable at first, but now it felt like a second skin. Like Batman was merely Bruce Wayne without the costume and utility belt.

Charlotte left messages again, so Della was going to her room for breakfast before she went to bed, and she had a ticket in the cheap seats for Charlotte's show in the evening. Amelia could chew her out later for taking two hours off.

She hadn't had a break since Christmas Day.

Friday

Walking into that hotel was a step into a world that fit as well as a watermelon for a shoe. The wealth implemented intimidated her in her tee and shorts. May in L.A. was pretty warm, after all. She went straight to the elevator and up to her cousin's floor. The bodyguard grunted hello and let her knock.

"Good morning," Charlotte said. She had an elaborate spread already set out in the parlor. "Coffee, tea, juice?"

"O.J., please." The dishes were on the coffee table, so Della had a seat on one of the sofas. "Sorry I couldn't drop by yesterday."

"It's okay. I was pretty busy, myself. Had a delightful dinner downstairs, though."

"Food good?"

"It was excellent, but that wasn't the good part." She wore a smile as she served.

"You met someone."

Pink cheeks joined the smile. "The company was pleasant, yes."

"Well, tell me about him. Assuming it's a him?" Della's plate was piled with scrambled eggs, bacon, sausages, and fresh fruit.

"Yes, it's a *him*. We were both eating alone, he asked to join me, and it was very nice."

"Are you going to see him again?"

"I'm going to be up here except for going to the hall, so I guess not."

"If he's staying in the hotel, Charlotte, look him up."

"I'll see what Nicholae has on my schedule after tonight."

"You always do what this Nick guy tells you to?"

She blinked. "He's my manager."

"Yeah, and I've heard they're supposed to work *for you*. Last I knew, you were an independent woman, Cuz."

"The arrangement works, okay?"

She surrendered. "Fine. I'm comin' to see you play tonight. The nosebleed section wasn't sold out, yet."

"I hope you enjoy it."

"Hey, you're family. Of course I'd come."

Breakfast continued, and they compared lists of visited cities. They'd been to a comparable amount of states, though Della's work usually took her to the rural areas, to towns easily picked on. All of Charlotte's stories had a recurring theme of Nicholae guiding her this way and that, and Della couldn't help thinking he was pretty controlling. Why would a gal as capable and independent as Charlotte go along with everything this man said? She didn't love him, so unless it was some kind of daddy complex thing, Della didn't understand it.

She feigned a yawn as an excuse to leave.

"You've been up all night and here I am blabbering on and on. Della, it was so sweet of you to come over when you must be ready to drop."

"Think nothin' of it." Della hugged her. "Break a leg tonight."

"Thanks. Drive safe."

She nodded and left. Once back in the car, she pulled out her company cell.

"Amelia, run a background check on Nicholae Dragomir." Della spelled out the name using the NATO alphabet.

"Who's that, Seven?"

"My cousin's manager. Could be nothin', but I have a bad vibe."

"Supernatural?"

"Haven't met him, so I don't know. Thanks." She hung up and pulled out of the parking garage.

She was yawning for real when she parked in the driveway of the minister's house hosting her stay. It *had* been a long night.

Didn't travel with skirts or dresses, so she wore the newest pair of jeans and her best shirt to the concert hall, with her hair in a neat French braid. Several other patrons looked sideways at her, but hey, sittin' way up in the top tier wasn't a dress to impress location, anyway. All eyes would be on the stage.

Fancy her surprise at feeling a vampire walk in just after the curtain rose.

The audience clapped for the orchestra starting to enter and she searched in the dim light for where the tingle down her spine came from.

There.

In the back of the balcony. It was too dark to make out features other than pale skin and a tall frame, but her Spidey sense didn't lie.

Crap.

Charlotte was taking her seat at the piano, too. As soon as the audience went silent, the acoustics would carry any ruckus we made throughout the auditorium.

Della darted out of her row and up the aisle. The entry walkway behind his row gave her clear access to sneak up behind him. As the vamp sat down, she touched a fingertip to the skin above his collar. He froze. A puff of smoke started to rise from the contact.

Chapter Five
Adam

"Outside. Now. Quietly," the female paladin whispered, and walked out to the lobby.

"I hope you have a good reason for bringing me out here, miss. The pianist has started to play," he said.

"Really? You're gonna play the inconvenienced music patron? We both know what you came for."

"And what is that?"

She waited for a passing usher to get out of earshot, then said, "I know you're a vampire, and from that burn mark on your neck, you know what I am, too. Let's leave the nice innocents be and take this outside."

He stepped closer. "You have me all wrong, paladin. I came for the music by recommendation of a friend, and that's all. I'm Adam. And you are?" He would've offered his hand had she not possessed the power to burn it off.

"Not givin' you my name. You really want me to believe you didn't come for a snack."

He shrugged. "It's the truth. Do you think I want blood on this shirt? It's expensive."

She stared at him.

"Look, sit next to me and babysit if you wish, but I'd rather not miss more of the performance than I have, so—" He turned to go back inside. She grabbed his arm and he put her back to the wall, held her pinned there by the shoulders. "Listen carefully, paladin. I will say this once. I am not your enemy unless you force me to be."

"You're *all* the enemy. Swear on a Bible you've never killed a human for food and I might believe you."

He gripped the cross pendant she wore. "I have *never* willingly killed a human for blood." Then let go and went back in the auditorium.

She came back to sit two seats away. Watching.

"It's impolite to stare, paladin," he murmured.

"It's unnatural to still walk the Earth, vampire."

"Would you two shut up?" Simon said.

"Make me," they said in unison, then looked at each other. Adam winked at the girl.

He couldn't resist riling up a redhead.

An usher appeared at the end of the row. "Please be quiet or you will be asked to leave."

The paladin mimed zipping her lips shut.

The lights came up at intermission.

Simon stood. "Can we get through one more hour like adults, please? I came to watch a pretty lady play and you two are a right buzz-kill."

"Your *friend* runs the risk when he comes out of his coffin," she said.

"Please, that's so two hundred years ago."

Simon moved between them and offered his hand to her. "Hi, I'm Simon. And you are?"

"Not giving that information."

He dropped the hand. "As is your right. For the sake of peace and my sanity, I propose this site be accorded neutral status for the duration of the evening."

"Boundaries?" she asked.

"The parking lots."

"Deal," Adam said.

She nodded. "I agree to your terms."

"Thank God. You may resume your original seat, paladin. Adam, here, will be frightfully boring the rest of the night. *Won't you?*"

"Hey, she started it."

"And I told you I didn't need company, but you insisted, anyway."

"You bicker like old marrieds," she said. The lights flashed on and off to warn everyone back to their seats.

Simon smiled at her. Adam glared at both of them.

When Charlotte's concert ended, the paladin followed him when he left. He walked through the crowd at the same pace as the humans. He never bothered looking over his shoulder until outside, where he turned around and waited for her to come through the door. "Got trust issues, don't you, girl."

"Why are you waiting out here?"

"Figured you won't be satisfied until you see me get in my car and drive off."

"Where's your friend? Or should I say minion?"

"Simon is a *friend*, and he's off trying to congratulate the pianist. He's a fan."

"She doesn't need fans like you."

"Every artist needs a ticket buyer." Adam turned for the parking lot.

"You are the most irritating creature I've ever met," she yelled, running ahead of him.

"Thank you." He grinned and kept walking past her. The girl was cute when she got mad.

"Why can't you act like a normal vampire?"

"Never been one. Besides, this is more fun."

"And 'fun' is what you're about?"

He sighed. "Fighting boredom is what I'm about, paladin. I don't fancy a sun-soaked suicide, so I live."

"And not on people." She crossed her arms under her breasts, one hip cocked to the side.

"Yup. No biting humans."

"Why are you in L.A.?"

"Why are you?"

"You can't answer a question with a question!"

"Just did. You want to play Twenty Questions. I don't."

"Where did you park, the back?"

"It's right there." He took out a key fob. The alarm chirped and the lights flashed. A Lincoln Towncar. "It's a rental, so don't get any funny ideas, please."

"Me? Your kind are the ones known for *destruction*."

"You know nothing of 'my kind', child. I happen to be undead and require blood to survive, but that's where the similarity ends. I won't say it again." He opened the car door.

"Why should I believe anything you say?"

"Read my file. I'm sure your Agency has one."

While Simon could find his own way home, Adam didn't want the earful he'd receive if he ditched him, so he circled the parking lot until he was sure the paladin was gone, then parked in a different spot and waited.

Didn't take long. Simon came out with hurried steps. Opening the passenger-side door, he said, "Hotel."

"Struck out, eh?"

"They don't allow audience members backstage and she didn't come out the front."

"It was a long-shot."

"I can still run into her at the hotel. The night is early."

Adam sighed. "Maybe you do. Maybe you have dinner and charm her socks off. Then what? This concert was one-night-only, so she'll be off to another town."

"So? We'll follow her."

"What if she doesn't like you?"

"That only happened once."

"Which doesn't rule out a second time. If you stalk the girl she'll only call the police on you. Again."

"Bloody hell, Adam, it's like you don't want me to be happy!"

"That's absurd and you know it. I'm counseling you to take it slow. A modern girl in her twenties knows to be wary of strange men. Exchange numbers or e-mail or something. Court her properly, or she'll never fall in love with you and we'll be doing this all over again twenty-five years from now."

Simon went silent. An acknowledgement he was right.

He parked the car at the hotel. Simon was out and heading inside as soon as Adam turned the engine off. He wouldn't see Simon again until he got his answer.

Upstairs in their room, he checked in on Darius by phone, then searched through the TV channels until he found something palatable. L.A. wasn't a city he could wander around in if he valued his hide, so he'd be glad to move on.

Staying cooped up wasn't his style. With any luck, the next city would be cloudy and wet. He didn't understand why any vampire would choose to live in Southern California with all this sunshine threatening to reduce them to ash.

Shortly after ten, Simon came in. By the droop of his shoulders, he had bad news.

"What happened? Did you see her?"

"No."

"Maybe you haven't waited long enough."

He shook his head. "I had the front desk clerk ring her room. She turned in for the night." He took off his boots. "Must've entered a different way. I was sure she'd come down to eat..."

"Tomorrow is another day."

"The clerk said she's scheduled to check out tomorrow."

"Oh. Let me guess, during daylight?"

"Got it in one."

"Look, now you have her name, we can call Darius and have him search the Web for her concert schedule. The hunt has just begun."

"What happened to your cautionary speeches?"

"I want you to be careful, not give up."

"Now you tell me."

"Go on, then. You don't need me to find the woman." Plenty of Simon's searches before and after they met had been carried out alone.

"At least I have a woman to look forward to, mate."

Not this tune again. "Oh, no. I have no interest in a wife. Don't even start."

"Darius won't be around forever, eventually I'll be free of this curse, and then you'll be alone again. And that wasn't a pleasant Adam."

"I can fill my time without the company of females, mortal or otherwise."

"Just think on it? Immortality is a lot of years to fill. Believe me."

Of course Adam knew that. But Simon spoke from the heart of a man in love and couldn't understand his comfort with solitude.

Vampires were good at it. As a species, they rarely got along with anyone—not that he had much in common with them beyond physical requirements—and generally couldn't be trusted. He despised his kind for good reason. Other supernatural beings? There were allies, acquaintances, even a couple he would call friends, but no one he would enter into a relationship with. And mortals were out of the question.

Simon had snatched the remote. Adam groaned at his selection. Simon had a penchant for obnoxious reality shows. Adam took the remote back and turned the TV off.

"Call Darius. Faster I unload you on your reincarnated wife, the better."

Simon laughed.

Chapter Six
Della

Adam started the engine, closed the door, and drove away.

Round two: Vampire — 1. Della — 0.

She called Amelia from the car. "Any luck?"

"Not on your first request, but there is an Adam in the archives."

"Hit me."

"A vampire with that name popped up around 1730, following the razing of a monastery in Northern Italy. But I doubt the one here would have let you leave unscathed."

"Why not?"

"He's said to be in Juliet's family."

"Oh." Yeah, that would be a bad run-in. "But how can an old vamp with the name of Adam be in Los Angeles by coincidence?"

"I...can't answer that. Perhaps this can be included in your surveillance. *Carefully.*"

"Yeah. I'll sleep on it. I'll check in later. Seven out." Della ended the call and started the car, pondering the mystery that was Adam.

It would've been nice to find her cousin to congratulate her, but duty had called, as always.

Sitting on that rooftop, she went over the conversations with Adam again and again, looking for some clue she'd missed the first time. But... Nothin'. A perfectly outstanding citizen outside the lack of a heartbeat. He hadn't even sped in the parking lot.

She headed home from another bland night of watching the vamps, left a report for Amelia, and went to bed.

But she couldn't sleep that morning. She called Charlotte.

"Della? I'm surprised to hear from you at this hour. Are you okay?"

"I'm fine. I forgot to ask you how long you're staying in L.A."

"Oh! We're leaving for Portland today." Thank God.

"Oh, do you play there tonight?"

"Yes. Hey, I'd love to chat, but I have to go. It was great catching up. Keep in touch."

"Sure. Safe travels, Charlotte."

"You, too. Bye!"

Thank the Lord for small miracles. Charlotte would be safely out of town and away from all these vampires. With any luck, her time in L.A. was up, too.

PART TWO

Nicholae overplays his hand.

Chapter Seven
Charlotte
May 2008

As always, Nicholae had red roses waiting in Charlotte's dressing room. It was the other vase of flowers that made her pause—a simple bunch of pink peonies, the fat heads giving off sweet fragrance. No card accompanied them.

"The pearls again," Nicholae said, shaking his head. "Why won't you wear the diamonds I gave you?"

"My mother gave them to me." She wore an inexpensive necklace and earring set of white freshwater pearls with her standard black dress.

"Yes, thirty dollars out of a catalog. You're better than that, Charlotte. They don't compare to your beauty."

"Nicholae, they wouldn't show with my hair down, anyway. No one's going to be looking at my jewelry when my hands are at work. Do we have to have this argument every time?"

"Only because you insist on leaving my gift in its box."

"You spend too much on me as it is. I'm not trying to be unkind, but they're too extravagant." And too much like what a husband gives his wife.

He rotated her chair so she faced him instead of the mirror. "You'll wear what I ask you to wear, hmm?"

The sparkle *was* pretty. "Hand me the box, please."

He did. "Good girl."

She put in the diamond studs and he clasped the pendant around her neck. The stone glinted in the light.

Nicholae pulled her hair back. "How about we pin this up, too?" He twisted her curls into a bun.

"Okay."

"There, that's better. Let's get you to the stage door." He turned to leave the dressing room. "Charlotte, what are these pink flowers doing here?"

"I don't know. No card."

"Hm." He reached for the vase.

"Please, leave them. I like pink."

He smiled at her. "Of course, my dear. After you."

She nodded, and walked through the corridors to her mark to wait for her cue. The conductor would escort her on stage and introduce her.

Don't be nervous.

It's just like every other show…

Nicholae was right there when she walked offstage when it was over. He kissed her cheeks. "Bravo, Charlotte. Not one missed note. As a reward, you may have the rest of the evening to do as you like in The Biltmore."

"Thanks. Goodnight."

She collected her belongings in the dressing room and Reed escorted her to the limo, carrying the vase of roses. The little bouquet of peonies fit in her hand.

Always famished after a show, she dropped off her things in the bedroom and went down to the restaurant.

"What perfect timing," she heard behind her.

"Simon! A year later and we're in the same hotel again. How are you?"

He took her hand. "You played wonderfully. Catching a bite?"

"Yes. You were at my performance?"

He grinned. "Wouldn't've missed it once I learned you were here in Los Angeles again."

"Flatterer." She'd listen to more, though. She hadn't felt so instantly at ease with someone in a long time, if ever.

"Two?" a hostess asked. On Charlotte's nod, she took them to a table.

"So, were you at the hall alone?" she asked Simon.

"My friend tagged along, unfortunately."

"Oh?"

"You were much more interesting, I assure you. Did you start lessons as a young girl?" He pulled out the chair for her.

"Not until I was in school. We didn't have money for private lessons, but my elementary school had a music teacher. My choir teacher in high school helped me get the materials I needed to study to get college credit, and I won a few small scholarships at competitions."

"On the piano?"

"No, voice, but I accompanied myself when it was allowed. For college, I chose the practical side and went with the music teaching degree. The concert stuff has been going on less than two years."

"With the help of your friend."

"Yep."

"Only a friend?" he asked.

The interest made her blush. "Yes." *Kind of. Nicholae wasn't a friend in the traditional sense — we didn't share anything personal with each other.* "It's been a bit lonely on tour, actually. I don't know when I last had a normal day out."

"Is there a Charlotte Taylor home somewhere?"

"If you count my parents."

"And that's not the preferred option."

She laughed. "No. I love them, don't get me wrong, but Mom gets way too involved in my life. My apartment building got condemned two years ago and I've been living out of suitcases ever since."

"Do you miss having roots, yet?"

"Yeah, I actually do." It was something she wouldn't admit to Nicholae, but it'd be nice to have some time off for a while, to have a routine again. "Lucky us, wandering in the same direction."

He smiled, and butterflies fluttered in her stomach. "Glad you feel that way."

Is this what it felt like to start a relationship? Her last date was in college, and she wouldn't describe it as a night with sparks. Leaving L.A. soon suddenly seemed like a crappy idea.

They might've sat making googley eyes at each other all night if the waitress hadn't brought their food. It was another gastronomic delight, but she would have been just as happy eating at McDonald's with the same company.

"Any luck finding what you're looking for?" she asked over dessert.

"Getting closer."

"That's good…unless it means you'll be heading back to England this weekend."

He laughed. "No chance of that, Charlotte, I promise."

"Even better."

The check came—his hand was faster—and they prepared to leave La Bistecca.

"Luck continues to favor us," he said.

"How so?"

"It's Friday night, otherwise known as the weekend, which means a live band is only a few steps that way. Unless this is too late for you."

"I'll have you know I closed many a club once upon a time." She put her hand in his. "Lead on, sir."

She expected him to rush off with her, but he surprised her again by taking her hand, placing it on his arm, and strolling to the bar like a gentleman. Some guys displayed manners merely to win points, but Simon had nobility that made his chivalry look very natural. He'd treated her as something special since the moment they met.

The band was playing some slow jazz when they entered The Cognac Room, a song that was both romantic and melancholic.

"My lady, it would be an honor if you would dance with me."

"I'd love to," she said. He held her very properly, reminding her of junior high dances and teachers moving kids six inches apart. She put both hands on his shoulders, but he still didn't bring her any closer. Ah, well…baby steps. At least something made him nervous. It made her feel on more equal footing. "So, we've talked about my life. What do you do when you're not searching for lost heirlooms?"

"Oh, same as everyone. Bit of reading, bit of the television…"

"Just books and TV?" she teased. "What about school?"

"Self-taught, mostly. I served my village before my, uh, quest."

"You don't want to talk about your past."

"There are things I'd rather not dwell on."

"Why?"

"Nothing personal, Charlotte."

"Sorry I asked." She broke from his arms.

Knew there had to be some big flaw. In her experience, nice guys always turned out to have issues. So did the not-so-nice. A moratorium on dating was probably a good idea. No one was what they seemed.

"I had a wife once." Simon sat next to her. "She was everything I could want, and she was taken from me. Every memory before I left England is tied up in her and it's hard to think about the past."

"Oh." Definitely a ton of baggage. "What happened?"

"It was my job to protect my village, my birthright. She paid the price for work well done."

"But it's not your fault some people are evil. I'm sure she was proud of you keeping everyone safe." Poor man…tried to be a good cop and lost his love. She wanted to comfort him, but she knew words couldn't wipe away the guilt he obviously felt…he'd have to let that go on his own. "How did she die?"

He swallowed before he replied, "Painfully."

"I'm sorry."

He looked down at her hand covering his, then into her eyes. "I know."

She kissed him, a soft and gentle press of the lips, receiving a shaky sigh.

"Don't do that because—"

"I'm not." Ducking her head, she added, "Your beard tickles."

One corner of his mouth lifted, and he started to laugh. "Thank you."

"I like your smile."

He kissed the hand he held and they sat shoulder-to-shoulder watching the band.

They were pretty good, a surprise in a hotel. Very professional. Then again, The Biltmore wasn't cheap. The band consisted of a string bassist, a drummer, the pianist, and a guest on sax.

"I love the saxophone," she said.

"Really."

"It's a very moody instrument, from sexy and sultry to lively and bouncy, and everything in between. Not all instruments work in a room by themselves, but a sax can."

"What else do you like?"

"Watching a guitarist's hands." The statement made her blush to admit it and she was glad for the dim lighting.

"Does someone have an inner rock groupie?"

"Shut up."

He caressed her cheek. "I like your smile, too."

She thought he was going to kiss her, but he just…looked, his hand cupping her cheek. The first kiss was an uncharacteristic move on her part. Did she dare risk another?

Before she could decide, he dropped his hand and turned his head back to the stage. She sighed.

They shared a couple more dances to slow songs before the room closed at twelve-thirty. She hadn't been up past midnight in a long time; in spite of having a good time, she was stifling yawns. Simon walked her to her door.

"I had fun tonight," she said. They'd been holding hands all the way up in the elevator.

"Glad to oblige. Tomorrow night, same place?"

"What about lunch?"

"I'm not free until the evening, I'm afraid. Does that change your mind?"

"No…it's just disappointing," she said, pouting a bit.

He grinned. "You're used to getting what you want, aren't you?"

"Eventually. One of these days we'll have to do breakfast."

He tucked a stray tendril behind her ear. "Maybe even leave the building. Goodnight, Charlotte."

"Goodnight, Simon."

The second kiss finally came, the sweetest little brush of his lips against hers. Her tummy fluttered again. "Sweet dreams," he said, and left for the elevator.

She had the sudden urge to call Della and babble about a boy like she was sixteen.

Reed had left a lamp on, but the rest of the suite was dark. She went to her room.

Someone shoved her against the wall next to the door.

"You little slut! I generously give you time to relax and you spend it with a stranger?"

"Nich—?"

He covered her mouth. "Shut up. You are *mine*, do you understand?" His grip on her arm was too tight.

"You're hurting me," she tried to say behind his hand. She didn't know what had gotten into him, but it scared her.

"No more indulgence!" He grabbed her and shoved her to the floor.

Due to his force, she landed awkwardly on her hand. Pain shot through her palm and up her wrist. "Please…" *Why is he hurting me?*

He rolled her on her back and sat on her hips, grabbing her face so she had to look at him. "Listen, Charlotte—"

"Get. Off. Me. I think you broke my hand, you bastard." She'd been cradling it to her since she felt the pain.

He grabbed it and forced her fingers straight. She screamed at the unexpected agony. Why wasn't Reed coming out at all this noise?

"*Dammit.*" Nicholae bent so they were eye-to-eye. "Listen, Charlotte. You will get up and go into your room. You will turn the water on in the shower and prepare to bathe. A few minutes later, you will call my room to say you slipped in the shower and think you broke your finger. Do you understand?"

I broke my finger in the bathtub. "Yes, Nicholae."

He petted her hair. "Good girl."

It was so embarrassing to sit in the ER in the middle of the night for a broken finger.

"I'm so clumsy sometimes," she said to the doctor wrapping her hand.

"You should think about traveling with one of those traction mats for the tub, Miss Taylor." He secured one more piece of tape. "There you go. The nurse will get you care instructions, and here's a scrip for a few days of pain medication."

"Thanks. Hope you don't think I'm a total wuss."

He smiled. "A lot of patients complain a lot more, believe me. Have a good night."

Six weeks with a giant bandage on her right index finger. So much for piano. Nicholae sat in the waiting room looking like Oscar the Grouch.

She held up her damaged hand. "Sorry."

He sighed. "Accidents happen. Let's get you to bed. I have a lot of calls to make in the morning."

She winced. "Postponing concerts. Again, sorry."

He shook his head, tight-lipped, and led her to the car. They were losing at least two months of performance dates and she felt like the biggest idiot. Who hurts their hand in the shower?

****

Between the nightmares and ache in her hand, she was just having breakfast a little before eleven. Around seven, she'd finally given up on drug-free sleep and popped one of the pills the doc gave her. Still be asleep if she wasn't starving.

"Hey, Del, I'm staying in L.A. longer than I thought, and you'll never guess why. If you're in the area, come over. I'm in the Biltmore again." Message sent, she hung up and changed the channel on the TV again.

Calling her cousin was her second choice. Her first impulse had been Simon, but one, she didn't want to appear needy, and two, he wasn't available anyway. She didn't know his room number, but it'd be easy enough to ring him through the front desk. Truth was, she wanted friendly company and the suite didn't feel safe anymore.

There wasn't a tangible reason to think that way, but the night of bad dreams had given her a definite unease in the room. Once she woke up a bit more, she was going to look for a nice apartment she could rent month-to-month while she healed. Nicholae seemed to think everything needed to be arranged for her, but she'd been on her own for years before they met.

Simon's eyes immediately zeroed in on her hand when they met for dinner. "Charlotte, what happened?"

"Shower accident. I feel like a dork."

He placed a feather-soft kiss on her bandage. "Does it hurt?"

"Aches. They gave me some nice pills. Do you think we could go someplace different for dinner? The hotel is lovely, but I've been eating here for days."

"Of course. Do you have a car?" He moved to walk on her left side so her hand wouldn't get accidentally bumped.

"Nope."

"We'll ask the desk for a taxi, then."

It was only a few minutes wait, then they were off to eat. The driver was happy to hear they wanted to go "that way" until they saw where they wanted to stop. For once, she didn't care about the meter. When she saw where Simon said to drop them off, she was relieved—finger food.

Do you have any idea how hard it is to hold a utensil without using your index finger?

"Not exactly gourmet…"

"Fish 'n' chips is perfect," she said. "This stupid finger has gotten in the way all day."

"What happens to your concerts?" He opened the door for her. The scent of fried fish made her mouth water.

"Postponed until I'm healed. Some of them might have to cancel entirely, I don't know. It sucks."

"Are you staying in L.A., then?"

"Subtle." The line moved forward.

"Can't blame a man for asking." He tugged one of her ringlets. "I like your hair down."

"Don't have many options right now, but me, too. It's heavy to have up. It was a frizzy mess 'til I reached high school."

They ordered, paid, and found a table. The girl at the register took a couple tries to get it right once she heard Simon's accent. Yeah, he was charming and nice to listen to, but geesh. In a city of tourists and immigrants, accents were a dime a dozen.

"Does that happen every time you speak to an American female?"

He laughed. "Often enough. It's an advantage and a curse."

"A curse. *Right*."

"Really! Some attentions are unwanted, is what I'll say."

"Ohhh. I see."

"Did I just walk into trouble?"

She propped her chin on her good hand. "Not yet."

And employee called their number, he went to the counter, and they moved to sit at the tables outside. Believe it or not, it was less noisy out there. She car-watched, picking at fries until the fish cooled a little. Wishing she could see him in sunlight—his hair was black, but did it show other colors in daytime...and his eyes were light-colored, but she couldn't tell what hue.

He touched her uninjured hand and she looked at him. "Where did you go?" he teased.

"Sorry…observing. I rented a place today."

His brows rose. "Did you?"

"Well, I'm not going to be playing for at least six weeks, and I lived here before, in California."

"For only yourself?"

"Not for two more weeks. A friend of mine; it's hers. Guess you could say it's a sublet, but there's decent space and she'll be off home for the summer as soon as her class ends. I haven't told anyone, yet."

"Then I feel very privileged. And I think the arrangement is a good idea. Safe."

"Can't go wrong with the buddy system. Anyway, I'd ask you to help me move in tomorrow, but I know you'll say you're busy until the evening, so my cousin can be the pack mule."

"Hooray for your cousin?"

She laughed. "It's not much, really. I've been living out of suitcases!"

"A bloody shame, that's been. When your schedule resumes, what then?"

She stirred a fry in the pool of ketchup. "I don't know. I was booked to the end of the summer already, so some are still open to me, but after that?" She shrugged. "Anyone's guess. Canceling shows doesn't look good."

"But you can't help that, Charlotte…you're injured. You'd play if it was a toe instead."

"*I* know that, but they don't have a reason to… I barely have a track record, yet. And there's no CD to hawk. There's always teaching, public or private…"

"Hey, a broken finger is not the end of the world, alright? You'll be fine."

"Thanks, but, how do you know?"

"I just do. Trust me."

"Thanks." Figuring she'd moped enough, she stuffed a filet in her mouth and chewed.

Simon was so different than Nicholae. Where her manager treated her like a prize-winning poodle lately, she had the impression Simon would support her trying anything as long as it wasn't dangerous. His late wife was a lucky woman if he was the same way then.

As little time they'd spent together so far, she did trust him. A feeling in her gut that she absolutely could. She'd always been pretty intuitive, so the instinct was a good sign.

"Ugh, what is *that*?" referring to the black liquid he was sprinkling on his food.

"Malt vinegar. What of it?"

"That smell is revolting!"

"Huh. Breeze must've changed. It's good, though. Tangy." He moved to her other side and the smell lessened intensity.

"It's so strong…how can you even taste the fish?"

"Sensitive palate." He winked and took another bite soaked with vinegar. "What would you like to do next?"

What was Daddy's line – oh, yeah – men like food with results. "I'm not done here, yet."

"I know, but I can plan ahead, can't I?"

"What do *you* wanna do?"

"Don't start."

She grinned, unabashed, and he couldn't glare at her for long, smiling back. The smiley twins. Of course, staring into his soulful, twinkling eyes, she wanted another kiss.

She went to work finishing her last fish piece instead.

Not sure how they ended up at the coffee bar later. Sometimes wandering lands you somewhere. It was a cozy place filled with overstuffed chairs and sofas, young people, and shelves of books. Like a commercialized living room. A hopeful starlet-in-the-making was crooning her heart out with some folk tunes and a guitar in the corner.

"It's May and I'm drinking hot chocolate," Charlotte mused. "Contradictions follow you, don't they?"

"Don't know about that, but the unexpected can be fun." He touched her nose. "Whipped cream." She rubbed the tip dry, feeling ridiculous. He grabbed her hand and lowered it to her lap. "Stop. It was only a little speck, and it was adorable."

They sat on a loveseat to the side, a half-height bookshelf giving them a bit of seclusion. "It's silly on anyone over the age of ten."

"Well, you've got the height right."

Her jaw dropped and she hit his arm. He laughed. "You think you're so funny! I'm beginning to side with your friend."

"Oh, now that's mean."

"Don't dish it if you can't take it, bud." She knelt on the sofa with him trapped in the corner.

"I can take quite a lot... Short-stuff."

"Shut up," she said, and kissed him. Hey, she was already close enough to, so, why not?

She'd never made out in public before…though the term hardly applied to this. They didn't kiss with the frenzied lust of teens or get-a-room lack of decorum of exhibitionists. She doubted anyone else even noticed them.

But she was falling with each tender touch. He seemed so grateful, like he hadn't had sweetness in years. When the kiss did end, their foreheads remained touching, and she guessed neither of them was ready to disconnect, yet.

"I should get you home," he whispered.

She swallowed the "why" that came up first, and nodded. The gentlemanly wooing was preferable to the ham-handed attempts of college boys in the past.

At least, I think I'm being wooed.

****

The night had been so nice. She didn't want it to end. "It's not even midnight, you know. I promise I won't turn into a pumpkin if I'm not in my room."

"Tomorrow is your moving day, Charlotte." He pressed the *close doors* button for the elevator at the hotel.

"Which consists of two suitcases and a carry-on, and my cousin is doing the heavy lifting. I don't need to go to bed early for grocery shopping. Do you have an early appointment?"

"No…"

"Then there's no rush, is there?"

"Fine, you win." He pushed a button for a lower floor. "Pardon me for wanting you to get some healing sleep."

"I'll take full responsibility, Doctor."

He unlocked the door to a standard two-bed room, which in the Biltmore was still pretty nice. One bed was neatly made, the other in shambles with the covers half on the floor.

Simon sighed and attempted to make the bed less of an eyesore. "Adam."

"Ah..."

"He leaves the room like this only to annoy me. His house could pass white glove inspection."

"Sound like brothers." She sat on a chair.

"Long-time mates." He glanced in the bathroom and she heard another sigh, then the faucet running. "But close enough. Never had a brother."

"Sisters?"

He came back out and shut the door. "One. Influenza took her when she was nine."

"I'm sorry."

He nodded. "It was a long time ago." He sat in the other chair, the small table between them. "Unless you fancy a bit of telly, there's not much to do in here."

"We've done pretty well at talking so far." It was warm in there, like the AC hadn't run in hours. She started removing her thin cardigan, sliding the right sleeve off over the bandage.

"What is *that*?" he asked a bit harshly.

"What?"

Simon got up and moved her left arm into the light. "*This*."

A black bruise was on her upper arm. "I must have—"

"These marks aren't from impact, Charlotte. Who did this?" The question promised a world of hurt on the culprit, and for a moment it scared her.

"I don't remember getting a bruise at all. Simon, it has to be from when I slipped."

"Were there any other bruises from the shower when you got dressed? Your knee or hip? Elbow? Anything sore from falling?"

"I don't know. I've been focused on this, I guess," and waved her damaged hand.

He brushed his fingertips over the bruise. Now she knew it was there, it stung, and she winced at contact. "Simon, I'd know if someone hurt me."

He didn't look convinced, but let her arm go. "I have some arnica salve. It'll help it heal faster." He stood and went into the bathroom.

She followed him to see the mark in the mirror. "Gee, that's some nice colors," she said, turning to see the back of her arm, too. "Cold!"

"Sorry." He gently massaged the balm into her skin, which frankly stung quite a bit.

"Smells better than I expected."

"A botanical thing. Arnica, wild yam, other bits of this and that. Nature can be pretty handy." He rubbed it in until it was dry. "Charlotte, if there is something going on, you can tell me. You're safe with me."

"That's sweet, but aside from a broken finger, I'm fine. My life is actually kinda boring."

"It's…when you ran off the other night, before, you seemed afraid of being caught in the lobby. And no offense, but your manager has sounded a might controlling. Then, this…" He stroked her arm, raising goose pimples. "I have to ask."

She touched his cheek and looked into his eyes. "I'm not a battered woman. I promise."

"If you ever do feel in danger, you'll tell me?"

"Cross my heart."

Simon pulled her into a hug, which felt really nice. Warm. Safe.

She could feel his fear that something would happen to her. Guess it made sense with what happened to his wife, but poor guy...how many times had he not entered a relationship because of that fear, or on the flip side, driven a woman nuts with over-protectiveness?

He loosened the embrace, but only to dip his head and kiss her. She wrapped her arms around his neck and he sat her on the counter—hey, no kink in her neck from looking up—tilting his head to deepen the kiss.

And broke away a second later. "Sorry. Got carried away," he said, breathing fast.

"I didn't mind." His brows rose in surprise and she added, "Hey, I'm not gonna throw down on the bathroom rug with you right now, but making out works. Haven't you figured out I like kissing you?"

He smiled, looking a bit embarrassed. "I did, yes."

"Then don't apologize."

"Never again...until you change your mind."

She grabbed his shirt and pulled him closer. "Not gonna happen."

Charlotte went back to her suite a little while later accompanied by her new beau. He looked around the main room under the guise of seeing what was different than his, checking that it was safe. The suite was empty. She sent him away with a kiss and promised to call once she was at the apartment to give him the new address.

Sunday was Reed's day off, so he wasn't there when she woke up, and she didn't see Nicholae or receive any calls before Della showed up and she checked out.

It was the least stressful moving day she'd ever had.

Chapter Eight
Della

L.A. again. Her third time in this city, and the first since…well, she didn't think about Solstice night. Activity was down, and if Juliet was still in town, she was laying low.

Last night was morgue duty and Della was in a crappy mood. She hated going into the body storage and staking vamps-to-be, especially when a couple of them were children.

Drove to the Biltmore late morning and knocked on Charlotte's door. They got her luggage, which she had already packed, she checked out, and they started for the apartment she was directing Della to.

"You're smilin' an awful lot today."

"No more than usual," Charlotte said.

"Uh, ya-huh. New boy?"

"*Grown man*, and yes, if you must know. He's sweet, charming, and makes me laugh."

"Sounds too good to be true," she said, taking the turn into the complex's parking structure.

"He's *not*. Just a genuine good guy. They do exist, you know."

Della did. Thirteen was a great guy, and Lev was still a good friend. "Yeah. I just don't expect to find 'em in California." Not with Vampire Underground Central owning L.A.

"You can't judge an entire state by one city, Della. Anyway, Simon's not from here, so he doesn't count."

"You met him at the hotel? Oh, honey, don't hook up with a wanderer…"

"It's not a *fling*. We're building something. I can feel it."

"Alright, alright…I hope that 'feeling' doesn't get your heart broken." She turned off the engine and popped the trunk lid.

They took the lift up four floors and found Charlotte's friend's place.

"Hey, Charlotte!" They hugged. "Who's this?" The friend was a big girl, at least six feet tall.

"My cousin Della. Del, this is Carrie. We did teacher's training together."

"Nice to meet you. Char's room is this way, where you can drop that heavy luggage." Carrie led them past the living room and kitchen and turned down a hall. "Each bedroom has a bath, so you'll have total privacy."

"Wow, private school is paying you well," Charlotte said.

"Well, that, and my grandmother's inheritance, but thanks. I've tried to make it really homey."

Della dropped the bags in Charlotte's room and left the hall. It seemed like a nice building, but she wanted to check out how safe this unit was, and ended up on the balcony.

"Del? What are you doing?"

"Checking the view. Figured you'd want to catch up."

"Well, thanks, but we weren't going to exclude you. I didn't ask you along only for your arm strength."

She turned and leaned her back on the rail, one leg crossed over the other. "I know…don't mind me. It's been a crappy weekend."

"Rough time at work?"

"Kids doin' stupid stuff, and they won't stop just because you tell 'em to."

"Wanna talk about it?"

Not with a civilian. No innocent should have to know what can really be found in a morgue at night. "Nah. Tomorrow's another day."

"Well, I'm glad you could come, you know, had the day off."

Della smiled at Charlotte, much of one as she had energy for. "Yeah. Thanks."

They hugged and she left. Charlotte had to unpack, she and her friend looked on the verge of a bond-fest, and Della didn't fit.

Sunday was her day/night off. Barring a crisis, even The Agency recognized people needed downtime to stay sane, so agents were allowed the respite if they could take it. Since her official orders were to watch vamps move around behind curtains all night, she wasn't going to miss much.

Only drawback was she had nothing to do.

Chapter Nine
Charlotte

Charlotte got out of the car and chose to ignore that comment. Della had been suspicious of everybody since they met up in L.A., so Charlotte guessed that's how she operated now. Walking into the building, Della sized up every person she passed like a potential threat. Charlotte wondered what that aid organization had really trained her to do.

Up the elevator four floors, down the hall five doors, and she knocked on Carrie's.

She opened it right away. "Hey, Char!" They hugged. "Who's this?"

Carrie was a tall blond with short curly hair—not the model type, but a really sturdy gal, like the kind they might have made Amazons or Valkyries out of. She was also the most eternally-positive person Charlotte knew.

"My cousin Della. Del, this is Carrie. We did teacher's training together."

"Nice to meet you. Char's room is this way, so you can drop that heavy luggage." Carrie led them past the contemporary living room and kitchen and turned down a hall. "Each bedroom has a bath, so you'll have total privacy."

"Wow, private school is paying you well."

"Well, that, and my grandmother's inheritance, but thanks. I've tried to make it really homey."

Della dropped the bags in Charlotte's room and left the hall. "She's not trying to be anti-social," she whispered to Carrie. "I think she's just worried about me since I busted my finger."

"I can install bumpers and child locks if that'll make you more comfortable." Carrie turned on the light in each lamp.

"Oh, shut up. It's the first broken bone I've ever had, not a trend."

"If you say so." She opened the closet and bathroom doors. "Do you like it?"

The room was in a soft shade of blue with accents of cream. "It's great. Thank you so much for letting me crash on short notice."

"Hey, it saves me looking for a stranger to sub-let to. Even a background check doesn't tell you if they're a slob."

"No kidding." They walked back to the living room. Della was on the balcony looking over the rail.

"Let me show you where everything is in the kitchen. I already cleared a shelf in the fridge for you." Carrie opened all the cabinet doors, though the frosted glass gave Charlotte some clue to their contents. "Don't feel like you have to memorize the place today. Feel free to ask."

"I will." She got through college with one bowl, one pot, and one set of silverware, so her home cooking wasn't fancy. As long as she could find soup and cereal, she wouldn't starve. "Let me see what she's doing out there."

"Okay."

She went out on the balcony and shut the sliding glass door. "Del? What are you doing?"

"Just checking the view. Figured you'd want to catch up with your friend."

"Well, thanks, but we weren't going to exclude you. I didn't ask you along just for your arm strength."

Della turned and leaned her back on the rail, one leg crossed over the other. "I know…don't mind me. It's been a crappy weekend." There was a thin cut on her arm, a long scratch.

"Rough time at work?"

"Kids doin' stupid stuff, and they won't stop just because you tell 'em to."

"Wanna talk about it?"

"Nah. Tomorrow's another day."

"Well, I'm glad you could come, you know, had the day off."

Della shared a crooked half-smile, and Charlotte thought she looked older than twenty. "Yeah. Thanks."

****

Have to say, putting clothes in a closet and toiletries in a bathroom she knew she wouldn't have to leave for a couple months was a thrill. Once it was all settled, she called her mother.

"K.T. speakin'."

"Hi, Mom."

"Charlotte May, where have you been? I haven't had a phone call in forever."

"It's only been a few days, Mom. I called when I landed in L.A., just like with every other town." Starting with the drama — yay.

"Della said you've been under the weather?"

"Sort of. I pulled a klutz maneuver and broke a finger."

"A bone! Oh my goodness, did you need surgery?"

"Mom, calm down…it's only a little clean break that'll be gone in six weeks. I'm fine."

"But what about your career, honey? You really should've been more careful. All those disappointed people with worthless tickets…"

She let out a long breath. "They're getting rescheduled for a new date, Mom. No one's being left high and dry."

"Still, what've I said about carin' for your hands—"

"I do my best, Mom. Accidents happen, okay? Everything fine at home?"

"Oh, yes…same ol', same ol'…though your uncle lost his shirt gamblin' again."

"Again?"

"Well, literally his shirt, this time. It's a long story…"

Charlotte zoned out as Mom started to drone on about everything that led up to the incident. Calling home was always potentially dangerous to her cell phone bill.

Carrie walked in, softly tapping on the door. She mimed eating some food, then pointed at Charlotte. She nodded. "Hey, Mom, gotta go. Food's here. Bye! Love you!" She hung up before Mom could protest. "Thanks. My ear was going to fall off before she was done."

"Any time. I don't actually have food ready, though. I was asking if you're hungry."

"Oh, I know. But it was a good excuse."

"I'll keep that in mind for future reference." She took a stack of take-out menus out of a drawer. "Sorry your cousin couldn't stay."

"Me, too. I think some normal socialization would've been good for her."

They ordered Chinese delivery, then Charlotte called Simon's room. It took three rings before someone picked it up, and the male voice wasn't his.

"You must be Adam. Is Simon in?" she asked.

"He's indisposed at the moment, but I can take a message, Charlotte."

"Hey, I hadn't given you my name, yet."

"No, but the only woman calling for him would be the only one he's been talking about for days, so it was a simple deduction."

"He talks about me?"

"And little else."

"Give me that!" Simon's voice cut in. She heard a struggle on the other side of the line and imagined them wrestling for the phone. There was a deeper laugh that must have come from Adam, then Simon said, "Hello? Charlotte?"

"I'm here. What was that about?" she asked, amused.

"Roommate boundaries. What did you need, love?"

It was the first time he'd called her that. "Um, I'm at the apartment, so…"

"Right. Pad and pen, pad and…aha! Ready."

She read off the address, slow and clear, and gave him Carrie's landline and her cell. He read the info back to her, pausing twice to tell off Adam again.

"Do you have plans tonight?" he asked.

"We're waiting for Chinese food."

"Oh. Alright."

"Maybe later, though…call me."

"Okay," he said, and she could hear the relief in his voice.

Charlotte knew how he felt. She'd been thinking about him all day. "Bye, Simon."

"Until later, Charlotte. Enjoy your supper."

"Thanks." She hung up with a sigh.

Carrie grinned when Charlotte walked back into the living room.

"What?"

"You've got 'my boyfriend's so dreamy' face."

"I do not! And he's not my boyfriend. Yet." She plopped on the sofa. "Maybe."

"Uh-huh. Well, whatever he is, you're obviously smitten, so, spill."

"It's been really nice so far, and that's all I'm saying."

"Aww, come on!"

"I feel good about it, but we're both in temporary places, you know? So I don't want to jinx it with labels. But he's pretty great."

"And…?"

"And…a really good kisser."

She held up her hand, and they high-fived. "There you go! Chemistry's half the battle."

"I wouldn't say *half*…but yeah, it's there, in a really good way."

"Like knockin' boots kinda good?"

"*Nooo*…gutter mind much? It's…healthy, I guess. Like, I can feel that I'm safe with him. Not pressured. That he's just as hopeful about this working out as I am. There's attraction, definitely, but I'm not in this mad rush to get his clothes off, or mine."

"And that's better than…?"

"Way better. Imagine falling with a clear head."

She thought about it. "Whoa…"

"*Yeah*. It's not scary, except for the chance that it won't work out."

"And that's always there, anyway, so that's normal."

"Yup."

"Oh my god, I am so jealous of you."

The doorbell rang. They looked at each other, and burst into giggles. Man, it was so nice to hang out with a good friend again.

****

When Simon walked into the lobby, Charlotte was waiting. He greeted her with a brief kiss and she showed him to the elevator on their side. "Nice building."

"I think so." She took his hand with her left. "Adam give you much trouble?"

He groaned. "How much did you hear?"

"Enough." She grinned. "He has a nice voice."

"Don't tell him. He's vain enough already."

She wrapped her arms around his neck. "It's okay. I already like you better."

They were an inch from kissing when the elevator doors opened. She led him to the apartment and opened the door.

"You didn't lock it?" Simon asked.

"My roommate's here. So, this is my new home."

"It's lovely."

She turned him to look at the wall next to the door. "And see? Alarm system."

"Had to point that out, eh?"

"I value your piece of mind. The building comes with a pool and gym, which is pretty nifty, and my bedroom also has a bathroom so Carrie and I don't get in each other's way. Speaking of…"

"Don't mind me. Just getting a drink." Carrie opened the refrigerator and grabbed a soda.

"Carrie, this is Simon. Simon — Carrie."

She came to shake his hand. "Welcome. I'll be in my room with headphones on." She went back down the hall.

"She's kidding," Charlotte said.

"No, I'm not!" she yelled, and they heard her door shut.

Simon's face twitched as he tried not to laugh. She shook her bandaged finger at him. "Don't encourage her."

"Yes, ma'am." The mischief in his eyes betrayed the obedience in the reply.

"Continuing the tour, the balcony is behind that curtain, and my bedroom is across from Carrie's." She led him to look. "Feel free to use my bathroom if you need it."

"Seems a bit odd not to include a powder room in this floor plan."

"Oh, there is one, but it's under renovation. Carrie says don't ask."

"Ah." He looked at the picture frames Charlotte stuck on the dresser. "All family?"

"Yup." She had this accordion-folding photo holder thing that stretched out to display all of them. It was only painted cardboard, but it fit in a suitcase. She made it back when they couldn't afford to buy real frames. "Are you thirsty or anything?"

"I'm fine, Charlotte."

They went back to the living room and picked out a movie.

When she checked her phone before bed, there were four messages from Nicholae.

Chapter Ten
Nicholae

It had taken immense restraint to not tear apart the hotel when Nicholae discovered Charlotte checked out. How could she take such initiative? And not only to leave, but to not tell him where she went? He thought he had her so well-trained by now.

His mother's minions parted instinctively to let him pass as he made his way through the mansion. Suppose he was carrying around a dark cloud above his head at the moment.

"I wasn't expecting you," Juliet said when he walked into her office.

"She's gone!"

"Who, childe?"

"My charge. She scurried off during the daylight."

"I see. I thought I taught you better, Nicholae. Your will must be absolute. Have you gone soft for the girl?"

"Nonsense, my Lady. A mere underestimation of her impulsiveness. It won't happen again."

His maker's red-lacquered fingernails drummed a rhythm on the desk. "I hope not. I have allowed you enough time with this…distraction. If you're so convinced the girl is special, carry out the ritual and be done with it."

"My humblest apologies. I am. She will be worth the wait. Thank you for your patience."

A dismissive wave of her hand was her only reply. He could go without punishment.

But his queen was right. This had gone long enough. He needed to regain his hold on the little bitch and finish the plan.

A mission that could seal their victory in this war with the paladins.

Chapter Eleven
Charlotte

Charlotte waited until morning to call back to approach this with a fresh mind.

He started lecturing her the second he recognized her voice.

"Nicholae, I haven't bailed on you—

Let me explain—

Just stop for a minute—

Nicholae, I'm going to hang up if you don't calm down, and then you won't have your answers."

"Proceed," he said through clenched teeth.

"I left a note with the front desk for you, but I'm staying at a friend's while my hand heals. I needed a break, a steady time. I'm very grateful for the life you've carved out for me, but it doesn't include a home. I need some time off from playing gypsy."

"If you wanted alternate accommodations, I would have arranged it. Where are you? We can put this behind us and get you pampered like you deserve."

"Nicholae, I don't need you to 'fix' anything. There's nothing to fix! I'm comfortable here, I'm catching up with an old friend, and it's all temporary, anyway. Take some time for you, okay? You've worked hard this year, too."

"Let me take you for refreshment, then. We can make up and be friends again."

"I'll get back to you. Bye." She disconnected the call, not willing to succumb to a guilt trip today.

There was nothing logical to explain it, but seeing Nicholae in person right now was an uncomfortable idea. Her gut instinct usually served her well, so even though it didn't make sense, she was going with it.

Besides, she wanted to spend time with Simon while he was here before responsibilities called them away. It bugged her that he was only available at night. One of these days, she was going to surprise him and see what kept him so busy. It was nearly *summer*...full of ice cream in the park, beach trips, and baseball games, barbeque and dips in the pool.

"Hey, Space Cadet. Thinking about the distinguished Englishman again?"

"Summer, actually. Off to work?"

Carrie shouldered her messenger bag. "Yep. Have fun being lazy."

"I intend to," Charlotte said, and Carrie left, locking the door from the outside. "Let's see what qualifies for daytime television..."

Uh-oh.

Four hours into the start of her vacation and she was already bored out of her mind. Della would be asleep, so she called Simon's room.

The line connected on the fourth ring. "What?"

The growled question startled her. "A-Adam?"

"Yeah...who is this?" He sounded like she woke him up.

"Charlotte. Simon's friend?"

"Oh. He's not available."

"Why not?"

"Ask *him*."

"Then put him on the *phone*."

"He's unavailable." Then Adam hung up.

Well, *that* was rude. No wonder Simon complained about living with him. Was it so hard to answer a simple question?

She could go over there and straighten him out...or that could backfire when best-friend mojo beat girl-he-was-seeing. Or, Simon might be pissed his friend was rude to her and she'd get some answers.

Flip a coin, dummy, it's faster.

Tails. To the hotel, it was.

The bus schedule served her well and she made the journey with only a couple minutes to wait. Her hands got clammy on the elevator up. She raised her fist twice to knock before she actually did it.

The door opened to the extension of the chain, giving her a glimpse of a—admittedly gorgeous—man in boxer briefs. "Didn't order anything," he said, and started to close the door.

"Wait! I don't work for the hotel. I'm looking for Simon."

He rubbed his eyes and peered out of the dark room. "Charlotte. You're persistent."

"And you must be Adam. Is he here?"

The door closed in her face. She lifted her hand to pound on the door again, then heard the chain slide, and he opened the door. With a full glimpse from the light of the hallway, she'd swear she was looking at a model and wondered what the heck these two had in common.

"Charlotte."

"Huh?"

"Look, there's a reason Simon doesn't see you during the day, and it's not his fault."

"Then he shouldn't mind me knowing the truth...unless it's something illegal?"

"No, nothing like that, but—"

"Then if he's here, Adam, let me inside."

"I can't."

She folded her arms under her breasts, skepticism dialed to a hundred. "Can't?"

He straightened to his full height, still blocking the doorway. "Fine. Won't. Do you have feelings for him?"

"That's none of your business, no offense."

He smiled. "Then you'll let him court you his way. Now, if you don't mind…"

"Yeah, alright… I'll go. But Adam…try to improve your phone manners."

He laughed, and she left.

Out on the sidewalk, she called Della. She'd hurried out of the Biltmore, not feeling right until she breathed fresh air — well, as fresh as it got on a Los Angeles busy street.

"Hello?" Della croaked. Dang, she woke her up, too.

"Hey, it's me. Wanna grab a bite?"

"Where are you?"

"On 5th Street near the hotel. You can hear me okay?"

"Yeah…um, food, you said?"

"Yeah, how about it?"

"Charlotte, are you okay?"

"Yep, just hungry and a little bored. So?"

"Okay. I'll pick you up in Pershing Square in fifteen."

"Cool. See ya." Charlotte ended the call.

Fifteen minutes later on the dot, her cousin pulled up to where Charlotte was waiting. She got in the car and buckled the belt. Della pulled into traffic, stifling a yawn. "So what's the real reason you got me out of bed?"

"Lunch, just like I said."

"If that's the story you want to stick to…"

"Della, I think your job's made you paranoid, no offense. With this broken finger and few people I know here, I really do have nothing to do. Daytime TV sucks. Is it a crime to prefer your company?"

"Okay…"

Girl was entirely too perceptive. What happened to the sweet kid that took things at face value? They got through picking a place to eat, getting served, finding a seat, and halfway through Charlotte's burger.

"Ever seen something weird?"

Della's attention on her became intent. "Define 'weird'."

"You know…something hard to explain." She nearly squirmed in her seat, feeling like she was suddenly under interrogation.

"What happened?"

Charlotte sat back in her chair. "Okay, you're taking this way too seriously."

Della sighed and relaxed in her seat, too. "Fine. Sorry. To answer your first question: yeah. Going where I do, there's weird stuff."

"I don't know why I brought it up. Guess I shouldn't be allowed to get bored, huh?"

"Sure."

They found food very interesting then, and by the time they left, the weird conversation had been left behind. Della left her at the apartment, where Carrie was home to greet her.

Charlotte went to her room.

The sky got dark and her phone rang fifteen minutes later. Caller ID said it was from the hotel. She stared at it ringing on her nightstand until the phone went to voicemail. And jumped when it started to ring again. This time, it stopped before the caller would be prompted to leave a message.

Did she want to see Simon again? It wasn't his fault she went to his room, except that he'd triggered her curiosity. Maybe Adam was screwing with her somehow. Got one over on the demanding not-girlfriend. She probably deserved the ruse...it wasn't nice of her to pester his roommate with questions merely because she had them.

The doorbell chimed. Carrie probably ordered food again.

"Am I intruding?"

"Simon." Charlotte hopped off the bed. "Hi."

He looked at her in her shorts and t-shirt and bare feet. "Sorry for dropping by unannounced. Your friend said you were home and—"

"It's fine. I wasn't doing anything."

"Would you rather be left to...?"

She walked up and kissed his cheek. "It's nice to see you."

He grinned, his dimples not completely hidden by the beard. "Oh. Good." He took a small jar out of his pocket. "I brought more salve for your bruise."

"That was very thoughtful. It already looks better today." She twisted so he could see more of her arm. "See?"

"Better." He rolled up her sleeve and twisted the cap off the jar and applied the fragrant gel. The pressure of his fingertips didn't cause her to wince this time. "What do you usually do on a Monday?"

"Rehearse, travel, etcetera. Concerts can happen between Wednesday and Sunday, so I'm either moving or preparing. Truthfully, the only routine part of my routine revolved around the piano. Every week was different, and when it's busy, I'm usually more aware of the *date* than the day." She straightened her sleeve and sat on the corner of the bed. "So, there is no typical Monday."

"Well, we can do anything you like."

"What do *you* like to do?"

"It frequently ends up 'what does Adam like to do'. When I'm not on the trail for—"

"That thing you lost."

"Right."

"What is that, anyway?" An innocent enough question, but she hoped it'd get him to share.

"A private matter."

"Something of your wife's?"

Simon sighed. "I'm not going to play Twenty Questions on this, Charlotte."

"Well, sorry for trying to get to know you. I've answered everything you've wanted to know about me so far, so forgive me for hoping for reciprocation. I know we haven't known each other long, but you're this friggin' enigma!" Between him and Della, she was starting to miss her family's penchant for too much information.

He crossed the space between them and took her hands. "I want you to know me, but certain things aren't easy to explain, especially so soon. Please be patient."

"I don't know if I can be." She pulled her hands away and crossed her arms under her breasts. "What could possibly be that secret and mysterious? You're James Bond?"

"Don't be ridiculous."

She went around him and closed the door so Carrie wouldn't hear them. "How about I make it easier by saying I met Adam today?"

"You...what?" His face went pale.

"I talked to Adam." She stayed in front of the door. He'd have to move her to escape.

"H-He sleeps during the day."

"I gathered that. He was pretty grumpy both times I woke him up."

"Both?"

"Yep. Once on the phone and once knocking on the door to your room."

Simon sat on the bed. She was not sure his knees would keep holding him up if he hadn't. "He didn't let you in."

"No."

He relaxed a little. "So you didn't see anything."

She went to him, draping her arms on his shoulders. "I didn't, except for Adam in his boxers. I think he was screwing with me."

"Likely."

"Are you two hiding something illegal?"

"Heavens no."

"Good. Now…" That was settled, so she chose something more pleasant: kissing him.

He wrapped his arms around her and kissed her back, holding her close, but not too tight. That was the awesome thing about kissing—nothing to debate about. Couldn't put a foot in their mouths. Her weight leaning on him made him fall backward and her hair came down around their faces, shadowing them behind a private curtain.

This was pretty comfortable. Simon was a thin man, but not bony.

He tucked her hair behind her left ear. "You're so beautiful."

A sudden sense of déjà vu entered her mind, a feeling of being in this position before hearing him say those words—except they'd never done this.

She sat up.

"Charlotte?"

She had a brief flash of being somewhere else, in a long dress, on a different bed, the air smelling like summer grass through the open window, and the fabric of Simon's shirt was different, coarser.

He looked up at her with worry, his brows knit together. She smoothed the crease in his forehead and kissed him again. Her world locked into place when their lips were touching. No fears, no doubts…no worries about tomorrow. It was the safest place she could be.

They did eventually go out to the living room and order a pizza. She learned that Simon didn't like mushrooms, so they were only on her half. Bellies full, they sat on the sofa watching a movie, her using his chest for a pillow. He stroked her hair occasionally and it felt nice.

Soothing.

She fell asleep.

A meadow. Running, being chased.

No, playing. I giggled, dodging my pursuer by darting around a tree. The line of trees gave way to open ground and I ran to the house, getting there first.

But not for long. My pursuer grabbed me round the waist, swinging me around and onto the bed.

"I let you catch me," I say.

"And I'll always let you let me." He kisses my neck and warmth floods my belly.

"You wouldn't be a hunter without the chase, my love." My husband.

I somehow know it's a rare day with little to do and we seize the chance to spend it in bed. His duties will call him away again soon.

Charlotte woke up lying on a warm body and snuggled in before the dream faded away.

Simon brushed her hair off her face. "Sleep well?" he teased.

"Mm…I didn't drool on you, did I?"

"No drool. But you did miss the end of the movie."

She sat up and stretched. "It's okay. I've seen it before."

"What were you dreaming about?"

"What makes you think I was dreaming?"

"The mumbling and giggling." He was so annoying when he had ammunition to tease her with, grinning in that way that made her want to hit him…or kiss him to shut him up.

Oh god… "Was anything coherent?"

"No…but you seemed happy, so I'm curious."

"Don't remember much, except it was nice," she said behind her hair. With her head down, he couldn't see her face unless he pulled her curls over her shoulder.

"Oh."

"Don't sound so disappointed, nosy."

"If you dreamed about me, would you tell me?"

"Ohh, so that's your angle. A nice dream could be about kittens or pink bunnies, you know." It was presumptuous to hope she'd dream about him, but cute.

Truthfully, she rarely remembered dreams in detail unless they were bad ones. The man in the nice ones lately was familiar, or at least some part of her recognized him, but she could never name an identity when she woke up.

"Still doesn't answer the question," he said.

She lay down again, propping her chin on her hands. "Hmm…maybe. But I don't think dreams are important to look at in the light of day."

"You don't."

"Nope. It's merely your brain going through its maintenance cycle. My grandmother claimed to have prophetic dreams, but I never believed her."

"Oh?"

"She never came up with a prognostication about the next president or something big…it was always rain next Tuesday or the neighbor's dog getting off its chain. Things that happened all the time, anyway."

"Things she could guess."

"Exactly. If you really had a gift to see the future, it'd be for something useful, like saving a kid from running in front of a car or preventing a murder. Helping people."

"I see. What about those who think they dream of past lives?"

"Wild imagination. Probably missed their calling writing for TV or something. I'm always me in a dream. Might be in a story instead of replaying a moment of my life, but it's me."

"You didn't pretend much as a child, did you?"

"Sure, I did. But I wasn't a princess or a fairy or a bride."

"What did tiny Charlotte want to be?"

"I was a brilliant mother to my dolls, a bird watcher, a teacher, a marine biologist, a famous singer…tried dance for a couple years. 'Course, living in Oklahoma, cowgirls were a popular idea and I had boots and clothes with fringe."

He smiled. "And the hat?"

"Two. In storage back home. Put away the country stuff when I moved to college out here."

"Why?"

"The Western phase went out of California with the '90s. I was eighteen and wanted to blend in."

"And concert pianists don't play in boots."

"Nope. Couldn't wear them as a teacher, either, except on Casual Friday. The voice lessons helped get rid of my accent and here I am. Just another chick walking around Downtown."

Mom didn't complain, since Charlotte was "livin' the dream" she never managed to achieve, but Dad snuck in comments about not knowing her every so often. He thought a person should make their big splash at home, where people that knew them could recognize it. Mom said she put up every postcard she sent on a kitchen wall and badgered her for every detail of New York City the first time she got there.

"You surprised me today. Didn't know you wore anything but long skirts."

She bent her left leg at the knee and wiggled her toes. "Yep. I even own jeans."

"Such variety. I'm impressed."

"Smart ass."

He grinned. "Better than being a dumbass."

"Shut up!" She dug a finger into his ribs. He jerked away from it. "Ohhh, someone's ticklish."

"No, no. Your nail is sharp."

"Really." She wiggled her fingers in the same spot and watched his face. He was biting his cheek to keep a straight expression. "Doesn't affect you, huh?"

"Okay, stop!"

Happy she'd found a weakness, she tucked her hands under her chin again, thankful he didn't try returning the favor. There were few parts of her that *weren't* ticklish to the right touch.

"You're trouble."

"And?" she asked.

"I like you anyway." Simon stretched his neck to kiss her. She slid up for easier reach.

Should've known the sneaky devil would use his lips to distract her. She was thoroughly melted into his kisses when his fingers wiggled along her sides, making her jump and fall off the sofa. Luckily, her bandaged hand didn't hit the coffee table.

He peered down at her. "Are you alright?"

"Yeah."

"You can come back up here."

"I'm fine where I am, thanks."

"The pout is adorable, but you had it coming, Charlotte."

Men... "Stop grinning like that and get me another soda."

He patted her knee and went to the kitchen. She claimed the remote and the sofa and rewound to the last scene of the movie she saw. He brought her the soda in a glass, set it on a coaster, and sat next to her.

Wasn't long before his right hand entwined with her left.

Simon lingered past one, then went home. It was sucky to have to stop cuddling. She wasn't ready to knock boots, yet, but she wouldn't mind if he stayed.

She had the wedding dream again. This time, they got as far as the cottage they'd share a bed in, when she woke up. Her groom had put her on his horse and led them the short distance home. The odd thing was that she never remembered if other people were there to watch or celebrate. Did they have family or friends?

"It's only a dream. You'll make yourself crazy over nothing," she muttered, and got out of bed.

Chapter Twelve
Charlotte

Nicholae left a message: "Charlotte, I arranged practice time for you with a piano. You can't let all your fingers atrophy. Be there." He included the time and address and the message ended.

Yay. It would be her luck he'd be there and want to have the location argument all over again.

Nicholae's Tuesday arrangement was at a private music school. They had the standard black Steinway seen in most schools that can afford a grand piano. At least it was in tune. Charlotte sat down to go through some reflex exercises since she couldn't play a full song with this finger.

"You look well."

She jumped and missed a note in the run she played with her left hand. "Hi, Nicholae."

"Don't let me disturb you, dear. I merely wanted to observe."

She kept her eyes focused on the music tray, but her senses were hyper aware of him in the room. Which was totally silly. He was her friend. He came to stand in the curve of the piano, tall enough to look over the top to see her hands. Her gaze dropped to her fingers, though she hadn't needed to see the keys she hit in years.

"Does the finger pain you?"

"Some. It's more of an ache, unless I bump it."

"And you like where you are staying?"

"Yes. Carrie's place is very comfortable."

"Perhaps you'll give a tour?"

"I'll have to ask her first."

"You need permission to have guests? That seems rather constricting."

"I don't need permission, but I do discuss it with her, since I'd be bringing a stranger into *her* home. It's just polite."

"I see. Charlotte…"

She stopped playing and looked up at him. "What?"

He locked eyes with her. "Give me your left arm, please."

She did. He turned her arm inner-side up and slid a small syringe into the vein at the crook of her elbow. She watched him draw a small amount of blood, then he withdrew the needle and pressed a cotton ball to her skin.

"Hold that there for a minute until it stops bleeding. Thank you, Charlotte." He capped the syringe and put it back in his pocket. "You may resume playing after that and forget what just occurred."

"Yes, Nicholae."

****

"Good practice, Charlotte. May I take you to dinner? We haven't socialized in a while," Nicholae said.

"I have plans, but maybe another time. Thanks for renting the space." She waved and walked to her new rental car she picked up this morning.

It was a current model compact and surprisingly easy to adjust so she could see out of it. One had no idea how hard it was to find a comfortable car when a girl was barely over five feet tall. She commended the rental agent on their selection.

Her honey was waiting in the lobby when she got home. She greeted Simon with a smile and a kiss.

"You're in a good mood."

"Happy to see you," she said. "So, where are we going?" They walked back out to his car.

"You'll see." He drove west.

"This is the way to the beach."

"Is it?"

"You can play coy all you want, mister, but I lived here for four years."

"I know."

He wore the usual button-down shirt and pants and she wondered how he could tolerate eighty degrees in long sleeves. She'd only avoided a tank top today because of the bruise still visible on her arm. "Well, if we are going to a beach place, it's a good time. Next weekend is a holiday weekend."

"What holiday?" he asked.

"Memorial Day is Monday. It's a national day off, the kick-off to the summer season. Anywhere fun around here is totally packed."

"Good to know."

When they entered Santa Monica, she knew he was headed for 3rd Street Promenade. It was lively on a Tuesday night, but not packed.

She had to laugh when she saw where he was leading her. "All of this available and you seek out the British pub."

"Everyone needs a bit of home now and again. One pint."

She held up her finger. "One."

Charlotte was a terrible lightweight and didn't drink, but she wouldn't begrudge him some homegrown atmosphere. From what she could guess, he hadn't been back to England in a long time. The smile on his face was worth the smell of beer.

After his drink (and a game of darts), they took to the street again to wander. It was good people-watching down here, and always a street performer or three. The Promenade glittered at night, with lights in all the trees and old-fashioned street lamps lining the sidewalks.

"You know they have ice skating here in winter," she said.

"Doesn't it melt?"

"Nah. It's not hot year-round — well, not most of the time."

"Perhaps you can teach me one day."

"You've never been on skates?"

He shrugged. "The opportunity hasn't come up. Getting hungry?"

"Kinda."

They wandered a while longer, window-shopping and stopping to listen to a saxophonist play a couple tunes. A booth of handmade jewelry caught her eye. "Do you mind?" she asked.

He smiled indulgently. "Not a bit."

Dangly earrings with crystals or shells, beaded necklaces, silverwork…it was so hard to choose.

Simon held out a bracelet. "What about this?" He fastened the silver clasp on her wrist and turned the bracelet right side up.

I wrapped my favorite leather hair tie around his wrist. My love was going away for a long time and I wanted him to have something for luck.

Whoa, where did that mental picture come from?

"Charlotte? Do you like this one?"

Huh? Oh. "It's pretty." Three flat pieces of white coral had been carved into roses linked by tiny pale green stone beads and the silver chain. "Never seen something like it before."

"There's a similar necklace that goes with it," the vendor said. She walked to another wall of the booth and took down a pendant. "The rose is carved out of reclaimed ivory and the leaves are green jade."

"Do you make all these yourself?" Charlotte asked.

"Most of 'em. My husband does the silver stuff and my daughter has an easier time handling the beads these days. If I'm not here on a different day, she's in the booth."

"A family thing. That's great."

"You can't say no, now," Simon whispered in her ear. Enabler.

"I'll take both," she said to the lady and handed her the bracelet. Luckily, she'd been to the bank this morning and had cash.

She wrapped the jewelry in tissue, bagged Charlotte's purchase, stapled it closed, and handed it to her. "Thanks. Come again!"

She nodded and they walked away to find dinner.

"You are very bad for my willpower, Simon."

"How can I resist seeing your eyes light up for pretty things? If you didn't get them, I would've."

"I really don't need more jewelry."

"Probably not. But you like it," he said, grinning. "And I like to indulge my lady."

"Am I?"

"What?" He stopped walking.

"Your lady."

"I hope so." By the look on his face, boy, did he. So vulnerable and open in the moment…how could she resist that?

She rose up on her toes and kissed him. He wrapped an arm around her waist and held her there a little longer than publicly appropriate. "Good," she said, and led him to food.

They left the Indian restaurant an hour later arm-in-arm.

"God, I'm stuffed."

"Told you you'd like it, didn't I?"

"I bow to your culinary expertise."

It was late and the closed street was mostly empty now, since this was a weekday. They headed for the car. The parking structure had lost a couple lights and the stairs to the second level were in shadow.

Charlotte stepped on flat ground first. Something spun her to the side and her back hit concrete, her head banging against the hard surface.

"Charlotte!" Simon yelled.

A man was in her face. "Aren't you a pretty treat?" He sniffed and his eyes turned red. "Smells really nice, too. What should we do first? Dinner and a fuck, or fuck, then dinner?" He pinned her to the wall and one hand slid her long skirt up her leg.

"Please, I'll give you cash. Just let me go."

He forced her head to the right. She squeezed her eyes shut when he dove for her neck. Mom was right—she was going to die in L.A.

Her skin was scratched by something sharp, then his weight was off her. She sunk to the ground, too terrified to run.

"Charlotte!"

Footsteps, then hands gripping her shoulders. She screamed and curled into a ball.

"Love, it's me. They're gone. You're safe. Did he hurt you?"

She chanced lifting her head and opening her eyes. "Simon…" She launched into his arms, knocking him over. He sat up and cradled her in his lap as she started to cry.

"Shhh, love…it's over, it's over…"

"What…how…"

"Breathe, love. It's alright." He stroked her hair and rubbed her back.

"How…how did you make them go away?" She looked over his shoulder, expecting to see unconscious men—and knew there had to be more than her attacker for him to have that much time with her—but the only thing on the ground was two piles of gray dust being scattered by the breeze.

"Let me see your neck," he said, and brushed her hair to the side. "Ah, good, only a scratch. I have a first-aid kit in the car."

She leaned back so she could look at him. "Why did he try to bite me?"

"What would usually bite a pretty woman's neck?"

"Simon, I'm not up for one of your jokes right now."

"I wish I *could* kid about this."

She pushed off his lap and got to her feet. "That's crazy. We're not in a *movie*. Some psycho talks about raping me and you're gonna call him a—"

"Charlotte, what else has fangs and leaves a dust pile behind when you stake them in the heart?" He pulled her to one of the piles. "That's ash, love."

"I can't... I can't deal with this. Take me home."

He let go of her arm. "As you wish."

Charlotte picked up her purse, wiped her nose, and followed him to the car.

So much for a nice date.

He opened the door for her. She nodded her thanks. He put the key in the ignition and activated the electronic locks, then started the car. She watched the buildings go by out the window. The radio came on to a classical station, the volume soft. She closed her eyes.

They were halfway back before she spoke again.

"You carry a piece of wood with you?" she asked.

"Yes."

"*Why?*"

"When I said before protecting people was my job; that was part of it."

"Carrying a stake."

"Yes."

"For..." She couldn't say it out loud, it was too ridiculous.

"Vampires. Yes."

"It's only superstition! Kids pretend to be vampires all the time and people play them in movies and on TV. This is L.A.—any freak could go to a prop store and look convincing!"

"What if I could prove they're real?"

"You can't."

"What if I could? Do you want to know?"

"No. I don't know. This is stupid."

"I'm sorry. I should've been more aware."

She wanted to curl up in the seat. "He would've grabbed the first person on the level whether it was you or me. That's what an ambush is."

"Thought I'd lose you. Scared me to death."

Don't cry, don't cry, don't cry.

"You saved me. Would've ended a lot different if I was alone, I know that. Just…stop talking about creatures of the night."

"Okay."

Charlotte was never so grateful to get in the bright lights of the lobby. Most of the lights were off in the apartment, indicating Carrie was asleep. She held her finger to her lips and Simon nodded.

She put a mug of water in the microwave for tea and went to her room to use the bathroom. He didn't follow.

Turning on the light and seeing herself in the mirror gave her a start. There was a small dry trickle of blood on her neck and her light blue top had dirt smudges on it, but it was her eyes that made her pause. She'd never seen herself look so haunted, not even after a bad nightmare.

Grabbing a washcloth, she cleaned the cut, then pulled clothes off and stuffed them in the hamper. Replaced them with a set of sweats and wiped the smeared make-up off her face. The Charlotte in the mirror looked better, then. Tired, but clean. Simon had already put a tea bag in the mug when she walked back into the kitchen.

"Thank you."

"You're welcome. Well, I best be going, unless you need anything." He looked so dejected, she hugged him. He hugged her back and dropped a kiss on her hair. "This isn't how I wanted the evening to end."

That made her laugh — well, snort a little. "Understatement."

"Are you alright?"

"I'll live."

He tilted her face up. "That isn't what I asked, love."

She shrugged halfheartedly. "I don't know. Ask me tomorrow."

"Okay." He kissed her forehead. "Get some sleep."

She nodded. It was too needy to ask him to stay and hold her. She saw him out, locked the door, and activated the alarm.

When she got in her room, she locked that door, too.

Chapter Thirteen

Simon

Once outside, Simon went hunting. Before returning to the hotel, he needed to expel all this negative energy. So close! Too close to almost losing her *again*. And slipping up by telling her about vampires? Unforgiveable. Maybe after five hundred years, he was going barmy.

Losing his marbles.

Edging toward senility.

"What are you doing out here?" Adam. He spoke from the roof of a warehouse to the right.

"It's too early to turn in." Damn vampire knew him too well.

Adam dropped to the ground, landing silently. "What happened?"

"Don't need you checking up on me." He walked away. "Got two hundred years on you, remember?"

His friend appeared before him. Those bursts of speed came so easily. "You won't let me forget it. But I know you, Simon. This isn't wise. We're in Juliet's territory. Frankly, we've stayed too long in this wretched town as it is."

"Bugger off, then. I don't need you to stay."

"Simon, what happened with the girl?"

He threw his hands into the air. "Fine! We were attacked by vampires tonight. She's well, but it was so close. Too close."

"I see."

"And I told her they were vampires."

"What were you thinking? Mortals don't take it well when you shatter their illusions."

"I don't know! I don't know. It just came out."

"How did she react?"

"Better than some, worse than others. Doesn't believe me, of course. We dropped the subject."

"And now you're afraid she'll never see you again."

"Yes. No. The night didn't end that badly, I just—"

"I know, friend. Come on. Let's find a pub where you can soothe your nerves."

Adam meant well, but Simon wouldn't feel calm until Charlotte smiled at him again.

Or remembered who they had been centuries ago.

If she died again, he didn't know if he could wait another twenty years for another chance.

Chapter Fourteen
Charlotte

I'm positive I'm being watched. I get out of bed. My neck throbs and there's blood when I touch it. A hand covers my mouth before I can scream and I'm pushed back on the bed.

His irises are luminescent red and he has fangs.

"What are you?"

"Isn't it obvious?" he says.

I feel pain in my neck. The suction as he feeds hurts and my skin burns where his fangs are puncturing me. He's taking so much so fast, I know I don't have long.

"Dammit." Charlotte reached blindly for the lamp on the nightstand. Once the room was illuminated, she started to calm down.

Another stupid nightmare.

The alarm clock said 4:00AM. She groaned and grabbed the empty mug to make more Tension Tamer tea. Her finger throbbed—must have bumped it or rolled on it while she slept. Took a pain pill, brewed tea, and carried the mug out on the balcony. The air was still and L.A. was eerily quiet. It got this way in the middle of the night and that always freaked her out, how a city with so much activity and millions of people could go dead quiet with barely a car passing by. Soon, the early morning commuters would be on the move, but for now, the City of Angels slept.

Wish my head was that peaceful.

Had she seen a real live monster of the non-human variety face-to-face? It didn't seem conceivable. Sure, people came up with all kinds of terms for things they couldn't explain, but that was before modern knowledge. They had medical explanations for people that grew too much hair all over, or ended up with weird growths. They weren't monsters, merely unfortunate. Magicians weren't performing real magic—only illusions. Smoke and mirrors. Animals had been demystified to merely interesting biological creatures.

Maybe there wasn't anything supernatural to the "vampire" at all…maybe it *had* been real, but only a product of mutation. Plenty of modern speculation they could be created by a virus or genetic experimentation. She could go with that…live with it…that the man had a biological issue making him violent and bloodthirsty. Of course, if there was treatment and he really was only a man and Simon reduced him to a pile of ash, then…

No, thinking of her boyfriend as a murderer was too far to go tonight. Granted, self-defense, but that was a sketchy gray area she didn't want to touch.

So. Until she knew different, she was willing to allow the possibility of a vampire-esque mutation in the world.

"And now that's sorted, crazy woman, go back to bed."

When Charlotte next woke up, she got proactive. Concert dates through summer were in her planner, so she looked up the persons in charge of scheduling each venue and sent a goodwill gift for the inconvenience of canceling the shows she couldn't make, and personal notes on good faith to the ones she could. Internet shopping was so convenient. Her last current show was in September, unless Nicholae was scheduling more without informing her, and she wasn't sure what she was going to do, or wanted to do, after that. This broken finger gave her a chance to take stock and she'd be a fool to ignore it.

Add a brush with death to that list, and she was ready to rethink how the rest of 2008 might go.

That took her to ten-thirty in the morning. "Now what?"

She could call home. Mom was always glad to hear from her…though she might wonder why Charlotte was talking to her twice in one week. With the chaos here lately, it was tempting to go back, though, even for only a few days.

"This was a lot easier when my mind was on teaching all day."

She really needed to get out of the apartment before she went crazy.

They looked at her weird at the movies when she walked back to the ticket booth for the third time, but they couldn't throw her out—she paid for every film she watched until sundown. Full of junk food, there was no reason to go out for dinner, and her cell had to be off in the theater.

Didn't prevent Simon from waiting for her in the parking lot at home, though.

"Hey."

He stood leaning on his rental by the door to the building. "How are you?"

"I went to the movies." She shut the door and locked the car.

"Not what I asked."

"Well, we don't always get what we want." She walked past him into the lobby.

"Charlotte—"

"Simon, just give me some space for a while, okay?" She ran into the elevator before the doors closed to escape, narrowly missing getting her boobs squished. "Yeah...definitely need to get out of town for a few days."

Chapter Fifteen
Charlotte

Carrie picked Charlotte up at the airport a week later. She was the only person Charlotte gave details to about the trip, with strict instructions not to share specifics with anyone who asked.

"How was home?"

"Like I remembered. Like, exactly. The 'burbs don't change."

"Your family was glad to see you, though."

"Oh, yeah. I'm surprised I still have a voice with being the center of attention for a week. Did you do anything fun for the three-day weekend?"

"Beach barbeque. The usual. Last day of work is Friday."

"Awesome."

"Yeah. It always feels weird to pack up for the summer, but I'm glad for the break. We can do girl stuff before I head to Washington."

"Wouldn't miss it."

June Gloom hung over the city when Charlotte landed, but the marine layer cleared out by noon and it was going to be another warm day.

She'd left her phone in her room and there were several missed calls. Carrie left hand-taken notes, as well. "Well, they can wait a while longer."

Her roommate popped her head in the room. "Ready for lunch?"

Charlotte grabbed her purse. "Starved."

"Did you see your mail?"

"Yep, thanks for leaving it on the bed. I'll look at it later."

"A fancy envelope came today."

"Fancy?"

"You know, like the kind used for wedding invites. Thick card stock inside."

Huh. "Well, I don't know anyone getting hitched, so I'm baffled." She shrugged it off. "Not important right now. Tell me about this long-distance boyfriend you're going home to."

Carrie's face lit up at the chance to talk about her love and she sat back in the seat to enjoy her friend's happiness while she drove. At least someone had it easy.

Somehow it wasn't a surprise to see Della sitting outside the apartment when they got back.

"Carrie, you remember my cousin."

"Of course. Hi."

"Hey." Della stood with her hands in her jeans pockets. She didn't look happy.

"Been waiting long?" Charlotte asked.

"Nope."

Carrie unlocked the door. "I'll give you two some privacy." She went inside.

Chapter Sixteen
Della

She sat outside the apartment waiting for Charlotte and Carrie to arrive. Mama had called about Charlotte being in Oklahoma City—a half-hour drive away from Guthrie—and asked why she didn't come with her. She'd sounded hurt until Della explained she didn't know her cousin was out there in the first place.

"Carrie, you remember my cousin," Charlotte said

"Of course. Hi."

"Hey." Della stood with her hands in her jeans pockets. This was going to get awkward.

"Been waiting long?" Charlotte asked.

"Nope."

Carrie unlocked the door. "I'll give you two some privacy." She went inside.

"Let's take this to the balcony."

Della shrugged and followed Charlotte in. "How was home?"

"You're jealous."

"Well, yeah. You could've given me a head's up, could've at least given me the chance to pass on a letter to my mother. I haven't been home since Christmas." Rarely been home in years.

"I'm sorry you're homesick, but it's not my fault. Look, Oklahoma usually isn't my first choice for a getaway, but I needed some stability, okay? Last week was crazy."

Della sat on one of the deck chairs. "It'd throw me off to be forced off work, too."

"Not just my finger, but yeah… I think you understand taking a break when you can get it." Della nodded. Charlotte let out a breath and took the other chair. "If it makes you feel better, I didn't get to Guthrie at all."

"I guess. Look, I know we don't know each other well, but I'm only asking for the courtesy of letting me know. It's my family, too."

"That's fair…but this really was last minute. I wasn't trying to hurt your feelings."

"I know. I'm annoyed, not hurt. But my mother called, so I had to say somethin'." She stood. "Well, I can't really stay, so…"

"No problem. Have a good night at work."

"Yeah. Thanks."

The call had ratcheted up anxiety she already felt. They never normally stayed in a city this long and she felt at times like she was being watched or followed. She'd changed routes since it started and been more cautious but she'd rather kill a creature than be stalked by it.

Would it make her feel better if it was Adam, a known quantity?

No. Even though he had yet to make an aggressive move.

Vampires were all alike. You either dusted them or became food.

Chapter Seventeen

Charlotte

Charlotte saw Della out, closed the door, and sighed. Poor kid. She sympathized, really, but she'd rather Della didn't drop her angst on her next time. She definitely liked home more than Charlotte did.

"All clear out here?" Carrie stuck her blonde head out of the hall.

She smiled. "It's safe. Teen drama has left the building."

"What'd you do to piss her off?"

"Went home when she's not able to right now."

"Oh. Big-time envy, then."

"Yup."

She headed for the fridge. "So…that Simon guy called a lot while you were gone."

"I saw."

"Didn't tell him you were skippin' town?"

"Sorta."

"Oooh. So why are you hiding?" She sat on the counter with a bottle of cream soda.

"I'm not."

"Uh-huh."

"I needed some space. That's not hiding." Avoidance, probably.

"Well, if he's that clingy, you probably did the right thing, anyway. Did you miss him?"

The entire time. "A little."

"Call him, then. Bet you can get Welcome Back perks."

Charlotte rolled her eyes and sat on the sofa, grabbing a pillow. "I'm not looking for 'perks'."

She laughed. "You big fat fibber! Every girl wants perks. Making a man earn his way back in is our prerogative."

"I don't play games like that. Besides, he didn't do anything wrong…specifically. I don't want to get into it."

"Okay…okay. It's your dating life, either way." She hopped off the counter. "Just know I've got your back."

"Thanks."

She went down the hall, leaving Charlotte with a sunny living room and way too many thoughts.

She looked at her mail.

Carrie was right about the one envelope. It was even closed with a wax seal. She carefully slid her finger under the flap to open it and pulled out the fine stationary inside.

Charlotte,

I'm hosting a party to welcome you back on Friday. A car will pick you up at seven. Expect a courier to drop off a gift between now and then.

I've missed you,

Nicholae

Not what she expected. A party? What kind of party, and where? And what's this about a gift? She called him.

The line went to voicemail. Of course he wouldn't want to be questioned.

She rolled her head on her shoulders and exhaled. Okay…it was only Nicholae making grand gestures as usual and it wouldn't hurt her to play along. Either he was apologizing for being irritable since she broke her finger, or wanting to show her off to perspective patrons. Perhaps both. She'd go and smile…then find a quiet moment to tell him the summer season would be her last for a while.

The rest of the mail wasn't important—merely a couple magazines and a sheet music catalog. Since she moved around so much, all of her bills were paid online.

And now all she had left was unpacking and calling Simon.

She unpacked.

When her phone rang at sunset, she answered it with, "Hello, Simon."

"Um...hello."

"I'm back in town, obviously, so you can stop pestering my roommate."

"I wasn't— Okay, maybe a little. Can I see you?"

"I don't know. Do your eyes still work?"

"Ha, bloody, ha. *May* I come call on you?"

"Hmmm..."

"Charlotte, please."

"I'll meet you downstairs at the hotel. You can see for yourself I'm alive and well. Bye, Simon." She hung up.

If this was going to be on her terms, she couldn't give him the chance to charm her. With nary a blemish left but her bandaged finger, she made the effort to look extra nice.

"Whoa. You pulled out the little black dress."

She glanced at Carrie in the mirror from where she was putting her earring on. "It's nothing new."

"May not be new, but it's certainly deadly."

It was a double-v-neck a-line dress, dipping low in front and lower in the back, though nothing Charlotte needed a special bra for. "It'll do." She added another coat of lip gloss then checked her teeth.

"He'll drool and you know it."

It really wasn't that special of a dress, except in how it fit. She spent less than fifty bucks on it years ago, and it was safe to throw in the washing machine. The dress just got along well with her curves. "I'm leaving now."

"Have fun. Should I wait up?" Carrie teased.

Charlotte rolled her eyes, grabbed her black purse, and got out the door. Her rental had been turned in when she left, but they gave her another car of the same model.

Had it really been two weeks since she first set foot in the Biltmore? Luckily for her stiletto-clad feet, there was a parking space up close. The admiring glances along the way to the restaurant were flattering, but there was only one man's head she sought to turn. She spotted him waiting in the doorway before he noticed her.

Simon checked his watch, stuck his hands in his pockets, then dropped them to his sides again. He was nervous. She made a point of letting her heels click on the tile and waited for him to look toward the sound. He looked. Blinked. Dropped his gaze to her feet and traveled up, and his mouth tried to work with no sound escaping.

"Good evening," she said.

"H-Hello."

"Is there a reservation?"

"Um…" He remembered he stood in front of a restaurant. "Yes. A table, yes."

She went to the host and told them they were ready to be seated. The host pulled her chair out for her — a good thing, since she didn't think Simon was capable, yet. He still appeared to be struck dumb.

Okay, she knew she looked kinda hot, but come on…

"I'm glad you came," he finally said.

"He *can* talk."

He blushed behind the beard. "You look beautiful tonight."

"Only tonight?"

"Of course not, you're—"

"Simon, I'm giving you a hard time."

"I knew that." He studied the menu.

It was cute. You'd think this was his first date ever. She didn't expect him to be this flustered. She thought…well, she thought he'd have more to say. Maybe the dress had backfired.

"I overheard the fish is good tonight," he said.

"Hmm." Small talk? Oy. "I had a good visit with my folks. And I missed talking to you."

"Really? I mean, that's good. Everyone is well?"

"Yup. Not much had changed since last time." The waiter came to take drink orders. She waited for him to go away. "It was nice to see some familiarity. Everybody wanted to know what I'd been up to. What I'd seen."

"Are you going back?"

"Right away? No." She shook her head. "No. Being the local celebrity isn't my cup of tea. I still wouldn't live there."

"Oh…"

The waiter returned with drinks and asked about food. Simon had an easier time talking to him.

"You're, uh, cousin is from the same place?" he asked next.

"Close by."

"Did she go with you?"

"Nope. Flew by myself. Have you lost the ability to talk to me in a week?"

"No! I… Give me a moment." He stood from the table, pushed his chair in, and walked away.

"What…" What the hell was that?

Fifteen minutes later, she was still alone. Did he go to the restroom or just flat-out leave?

Deserting her was not the way to win her heart.

The waiter arrived with salads.

"Could you ask the chef to put my order in a box? I don't think I'll be staying."

"Yes, ma'am."

If he comes back with dinner before Simon returns, I'm out of here.

She scared off her date…of all the scenarios, this isn't how she imagined it'd go. He just…didn't come back. She could have waited longer, she supposed, but it was humiliating sitting there amidst a dining room of couples after he ran away.

She left cash for her part on the table. It was only fair. Her supper sat in a container on the passenger seat as she drove home.

He could be calling now, but her phone was at home, and she didn't want to hear excuses. Maybe he got caught up giving an old guy CPR in the men's room, she didn't know, but right now…she didn't care.

L.A. wasn't her town, anymore. Once she was able to play again, she was moving on.

Carrie lifted her head from grading papers at the dining table when Charlotte walked in the door. "You're home early."

"Don't ask."

Her eyebrows rose. "Okay…are you okay?"

"Yeah. I'm gonna have a soak and turn in early. I'm still two hours ahead."

"Alright. Sweet dreams, Charlotte. And if you wanna talk…"

She smiled. Carrie really was a great friend. "I know."

She walked into her room and shut the door. The shoes came off first. She padded into the bathroom to play with the taps, then started peeling off her dress. It got tossed on the bed.

Just washed her hair this morning, so she stuck it up in a bun and removed make-up while she waited for the tub to fill. Water was slow to heat in this building and she was hungry. She slipped into a robe, retrieved a fork, and came back to sit on the tub rim and chow down.

Welcome back to L.A., kid.

The bath stuff she poured in the water was a Christmas gift from Nicholae. It made bubbles that were somehow creamy, and felt so luxurious. She was baby soft for days when she used it, but the soothing feel was more the point tonight. The tub filled, she stripped the rest of the way and sunk into steamy goodness.

"Oh, yeah...just don't fall asleep in here."

****

Knock, knock, knock...

"Charlotte? You have a visitor. Charlotte?"

Carrie's voice woke her up. She sat up in the tub and wiped bubbles off her chin. How long had she been in here? The water was barely warm.

"Charlotte? You awake?"

"Yeah! Um...give me a minute." She stood, pulled the stopper out of the drain, and hastily toweled off. With her robe on, she opened the door a crack. "What is it?"

"Someone's here to see you."

"At...this late?"

"I think he's pretty sorry."

She sighed. Simon. Of course. "Thanks. I'll deal with him."

He stood by the front door still dressed in the dark blue shirt and slacks from dinner.

"You should've called," Charlotte said.

He took three strides and kissed her, catching her off guard. His hands pressed into her back, holding her close, and she started to melt. He felt so good...

"I tried," he said. "You weren't picking up the phone."

"I was asleep."

"I'm sorry. I had all these things I thought I was going to say, then I saw you, and nothing would come out right. I just wanted to gather my thoughts, but...how long was I gone?"

"Long enough. Maybe I could've been more patient, but— In the future, running off really doesn't look good."

He stroked a stray lock behind her ear. "The first and last time, I promise."

"Guess I can forgive you this time."

He hugged her, bending his head down toward the crook of her neck. "You smell amazing."

"Better than normal?"

"Charlotte, you always smell good to me. I was only noticing what you're wearing right now."

"Oh. I had a bath."

He pulled back and looked at her in the short robe. "Are you—?"

"I'm going to slip into something a little less comfortable. Sit somewhere."

She made a hasty retreat to her room to, you know, not be naked, and added appropriate layers.

He was on the sofa when she came back out. "Didn't have to dress on my account."

"Think I did."

"Don't trust me?" He pulled her down to sit on his lap.

Don't trust myself. "What did you come to say?"

"That I missed you, and I hope the last night we saw each other didn't put you off me for good because I couldn't bear it. You have no idea how you've brightened my life, Charlotte. Before you came along, I can't tell you how long it'd been since I had a reason to smile."

Wow.

That was all but an *I love you.* Was she ready to handle that?

"You don't have to say anything, love. Just let me be a part of your life."

That sweetness was part of what endeared him to her. She knew he wouldn't push no matter how much he wanted to be with her and occasionally got a bit too intense.

"I think I can do that." The kiss was short and soft. "I did miss you, too."

He smiled. "Good."

She swatted his shoulder. "You're so full of yourself."

He grinned. "Not when it comes to you. You have me at your beck and call."

"Dangerous to admit that, Mr. Cole. I might take advantage."

"Do your worst, love." He kissed her neck, trekking up to her ear. "I'll always come back for more."

How did this go right back to sexy?

You sat on the man's lap and got flirty – what do you think?

But god...how he kissed made her feel like nothing was close enough. He might be able to pull off a poker face, but she could always feel what he felt when she kissed him. Thank goodness it was a tell no one else would be exploiting.

She pulled away breathless. "I'll see you tomorrow."

"Kicking me out?" he teased.

She stood and hauled him to his feet. "For now. It is late, and my body thinks it's even later."

"Alright." He kissed her at the door. "Sweet dreams, Charlotte."

"Bye, Simon."

When he was gone, she locked up and slumped against the door. "Woo boy…"

Chapter Eighteen
Charlotte

There was a knock on the door the next day. She opened it to find a courier standing there.

"Miss Taylor?"

"Yes."

He extended a clipboard. "Sign here, please."

"What exactly am I signing for?" she asked, writing her name on the delivery slip.

"Here," he said, handing her a large box. "I just drop 'em off, ma'am. Don't know the contents."

"Thanks." She shut the door. There was an envelope taped to the box.

Dear Charlotte,

I took the liberty of selecting something for you to wear. I think it will be exquisite on you.

Look forward to seeing you,

Nicholae

She shook her head. Rich men and their eccentricities. Normally, she'd bristle at the thought of being dressed by someone else, but he'd never been anything but a gentleman with her, and he did have great taste.

The box was labeled "Do not open until tomorrow."

Whatever. She had more urgent things to think about, like cooking dinner for her boyfriend.

"Sure you don't want help?" Carrie asked.

"I'm fine." The pasta water started boiling over. "Crap!"

"Okay…" She grabbed her purse from by the door. "Well, I'm off to the movies. Don't do anything I wouldn't do."

"It's not like that. Ow, dammit, hot!" This stupid bandage on her index finger made her clumsy. She couldn't grip anything properly. "Stop laughing at me and get out of here."

"Good luck, Char!"

Alone, finally, she focused on not letting the pasta get mushy or splattering sauce all over the stove. She already had a band-aid on her left thumb from slipping with a knife cutting veggies for the salad.

"What time is it...crap!" She needed to change before he got here. "Nothing burn down while I leave the room."

It's no big deal...breathe...it's only dinner.

She chose a pretty halter top and jeans, and let her hair down. Her new necklace completed the look. It'd been a surprise when she opened the bag to find the lady included matching earrings at no extra cost when she wrapped everything up. She was wearing those, too, though her hair hid them for the most part.

The doorbell chimed while she drained the pasta. "Just a minute!" She finished pouring it into the colander and ran to the door. "Hey."

Simon stepped forward, kissed her, and kicked the door shut. When she'd melted, he produced a rose from behind his back.

"Aww, I love pink roses," she said, and sniffed the bloom.

"I missed you." Both arms went around her and he kissed her neck.

"I saw you last night."

"So? Before that, you disappeared for a week." He stroked her mostly-bare back, sending shivers up her spine.

She gently backed out of his arms. "Dinner's ready." She looked for a vase for the rose.

"Can I help with anything?"

"You can sit."

He leaned against the dining table watching her fill plates. The salad was already between the place settings.

"The sauce is out of a jar, but I did get the fresh-made tortellini." She handed him his plate. "Sit."

"I'm sure it's delicious, love." He set the plate on the table, but stayed standing behind his chair.

She had water on the table, but suddenly realized there was only soda to offer him. "Sorry there isn't any wine. I don't drink, so I didn't think about—"

"Charlotte, what you have here is fine."

"Really?"

"Sit. Please. Unless you have more to do?"

She glanced at the table and shook her head. Not until dessert. This was as fancy as she got. She sat, then he sat. Always with the old-fashioned manners. A quick prayer ran through her mind that the pasta was the right tenderness as she spooned salad into her bowl. He watched her, grinning.

"What?"

"Admiring the view." Teasing her again.

"Well, eat."

He saluted with his fork and dug in. She normally didn't mind his teasing, but her cooking was a tender subject. Give her a barbeque grill any day. Just place meat, time it, flip it, time it, and done. She'd have to ask Carrie about putting a grill on the balcony.

This meal wasn't bad, though…as long as she didn't poison him before the end of the night, she could relax.

"Want to take in a show tomorrow night? I'll spring for popcorn," he said.

"I can't. There's a thing with Nicholae."

Some of the good humor left his eyes. "A 'thing'?"

"A party."

"Where?"

She shrugged. "A car is picking me up."

"I'll come with you. What is the common term…your plus one?"

"The invitation was only for me. But I'm sure I won't be out late. These things are usually boring little shindigs where he shows me off to business associates."

"'Shows you off'? Charlotte, you're not some trinket."

She sighed. "Not like that. I play a little, look pretty, and we get new patrons. It's harder to get bookings without the support of a label."

"But you can't play right now."

"No…but I present well. A little dinner, a little conversation, Nicholae makes some deals, and I go home. There's nothing to be jealous about."

"I'm not *jealous*. I have a bad feeling about him."

"You haven't met the man! Look, he's my friend and my manager, and I've known him for over two years. It's been a perfectly fine work relationship."

"Charlotte—"

"Back off, Simon."

He stabbed a tortellini with his fork. "Fine. Subject dropped."

"Thank you."

The silence that followed was tense and uncomfortable, the scrape of their utensils on the plates the only sound in the room.

His concern over Nicholae was so ridiculous, and completely unfounded. Nicholae was her biggest fan, her mentor, the first person that really believed in her talent. If he ever wanted to take advantage, he'd had plenty of opportunity to already do so.

She cleared the table and took dessert out of the freezer—two bowls of strawberry sorbet.

"Thank you," he said when she set his in front of him.

"You're welcome."

Her time with Nicholae was temporary, anyway. She didn't know where she was going to end up besides staying in one place for a while, but she was going to tell him the summer season would be her last for a while.

When their bowls were empty, Simon got up and took them in the kitchen.

"You're my guest. That's my job," she said.

He put them in the dishwasher before she could take them out of his hands. "I don't need to be waited on, love, but I appreciate the effort tonight. Don't worry about your cooking so much next time."

"Give it until tomorrow before you think about a next time."

He laughed and kissed her forehead. "Not getting rid of me that easily."

"Carrie's out for the evening, so you don't have to rush off."

"Sorry about earlier." He wrapped his arms around her middle. "It's...it's been a long time since there was light in my life, and I don't want to lose that." *To lose you* was implied.

"It's only a party," she said, making eye contact. "I can call you when I get home."

"Please."

"No more party talk." She took his hand and led him to the sofa. "You came for an enjoyable evening, yes?"

He smiled, and kissed her. Much better than talking. Heat spread inside her. He sat and she straddled his lap without breaking contact, or opening her eyes. His hands on her back were a mix of textures, soft and callused. They stroked her shoulders and arms, and down her back again, always wandering while pressing her closer to his chest.

She'd always thought making out with a bearded man would be abrasive, but the hairs only tickled when they brushed her skin.

"You could stay," she said when he let her breathe. His eyes widened. "To sleep," she hastened to add.

"Very tempting. But I can't stay 'til morning."

She played with his collar. "Forget I said it. I wasn't thinking."

"It's not that I don't want to."

"I get it. You have obligations."

He took her face in his hands. "Charlotte, I'd hold you for the next week if I could."

"I-I know. My mouth got ahead of my brain, is all." She moved off his lap to sit next to him. "You should go before the only people on the road are drunks."

"Love, it's nine o'clock."

"Oh."

He laced his right hand with her left. "I don't want to leave you. I have to."

"You're not making sense."

"One of these days you're going to have to admit some things don't fit in neat little boxes."

"Sure they can."

"Love, that's not how life works."

"Don't patronize me." She broke his hold.

"I'm not. I wouldn't."

"I think you should go."

"Charlotte…don't be angry. I wish I could explain, but it's complicated."

"Just stop, and leave my home."

"Charlotte…" She wouldn't budge. "As you wish," he said. He looked angry and frustrated, but he walked to the door without another word. It banged closed when he left.

The box from her manager still sat on the bed. Curious, she tore the brown paper off the box and lifted the lid. Packed carefully in layers of tissue paper was a white silk gown. Lifting the dress out of the box, she cooed in awe. It was pure white, like fresh snow. Illusion cap sleeves held up the embroidered empire bodice, giving the dress a strapless look. The skirt had layers, silk satin splitting open at knee level to reveal sheer chiffon. She carefully laid the dress on the bed and found a pair of shoes in her size.

It was a generous gift, one she wasn't sure she should accept, but Nicholae obviously went to a lot of trouble.

Guess you've made up your mind, then.

Chapter Nineteen
Charlotte
Friday

The driver arrived at seven sharp. Charlotte's eyes widened at the sight of the Bentley. She knew Nicholae was well off, but… "Is this Mr. Dragomir's car?"

"Yes, miss." He opened the door for her. "Please get comfortable."

"Thank you. It's quite…luxurious." She'd never felt leather so soft before. "Is it far to the house?"

"Not very. Just up in the hills, miss."

They drove up into one of L.A.'s most exclusive areas, where walls and gates and tall trees protected every house. Privacy was extremely valued in a neighborhood filled with mostly celebrities.

Finally, they turned down a private narrow drive that opened into a courtyard for an amazing house. Her jaw dropped. It was huge and looked more like a palace than a private residence. No other cars were here, though.

"Am I the first guest?" she asked the driver.

"I don't know, miss."

A young man in a white shirt and black vest and pants came down the steps to open her door. She took his hand and carefully exited the car, mindful not to step on the hem of her dress.

"Good evening, Miss Taylor. Mr. Dragomir is waiting for you."

The servant opened the front door for her and took her wrap in the foyer. He left as she heard another man's footsteps on the marble tile.

"My, you are a vision of loveliness," Nicholae said.

The foyer was a massive hall with many exits. She could get lost in the place. "Thank you. Are there many people here, yet? I didn't see any other cars out front."

He came into the light wearing a tuxedo and kissed her hand. "I must confess I lured you here with a ruse. I was unsure you would attend if you knew it would only be you and I. May I show you around?"

"You didn't have to go to all this trouble just to have dinner with me, Nicholae. We've known each other over a while. You're my manager. This dress, though…it's too generous."

"Nonsense. You are a beautiful woman who should wear beautiful things. Like this." He pulled a jewelry case out of his coat pocket and lifted the lid, showing her an exquisite antique sapphire necklace.

She gasped and shook her head in denial. "I can't accept that, it's too much."

"Only for tonight. Please. The piece is on loan, if that comforts you. The blue goes so well with your eyes, yes?"

"Well…" It really was beautiful. How many times in life would she get to wear something so fine? She sighed in defeat. "Just for tonight."

"Excellent. If you would turn?"

She complied, turning her back to him. Her hair was up in ringlets off her neck, so it was a simple matter to clasp the necklace. She shivered as his fingers brushed the fine hairs at her nape. The pendant dipped low. It would have slipped under her neckline if the dress wasn't so low cut. She'd felt a bit self-conscious about how much cleavage showed when she looked in the mirror at home. She was decent, but still felt…on display.

"Perfect. May I escort you to dinner now?" he asked.

She nodded, slipping her hand into the crook of his elbow. He led her into a ballroom with a table for two decked out in candles and two covered plates.

"You really went all out tonight. Trying to seduce me?" she teased.

He smiled. "Merely spending time with a beautiful woman. I have not entertained like this in a long time." He touched her cheek. "I thought you were special the first time I saw you. Have I told you that?"

Her cheeks warmed. "You've always appreciated my skill with the piano. So, uh, there's food?"

He laughed and led her to the table. "Indeed. A feast for two."

They engaged in small talk. He asked if her family was well. The food was exquisite, the same servant bringing five courses.

Nicholae checked his watch when they finished dessert. "Would you care to dance, Charlotte?" He used a small remote to turn on music.

"A waltz, hmm?"

He smiled. "Fitting, don't you think?"

"We are in a ballroom." She took his hand, rose from her seat, and allowed him to lead her to his chosen spot. "Nice frame. Where did you learn to dance?"

They naturally fell into step in the traditional hold.

"Here and there. The waltz in Austria. Perhaps I'll show you what I learned in Argentina some day."

"Well, tonight my dance card is empty."

She was drawn into his eyes as they danced; everything but the steps and the music fading away. It was nice to not think. He led her through complicated turns she didn't know, weaving a spell like she was hypnotized and bending to his will.

When the music finally stopped, she was out of breath, her breasts rising and falling against the gown. His lips found hers. He kissed like he'd been waiting years to do it and she didn't push him away. Her lips, her cheek, behind her ear, her throat…every touch left her burning.

"You taste so sweet, Charlotte."

She felt a sting in her neck, then the world went black.

****

Charlotte awakened on a bed of dark gray silk, feeling weak and woozy. "Nicholae? What's going on?" Her head spun when she tried to sit up. Was she drunk?

He came out of a side room dressed in black, the usual dress shirt and slacks. He paused, and sat on the edge of the bed next to her. "You really do look lovely."

"What happened? I don't feel well."

He brushed hair off her forehead. "That's why you're on my bed."

"Nicholae, you're making me nervous."

"Shhh, dear…there's no need to fret." His eyes locked onto hers, drawing her in.

She felt her will slipping away. "What—"

"You have a destiny, Charlotte. I want to give you a gift."

"A…gift…?"

"Sit up, darling." He helped her upright, and moved closer, holding her up. "I've always taken care of you, yes?"

"Yes."

"So you will trust me now."

"I-I'd like to go home."

One hand cupped her cheek and he locked eyes with her. "No, you don't."

"I don't."

"That's my good girl…"

Her eyes widened in horror as she watched his irises turn red, just like the man that attacked her in Santa Monica. "No!" She tried to flee.

His arms banded around her like strips of steel. "Stop struggling, Charlotte. This will only take a moment. Now, it's time for you to sleep."

"Don't do this, please."

He leaned into her neck. There was nothing she could do to prevent what came next. He bit her, and she screamed.

Simon, I'm sorry…

I lay on the bed in the suite at the Biltmore.

No, it's a different room. I don't know this place.

I'm positive I'm being watched.

I get out of bed. My neck throbs and there's a trickle of blood from two holes. Why am I bleeding?

I'm not alone in the room.

A hand covers my mouth before I can scream and I'm pushed back on the bed with dark gray sheets. I know it now.

"I'm going to give you a gift," he says.

It's Nicholae. His irises are luminescent red and he has fangs.

What are you? I think. His hand is still on my mouth.

"Isn't it obvious, my dear?"

I feel pain in my neck. The holes in my neck are his holes. The suction as he feeds hurts and my skin burns where his fangs are puncturing me. He's taking so much so fast, I know I don't have long.

Then, he's kissing me and filling my mouth with my blood. Lying down, I swallow against my will. The taste and texture are disgusting, unnatural. I should never know this.

"I'll always be in you, sweet Charlotte…"

Time blinks.

The bed is now surrounded by tall pillar candles. I don't have the strength to move. Didn't I die?

Nicholae stood within the circle of candles, his arms outstretched and eyes closed. He chanted something she couldn't hear or understand.

"Ahh, home sweet home…" a woman says at my side. No, not a woman – a demon. "You know, I do find your human world trying in some ways, but it's also a lot of fun. I bet you didn't know there's fun, **here**, too." Her lips don't move, but I hear her voice.

She touches my arm, and a scene unfolds before us.

I'm forced to watch as a man is disemboweled on a table, his screams deafening, until he succumbs to death. Then, it starts all over again. I try to close my eyes, but they won't obey.

It's dark, hot, and smells of sulfur – stereotypical, really, but no less disturbing. I finally manage to blink, only to find myself on the table.

The demon stands over me with a long curved knife. "I hope you'll scream for me. I must have my scream." The knife slices into my belly.

The scream forces its way out hard enough to make my throat bleed.

The scenery changes again.

Darkness. Isolation. Cold.

I get the profound sense I'm alone. Truly alone.

The demon's voice suddenly whispers, "You know what **real** hell is for the human soul? It isn't torture and fire and pain. It's **desolation.** To truly be deprived of any contact or comfort or even light." The voice shifts to my other ear. "It's what awaits you for being bound to me…"

"You lie."

The demon chuckles in such a way that I feel the bottom of my stomach drop out in dread. "You'd really like to think so."

Chapter Twenty

Simon

The door of the mansion swung open. The house was eerily quiet. Simon let the lady go first.

"I don't sense any vampires or demons," Agent Seven said, carrying her sword.

"Keep your eyes peeled."

Vampires rarely ran around solo, and usually had underlings.

The mansion was a maze. He and Seven had twenty or thirty rooms to search on the ground floor alone.

"I don't like this. It's too quiet," Seven said.

"We should split up. Check the rooms faster. They could be gone by now." He ran up the stairs to the second level.

The longer it took to find Charlotte, the colder his blood ran. A sick feeling settled in his stomach the moment they entered the house. He'd lost her so many times already.

They finally found the master bedroom.

"No!" He rushed in. "Not again…" Charlotte lay on the bed in a pristine white dress, her fair skin paler than normal. A small trickle of blood ran from the holes in her neck, and blood was on her lips. He cradled her body in his arms and wept. Once again he was too late.

Once again he failed her.

I'm so sorry, my love.

Another twenty years, or more…and not only was he still parted from Caroline, but Charlotte was gone, a woman he recognized yet still unique in her own little ways. He would've happily spent forever with her.

"I'm so sorry, Simon," Seven said. "Simon, you know what we have to do."

"What?" His face was buried in Charlotte's hair.

"She wouldn't want to be…we have to…to…"

"No."

"Simon, he turned her. You know what she'll become."

"I said no. You're not touching her."

"Alright…then you should be the one to—"

His bitter laugh cut her off. "You don't understand."

She tentatively touched his shoulder in support. "This isn't your fault."

"It's been my fault for five hundred years, only now there's no way to break the bloody curse." Another sob escaped his throat.

"She should be put to rest. Before—"

"Get out," he muttered.

"What?"

"Get. Out."

"Simon, any time now, the demon's going to set up shop in her body. Do you really want to see her as a vampire?"

"GET OUT!"

She held her hands up in surrender and left the room.

The girl didn't understand. Even as a vampire, he doubted his Charlotte would ever be a monster. Adam wasn't. He would endure the curse to spend every night with her for eternity. It was a better offer than he'd ever seen since Caroline died.

"Simon…" Adam said.

"Leave me alone, mate."

Seven stayed in the doorway.

"She's not dead," Adam said.

"*What?*" they exclaimed.

"Her pulse is slow and weak, but she's *not dead*. Simon, *she's alive*."

"Stop it."

"I'm telling you, I can *hear* her *heart*. She needs blood and a hospital!" He pulled her out of Simon's arms and carried her out of the room.

By the time Agent Seven had Simon downstairs, Adam had hooked up an IV to Charlotte's arm, the blood bag hanging from the handle above the door to the backseat.

"You don't know her blood type," she said.

"It's O-neg, don't worry."

Simon placed Charlotte's head on his lap. Seven covered her with a blanket Adam handed her and got in the front seat. He peeled out as soon as the doors were shut.

"Do I want to know why you had fresh blood in the trunk?" she asked.

"Can you be grateful I can help, for once?"

"If she lives through this." She braced for another high-speed turn.

"Watch the corners! She's not buckled in," Simon snapped. Bloody vampire and his crazy speeding. Some people in this car were *mortal*.

The ride to hospital took too long for his comfort. Then they wouldn't let him be with her. Didn't allow the paladin, either. He paced the hall. At least Adam stayed outside. Simon didn't need comfort right now. He needed information and then something to kill.

Minutes? Hours? Who knows? The doctors finally wheeled Charlotte out of the room and to the elevator. He followed Seven up to the ICU. So many tubes and wires. Would it take a miracle for Charlotte to wake again?

For the first time in a long while, he prayed.

Chapter Twenty-One
Della

Della's cell rang with an unknown number. "Hello?"

"Agent Seven. I need you." Adam.

"How did you get my number?"

"Not important. This is a matter of life and death. We need your help."

"We? Adam, what's going on?"

"My friend's girlfriend. He believes she's in trouble."

"Miss Seven. Please." A different voice had taken the phone. English accent. Familiar. "I believe Charlotte to be in serious danger."

Oh my God... "You're the...*what have you done with my cousin?*"

"Nothing! I love her! I'd never hurt a hair on her head. There isn't time to explain. Please."

"For her. I'll meet you at the hotel."

****

It was the first time Della failed and someone died. To have it be someone she knew, her own cousin, cut deeply. Tears tracked down her cheeks. Charlotte was family, and she would have to tell her parents.

Simon cradled her body in his arms and wept.

Della felt helpless. She didn't know if she could take Charlotte's head. A new vamp could rise anywhere from a few hours to a few days after they were turned and it was her duty to put that creature to rest.

When he yelled at her, she held her hands up in surrender and left the room, running downstairs.

Adam walked into the foyer.

"Nicholae?" she asked.

"Not here," he said. "Where are Simon and the girl?"

"Upstairs. She's..." Couldn't say it out loud, yet.

"Ah. I'm sorry."

She nodded. He started up the staircase and she followed.

"Simon..." he said.

"Leave me alone, mate."

Della stayed in the doorway while Adam went to his friend.

"She's not dead."

"*What?*" they exclaimed.

"Her pulse is slow and weak, but she's not dead. Simon, she's alive."

"Stop it."

"I'm telling you, I can *hear* her heart. She needs blood and a hospital!"

Thank God. It could only be a miracle...any vamp older than a night knew how to drain a human dry. She checked Charlotte's pulse, pressing two fingers to her throat. Adam was right, but she didn't have long.

He pulled her out of Simon's arms and carried her to the car in a flash. By the time Della had Simon downstairs, Adam had hooked up an IV to Charlotte's arm, the blood bag hanging from the "oh, crap" handle above the door to the backseat.

"You don't know her blood type," she said.

"It's O-neg, don't worry."

Simon pulled her head on his lap. Della covered her with a blanket Adam handed her and got in the front seat. He peeled out as soon as the doors were shut.

"Do I want to know why you had fresh blood in the trunk?"

"Can you be grateful I can help, for once?"

"If she lives through this." She braced for another high-speed turn.

"Watch the corners! She's not buckled in," Simon snapped.

Charlotte's heart had to be jumpstarted twice in the ER before she'd taken in a significant blood volume.

The wait was horrible before they knew she'd live. The doctors wouldn't let Della in the trauma room even with her credentials.

Adam stayed outside in the car.

They wheeled Charlotte to a private room in the ICU. Simon and Della watched them transfer her to the bed and hook up the monitors. A nurse handed her a bag with Charlotte's clothes and such. Simon sat next to the bed and held her hand, watching her chest rise and fall with slow breaths.

"You said you've been cursed every day for hundreds of years. What does that have to do with Charlotte?" Della asked.

"I was married when the demons wanted revenge. There's a reason so many stories have been told about tragic love. My wife and I are stuck in a loop. She never lives beyond twenty-five, the age when they killed her, and I only come alive at night."

"And you think my cousin is your reincarnated love?"

"I felt it when we ran into each other a year ago. That's how I know."

"Finding her can't be all there is to breaking the curse."

A sad smile crossed his face and he shook his head. "No, that would be too easy. She has to love me again. Only then will I see the sun and she'll know who I am."

"Five-hundred years and you've never gotten close?"

"Try searching for one woman among billions of people and see how quickly you succeed. Didn't make it to the Colonies 'til I met Adam."

"That's another thing I don't get. Why has he helped you?"

"Why wouldn't he?"

"He's a *vampire*."

Simon shrugged. "We keep the same hours."

"You were a *demon hunter*. He represents all you fought against!"

"I don't expect you to understand, Agent Seven, but he's my friend. The only friend I've had for a very long time. I'm entirely vulnerable during daylight hours. Adam can relate."

"Do you expect Charlotte to associate with the same kind that tried to kill her?"

He flinched. "I don't know how many times we have to tell you he's not like the others—"

"I won't let you court my cousin if he's in your life. *If* she has any interest in you in the first place."

"Think long and hard before you threaten me, young paladin."

"No, *you* better think," she said, poking him in the chest. "You're in this room by *my* permission. You're not family or Charlotte Taylor's spouse and hospitals have strict rules about who's allowed in ICU."

He stood and glared down at her. "You'd really bar me from seeing her."

"For her safety, absolutely."

"Sir, miss, I have to ask you to keep your voices down," the nurse said. Neither of them had noticed her opening the door.

"Sorry," Della said. "Long night."

"The patient needs her rest. You can come back in the morning." She stood holding the door open, so guess that was an order.

"Say goodbye, Simon." Della walked to the doorway.

The nurse went back to the station. He whispered something in Charlotte's ear, kissed her forehead, and left.

Della started to go, then turned back. "I'm sorry we didn't find you earlier, cousin." Charlotte's hand was cool in hers. "That bastard kept you for years and I hate that he got away with it. He'll pay, if it takes me ten years to find him, I promise. Just make it through the night, okay? I'll make sure you're safe." She kissed her cheek and covered her arms with the blanket.

The hotel manager let her into Charlotte's former room thanks to her ID. This particular suite had two bedrooms and she hoped Nicholae had stayed in one of them. She needed some kind of clue where he'd run.

"He won't have slept here." Adam.

"How did you get in?"

"You won't find any clues of Nicholae in this room. The only scent is human."

"One—eww, and two—then where is he, smarty-pants?"

"Staying with family. It's what's expected in Los Angeles."

"Yet you bunk with a statue."

He shrugged. "I'm a rebel."

She counted down from ten. He was so infuriating. Trying honey instead of vinegar, she asked, "Do you know where Nicholae is, Adam?"

"Probably, but you don't want to go there."

"I do."

"No you don't."

"Oh, I *really* do."

"No, you don't."

"Adam!"

"He's at Juliet's. I'm sorry, Della."

"Sorry?" The one place she couldn't go. Bastard knew it, too. Nicholae would always have bitten Charlotte in L.A.

"I know what it's like to have revenge denied from you."

"*Justice*. Revenge is fueled by hate. That's not me and never will be. Your kind doesn't get that."

"Will you stop painting me with the vampire brush? It's what I am, not *who*. Your cousin didn't ask to be turned? Well, neither did I! Your Agency doesn't want to tell you we have a soul, but we do, and *some* of us don't want to kill for food."

"Human blood doesn't tempt you."

"*Killing humans* doesn't tempt me."

"So, you're what, living on cows or whatever?"

"Donated blood."

"You steal from hospitals? Yeah, that's really helpful to mankind!"

"*Nooo*, I buy willingly donated blood from a private source. Don't need much at my age unless I'm injured. Look, I can't help what I need to eat to survive, but I'm not hurting anyone to get it. Need me to burn my hand again to prove it to you?"

"No thanks. I had to polish my necklace after the last time."

"You say you're not about hatred, but you hate vampires."

"I do not."

"Being this insistent that I have to be evil just because I got turned a long time ago—yeah, you do. I can understand after today—family is personal—but why before? Is that what The Agency trains you to be?"

"I don't hate you, or them. I don't *trust* you. You're the only one that hasn't tried to hurt or kill me yet."

"When did you start hunting?"

"Four years ago."

"That isn't right. You can't be more than twenty."

"My birthday was in April."

He swore under his breath. "How does a sixteen year-old fight monsters?"

"With practice. Same as everybody else does." She turned the light off, ready to leave. "Can you move, please?"

He cleared the doorway. "If Nicholae leaves Juliet's, I'll let you know right away."

"It's almost dawn. How will you know?"

"I have my ways. Goodnight, Agent Seven." He left the suite first.

There were only a few hours until she could go back to Charlotte, making sleep pretty much pointless, so she went to Amelia's to report instead.

Chapter Twenty-Two
Charlotte

Charlotte woke up screaming.

She was strapped to a bed and her arms and chest stung.

Della ran in. "Hey, you're safe, you're safe!" She turned on lights. Charlotte wanted to shield her eyes. Too bright. "Charlotte, you're in the hospital. It's okay." She came around the bed and started undoing the restraints. "You clawed at your skin in your sleep. We had to tie you down."

She tried to sit up. She had to pee.

"Hey, easy. You lost a lot of blood." Her arm was surprisingly strong holding Charlotte down. Or Charlotte was just that weak. "Let me get a nurse." Della pressed the call button.

The nurse looked to be around Charlotte's mom's age. She wore blue pants and a white pattered top.

"What day is it?" Charlotte asked.

Della looked like she'd been up all night. "Sunday."

Over twenty-four hours since she left the apartment. How did she get away from Nicholae?

The nurse suggested a bed pan, but Charlotte insisted she could walk the five feet to the bathroom. It took a while to get there, with all these tubes coming with her, and she wasn't allowed to lock the door for privacy.

"Can she eat? Are you hungry?" her cousin asked. Food for what ails ya; that was how their family healed.

"Just wanna get out of here." Charlotte got back into bed.

"You're in no shape to go anywhere, Miss Taylor," the nurse said.

She pouted. "Della, help."

"I need to make arrangements first. Follow orders until then." She left the room, pulling her cell out of her pocket.

At least Charlotte had a private room, whatever hospital she was in. Sunlight still filtered in through the blinds, so that was a good sign. Sun equaled safe.

Nicholae was a vampire, or thought he was, since vampires actually existing was too ludicrous to mention. But, if he could role-play far enough to drink her blood, then he'd also be afraid of sun rays and that was good news for her. She only had to spend the rest of her life surrounded by UV light.

Joy.

"What's going into me?"

"Hydration, nutrients, and a little pain medication. Your ribs will be sore for a while."

"Why?"

"They had to use the paddles twice. Personally, I don't know why you're alive with how much blood you lost." She finished writing on Charlotte's chart and left her alone.

Too alone. It allowed her to think.

What was she going to do now? Nicholae handled her whole career — the money, the contacts, bookings…everything. Could she do the summer tour without him? She definitely didn't want to crawl back home.

Did Della already call her mother?

"You're gonna get frown lines worryin' like that."

"Hey. News?"

Della sat on the end of the bed. She took Charlotte's hand without the IV in it. "I've got you a spot at a private retreat. Soon as they say it's safe, you're out of here."

"Thank you. So…what happened?" She gestured to the bandage on her neck. "Besides the obvious."

Della chewed her lip. "How much do you remember?"

"I blacked out sometime after Nicholae bit me. Never figured him for a total lunatic."

The mind trip of nightmares wasn't getting mentioned.

"We figured out where he took you and got there as fast as possible. Thought you were dead at first, but there was a faint pulse. Raced you to the ER and now you're awake."

"Who's we? How did you know where to find me?"

"It's what I do, Charlotte—help people."

"So they were colleagues."

"Not exactly…Simon and his friend helped me."

"Where is he? Is he here?" Wait, no, it was day. "Never mind. So he and Adam helped you come to my rescue?"

"Yeah."

Huh. She had no clue how he got in touch with Della, let alone met. "I'll have to thank him."

"He's glad you're alive."

"And Nicholae? Was he arrested?"

"Eh, no…he wasn't at the house by the time we found you. But don't worry. I promise he won't touch you ever again."

Charlotte didn't know how Della could give that guarantee, but she nodded anyway.

Della patted her leg. "I brought some stuff from your room, clothes and soap and all. Now that you're awake, they'll probably move you to a regular room if you have to stay a while longer. Are you hungry?"

"Not really. How many people know I'm here?"

"I, uh, told your mother you were under the weather today, in case she was expectin' a call."

She cringed. "Is she flying out as we speak?"

"Didn't mention it."

Maybe she dodged that bullet, then.

"Charlotte...you were unconscious, yet you tried to hurt yourself. What was goin' on in there?" Della pointed at her head.

Torture.

She didn't feel right, yet. The room was too bright and all the beeping and humming too loud. That hospital smell was nauseating, too. "I don't know. I was out, right?"

"Yeah. It doesn't matter. If you're here long enough to sleep again, I'll be here."

"Do you know if Simon is coming back?"

"He stayed until close to dawn, so I think it's likely. I'm not crazy about his choice of friends, but he seems smitten with you."

"Stubborn."

"Sure you don't want some Jello or somethin'?"

Charlotte pulled the blanket up to her chin. "Maybe later. Could you shut off most of the lights? They're giving me a headache."

"Sure." She carried that out, then filled the water pitcher and a cup from the bathroom sink. "Would you like the TV on?"

"I guess. If it's quiet."

Della handed her the remote. "These buttons control it."

"Thanks."

She sat in the chair in the corner and Charlotte flipped channels until she found a PBS station.

The nightmares continued to whisper in her head.

Charlotte blinked and the hospital room was visible again. Della slept in the corner and the TV was still on. She turned it off and sat up to get out of bed. The tile was cold to her bare feet. She didn't stir as Charlotte rolled the IV stand toward the door and left her room.

It could have been a hospital in Anywhere USA. The nurses' station was to her left, so she chose the other way. The painkillers must be wearing off—her ribs felt like one big bruise with every breath. She passed open doors and closed ones. Most of the patients in the ICU weren't awake.

The corner had windows. She looked out on the city. It was late afternoon, probably rush hour, and the streets were busy even on a Sunday.

"You should be in your room, Miss Taylor." A nurse had come up the other hall.

"Got a little stir crazy."

"Are you going to want supper?"

She wasn't hungry, but she should try. "I guess. Do I have to stay another night?"

"The night shift doc will check you out and make that call."

"Okay. Send them in when they get here."

She encouraged Charlotte back in the direction of her room.

Della opened her eyes when Charlotte opened the door. "Were you wandering around alone?"

"Just down the hall, and a nurse found me within a few minutes. I needed to move. You said something about bringing clothes?"

"Yeah. In that closet."

Charlotte opened the cabinet and saw her carry-on bag. It felt half-full. She grabbed what was on top and a pair of underwear and went in the bathroom.

Crap, how was she going to change with this IV attached? She pulled the needle out of her vein. *Yeow.* Her ribs made it pretty uncomfortable, but she managed to clean up a little and get dressed. She was still avoiding the mirror. The lighting in here was crappy and would only make her feel worse.

"I'll be glad for my own bed and a hot shower," she said when she came out.

"You almost look human now."

"Ha, ha." Charlotte looked for a comb. "You could use a brush and some concealer, yourself."

"It's hard work keepin' your butt intact." She stretched and stood. "They gave me what you came in with. The bag is in the closet, too."

"They cut the dress off, didn't they?"

"Sorry."

"Oh, well… I didn't pay for it. I suppose my purse is still at Nicholae's."

"Probably. My priority was finding you."

"Why did you all come looking for me?"

"Simon said you were supposed to call him. He got worried when it got late, and we tracked you down."

"Okay…but how did he find you? I've never—"

"Adam and I had met before."

"Oh. Lucky me, then. And thank you."

Della placed a hand on her shoulder. "We're family."

Charlotte sat on the bed to try to make her hair less resemble a rat's nest. Della took the comb from her hand and climbed up behind her.

"The nurse said they had to shock my heart twice. How long was I dead?"

"It was two separate occasions and your heart only stopped for a little bit. You weren't dead-dead. He, uh…he'd taken a lot of blood. It's a pressure system, you know, with the pumping and fluid, and there was barely enough to pump with. You're like a car with an oil change now."

"Should I be able to walk around by now?"

"Well, you had a transfusion, so it takes less time than the body restoring its own supply."

"Del, aside from my ribs hurting, I'm not tired or anything. If I was still teaching, I'd probably go to work tomorrow." She shook her head. "God, this was a weird weekend…"

"You're tellin' me. Look, you had a minor miracle. Be thankful. It doesn't need explanation."

"Divine intervention, that it?"

"Everything happens for a reason, cousin."

"He can keep the near-death experiences. I've had enough for one lifetime."

One that only has one year left, a voice whispered in her mind.

Great. Now she was being haunted. She had to get out of this hospital.

She popped to her feet. "You know what, I just need someone to sign me out and I'm going home. No sense in taking up a bed someone else could use." She left the room and approached the nurses' station. "I'm ready to check out."

"Miss Taylor, you—"

"Give me a waiver to sign or whatever, but I'm leaving."

"You realize this is against doctor's orders until he's seen you."

"Yep. I'm fully responsible and have no plans to sue the hospital. Hand me a form."

She sighed and started on Charlotte's request. Charlotte went back to her room to pack up and put on shoes.

"Charlotte, maybe you should slow down."

"Del, I'll heal faster at home where I'm comfortable and safe."

"Alright…"

By the time she finished tying her shoes, the nurse arrived with a clipboard.

Finally getting into Della's car allowed Charlotte her first breath that felt normal. She'd hated hospitals since watching her grandmother wither away for a year before death.

"I hope your roommate's here," Della said. "You don't have your keys."

"She doesn't go out on Sunday nights. Teacher habit."

Charlotte pressed the doorbell button, then knocked.

Carrie opened the door, surprise on her face when she saw it was them. "Char, did you lose your keys?"

"For the moment. Thanks." She walked inside pulling her luggage.

"No problem, but find them soon, or we'll have to have the super change the locks."

"Okay." She went to her room, Della in tow. Once the door was closed, she said, "You didn't tell her."

"It was a crazy weekend. I haven't seen her until now."

"Then how did you get my stuff?"

"It doesn't matter now. Get some rest, okay?" She opened the door and walked out.

"Del…thanks."

"Any time. Goodnight, Carrie."

"Bye."

That's her cousin…bail before it got mushy. Charlotte poured a glass of juice and took it into the bathroom. The temp dials for the shower adjusted, she waited for the water to heat and started to strip. The mirror fogged up and she sighed in relief.

The water was as hot as she could stand. It beat down on her hair and shoulders, muffling all other sound in the building. If she stood there long enough, she could wash away the whole week since she came back.

The water-logged bandage on her neck fell off.

A tap on the bathroom door made her jump. "Shit!"

"Charlotte? You have a visitor." It was only Carrie.

"Okay!"

Ugh. Couldn't she get some downtime? It was probably Simon, unless Della was back, but Carrie would've said so.

She dried off and combed her hair into a side braid to conceal her neck, then got dressed in a hoodie and sweats.

"There she is," Carrie said. She stood at the open front door.

It was Adam. "Hey, Charlotte. I found your purse."

"Oh. Thanks. I thought you'd be Simon when she said someone was here."

"Only me. Well, goodnight, ladies." He waved, and walked away.

Carrie shut the door. "Here you go." She handed Charlotte her clutch bag. "So, who's the hottie, 'cause *oh my god.*"

She checked everything was still in it. "Simon's best friend. I think he's single if you want to chase after him."

"Nah…out of my league. Any man that beautiful would be too high maintenance. Nice of him to drop off your purse, though."

"Yep. Well, I'm beat, so…"

"Sure. Goodnight."

It was sweet of Adam to drop it off. He must've gone back to Nicholae's, though why, she couldn't say...Nicholae surely wouldn't go back there after what he'd done. He was too smart for that.

She didn't want to sleep, yet, but she locked herself in her room with only a reading light on. A fun book was just the distraction she needed.

Chapter Twenty-Three
Della

It felt so good to be back in her armor again. They'd found Nicholae, and she was on her way with several lethal weapons strapped to her suit and in her coat pockets. She said a prayer she'd get there first.

No such luck.

Adam peered out of his car at his surroundings before getting out, senses alert. He grabbed a sword from the trunk and stuck a stake in his jacket pocket. "Very prompt. I'm glad you're taking this seriously."

"Don't antagonize her," Simon said. "Thank you for coming."

"Not doing it for you, just to set the record. This better be legit." She went first into the warehouse and light flooded the space. "Show yourself!"

"Ah-ah...that's not how this works, paladin." The tall accented vampire clucked his tongue.

The voice from the woods. He was the vamp that knocked her out three years ago!

She was going to *enjoy* this. "Sorry to disappoint."

Nicholae suddenly struck with a sword from behind, slicing at her leg. She'd heard the song of it cutting through the air and dodged in time for him to only nick her coat. Swinging around to attack, the battle was on.

Slice.

Parry.

Thrust.

Deflect.

The clash and clang of metal against metal echoed in the big empty chamber. Nicholae had speed and agility. He was as tall as Adam, but leaner, long limbs able to move in ways she couldn't. The heavy blows rattled her teeth every time their swords connected.

But she soon picked up the patterns of her opponent.

Hell with it. She shot his leg with a holy-water-filled bullet.

"You bitch!"

She shot his abdomen. "Now, now, no need for name calling. I thought you appreciated the art of playing with your food?" She feigned a move.

He reacted predictably. She slammed her bare fist into his temple. He stumbled to his knees, dropping the sword. She hit him again and kicked him hard in the abdomen. He rolled to his side and spit out blood.

She straddled him, a stake pressed to his chest. "Any last words?"

"You may kill me, but our message will live on."

She wondered at the ominous sentence a second before plunging the stake into his heart, dusting him.

"That was rather quick," Simon said.

"Nice job standing around, boys."

"You had him in hand. They trained you well," Adam said.

"Two years of it." She cleaned the blade before slipping it into the sheath concealed in her coat.

"It'll be best if everyone involved leaves LA," Adam said.

"Why? He's gone."

"Juliet and Vittore don't take losing family well."

"Who's Vittore?"

"A childe of Juliet. Older than me. In some ways, he's worse than she is which is why he's her right hand. Take the advice, Agent Seven." He turned around and left.

Adam had an annoying habit of walking away from conversations.

"He's only in the city for my sake, you see," Simon said.

"I'm surprised you let me do this."

"Bit surprised, myself, but this is your time. We were present to make sure he didn't escape."

She looked around the warehouse. "Wonder why he was here? I should call it in."

"It is curious, isn't it? Ground floor is empty. Well, I'll leave you to your paperwork before Adam makes me walk home."

He tipped an imaginary hat and walked out. Strange old man.

Activating her earpiece, she said, "Amelia."

"Seven." Amelia sounded both relieved and perturbed. "Where have you been?"

"Taking care of personal business. I have an address for you to check out. Send a forensic unit."

"What happened?"

"Nicholae Dragomir is dust."

"*You what?* How could you be so irresponsible to face him without backup?"

"I wasn't alone. He's dead, alright? I'm scuffing the ash pile with my boot as we speak. For his age, I wasn't impressed."

"Fine...but this is going on record. What's the address?"

Amelia was her guide, the real-life version of a Watcher, and bossy as hell. Her anger had nothing to do with Della's skills. She feared for her safety if she wasn't there. Didn't matter that Della had more dustings than any trainee in years or that she was one of only a few to graduate when she turned eighteen. It was Amelia's job to worry.

Della didn't tell Charlotte that Nicholae was dead—that would've gone over real well—"Hi, I killed your manager, yay?"—but she was assured he couldn't ever harm her again.

She wanted to stay at Carrie's. Considering the company Simon kept, Della wanted her nowhere near him or Adam, but she was determined to make her own choices.

Guess that's what I fought for, the freedom to choose.

To live.

To make normal, human mistakes.

Well, if Charlotte wouldn't allow her to put her somewhere safe, she'd have to put up with being watched. Her picture was in Della's report which went into a database all agents had access to, and The Agency had quite the team of nerds watching over the world. If she turned up in danger again, Della would know about it.

The adrenaline of a fight made her antsy, so as soon as the clean-up team got there, she bailed to blow off steam. If she had to leave LA soon, it was going to remember her.

They were going to fear the woman in black.

About the Author

Writer of supernatural badasses.

Vivian Lane is an American author. Born a Gemini, her interests fall under a myriad of subjects including classical music, American and World History; fantasy books, TV shows, and movies; travel, marine biology, and fashion.

Children of Ossiria

Ossiria is a land in an alternate dimension. A horrible event took place there that had reach on several worlds, including Earth. CHILDREN OF OSSIRIA includes immortals, vampires, demons, witches, paladins, and every-day humans, with love, loss, danger, torture, sex, and blood..

#0.5 - **The First Vampires**
#1 – Protector
#2 – Goddess
#3 – Outcast
#4 – Mate

Made in the USA
Middletown, DE
29 January 2017